Praise for the first novel in this sizzling new series
from *New York Times* bestselling author
CHRISTINE WARREN

Heart of Stone

"The opening of Warren's hot, new paranormal series
is a snarky, creative, and steamy success that delights
new and longtime fans alike."
—*RT Book Reviews* (4 stars)

"The sexual attraction . . . is palpable."
—*Publishers Weekly*

"Steamy scenes, mixed with an intriguing story line
and a hearty helping of snarky humor."
—*Reader to Reader*

"A rousing first act that sets the boundaries of this
engaging urban fantasy."
—*Midwest Book Review*

"Fast-paced with characters you'll love, and even some
you'll love to hate, *Heart of Stone* is another winner
for author Christine Warren!"
—*Romance Reviews Today*

NOT YOUR ORDINARY FAERIE TALE

"Warren has made a name for herself in the world of paranormal romance. She expertly mixes werewolves, vampires, and faeries to create another winning novel in The Others series. *Not Your Ordinary Faerie Tale* showcases Warren's talents for creating consistent characters with strong voices and placing them in a fantastical world."

—*Romantic Times*

"*Not Your Ordinary Faerie Tale* is a delightful read from the first word to the last. Christine Warren has created two amazing characters, given them an incredible plot, and laced the story with witty conversations, lots of snark, and a hefty portion of danger." —*Single Titles*

"Christine Warren merges lust, laughter, and intrigue magnificently in her latest installment of The Others. *Not Your Ordinary Faerie Tale* is a fun and fast faerie adventure." —*Joyfully Reviewed*

BLACK MAGIC WOMAN

"Excitement, passion, mystery, characters who thoroughly captivate, and a satisfying romance make [it] a must-read." —*Romance Reviews Today*

"Will capture your senses and ensnare your imagination. Another great novel from Christine Warren."
—*Single Titles*

"Sexy, action-packed romance!" —*Joyfully Reviewed*

PRINCE CHARMING DOESN'T LIVE HERE

"Christine Warren's The Others novels are known for their humorous twists and turns of otherworldly creatures. Like her other Others novels, *Prince Charming Doesn't Live Here* is an excellently delicious story with great characterization."
—*Fresh Fiction*

BORN TO BE WILD

"Warren packs in lots of action and sexy sizzle."
—*Romantic Times BOOKreviews*

"Incredible." —*All About Romance*

"Warren takes readers for a wild ride."
—*Night Owl Romance*

"Another good addition to The Others series."
—*Romance Junkies*

"[A] sexy, engaging world . . . will leave you begging for more!"
—*New York Times* bestselling author Cheyenne McCray

BIG BAD WOLF

"In this world . . . there's no shortage of sexy sizzle."
—*Romantic Times BOOKreviews*

"Another hot and spicy novel from a master of paranormal romance." —*Night Owl Romance*

"Ms. Warren gives readers action and danger around each turn, sizzling romance, and humor to lighten each scene. *Big Bad Wolf* is a must-read."
—*Darque Reviews*

YOU'RE SO VEIN

"Filled with supernatural danger, excitement, and sarcastic humor." —*Darque Reviews*

"Five stars. This is an exciting, sexy book."
—*Affaire de Coeur*

"The sparks do fly!" —*Romantic Times BOOKreviews*

Also by
Christine Warren

Heart of Stone
Hungry Like a Wolf
Drive Me Wild
On the Prowl
Not Your Ordinary Faerie Tale
Black Magic Woman
Prince Charming Doesn't Live Here
Born to be Wild
Big Bad Wolf
You're So Vein
One Bite with a Stranger
Walk on the Wild Side
Howl at the Moon
The Demon You Know
She's No Faerie Princess
Wolf at the Door

Anthologies

The Huntress
No Rest for the Witches

Stone Cold Lover

Christine Warren

St. Martin's Paperbacks

This is a work of fiction. All of the characters, organizations, and events portrayed in this novel are either products of the author's imagination or are used fictitiously.

STONE COLD LOVER

Copyright © 2014 by Christine Warren.

For information address St. Martin's Press, 175 Fifth Avenue, New York, NY 10010.

ISBN: 978-1-250-01266-1

Printed in the United States of America

St. Martin's Paperbacks edition / September 2014

St. Martin's Paperbacks are published by St. Martin's Press, 175 Fifth Avenue, New York, NY 10010.

10 9 8 7 6 5 4 3 2 1

In memory of my grandmother, who taught me to curse
in Lithuanian, but never told me how to spell any of
it. You knew I'd look it up one day, didn't you, Grandma?
And I bet you were looking down laughing when
I read those *real* definitions.

Oh, if only I had known what I was really saying all those
years. Life is much more interesting because of you.

Thanks.

Stone Cold Lover

Chapter One

Orange was so not her color.

Felicity Shaltis knew this, knew it even as she slipped the purloined key into the heavy antique lock and committed her first felony. The knowledge made her hands shake, but it didn't stop her. She couldn't stop; all she could do was hope she went to one of those progressive Canadian prisons where they let the inmates wear blue. Or black. She looked decent in black.

If she got lucky, maybe Ella would visit her.

Ella Harrow: long-lost college pal, kindred spirit, and—Fil was beginning to think—possible art thief. It was Ella who had steered Fil down this new road to a life of crime, and she had managed it with one phone call—one request for a seemingly trivial favor. At the time, Fil hadn't seen the harm in helping her old friend locate a gargoyle statue similar to the one that had made the news when it had disappeared from the museum where Ella worked. Now Fil wasn't so sure.

Of course, if Fil had stopped at revealing the statue's

location to her old friend, she might have gotten off easy as a simple accessory. But, no. She could hardly continue to call herself an accessory to a theft when she was the one committing unauthorized entry, criminal trespass, and what she herself could only term felony stupidity, all because she couldn't get that damned sculpture out of her mind.

Around her, the grounds of the Abbaye Saint-Thomas l'Apôst lay in quiet contemplation under a blanket of stars. On this hill above the bustling center of Montreal, the lighting was dim enough that she could actually see the bright twinkling, especially given the lack of moon. But Fil still felt as if there were a Broadway spotlight shining directly on top of her.

Hurrying, she fumbled and cursed, then heaved a grateful sigh when the ancient, rusty lock finally disengaged. Easing the door open, she squeezed through the bare minimum of space and quickly closed it again, sealing herself in the rear of the abbey's old chapter house. Before she so much as had the chance to draw breath, her gaze moved involuntarily to fixate on the limestone giant in the center of the chilly room.

Her heartbeat quickened.

In the back of her mind, her rational self kicked and screamed and called her all sorts of really quite hurtful names, but Fil ignored them. To be honest, she barely heard them. Her ears rang with a strange, powerful buzzing noise, and her focus had condensed down into a kind of tunnel vision. The rest of reality faded away, leaving just the statue and the surge of adrenaline that propelled her toward it.

She'd experienced this same weirdness the first time

she'd seen the sculpture, but she'd tried to ignore it. That glimpse had been brief, just enough for her to report back to Ella that she had verified the item's existence and its location.

Even then, she'd felt an odd compulsion to look closer, to stare, even to touch, but it had been the middle of the day, and the abbey had buzzed with the activity of employees and tourists. Even behind the scenes in the storage areas only someone with her credentials could easily gain access. Fil had forced herself to leave, to push the fascination to the back of her mind and go about her business.

That had been two and a half days ago. By this afternoon, she'd felt like a junkie detoxing from a long and brutal high. Her skin had buzzed and crawled, her attention had constantly wandered, and she'd vibrated with some kind of restless energy that had urged her— hell, it had *compelled* her—to return to the abbey, to get one more look at the statue that had her old friend in what had sounded like a heck of a tizzy.

Shadows drifted past Fil as she slowly crossed the room. In the dark silence, even the cushy rubber soles of her boots made quiet padding noises against the polished marble tiles. The stillness made her soft breaths echo in her own ears, but she continued to move forward. She couldn't stop.

Maybe she should have asked Ella a few more questions when her friend had first called, part of Fil acknowledged. Maybe her friend knew something about the statue that would explain this weird power it seemed to have over her. Then again, how exactly would Fil have phrased that question?

So this gargoyle you're looking for, she could imagine herself saying. *It wouldn't happen to have freaky magical powers, or the ability to devour human souls, would it?*

Sure. That would have made her sound perfectly sane.

Of course, there was always the possibility that insanity would serve her well when she went on trial. Maybe if she pulled it off, the judge would just lock her in a loony bin for a couple of years instead of throwing her into prison.

Look on the bright side, right?

Insanity might be the only logical explanation for why she was here, creeping illegally around a semi-operational historic monastery in the dead of night just to get a private, uninterrupted look at a piece of art that really wasn't all that artful.

Medievalism had never been a favorite style of Fil's. As a professional art restorationist, she'd studied or worked on creations from various historical eras, though admittedly her work focused on paintings, rather than sculpture.

Still, even paintings from the medieval era didn't float her boat. The figures were too stylized; they lacked the realism and dimension that the Renaissance had brought to the medium. And while she was hardly an expert in sculpture of the period, even less in architectural statuary, she'd never been a fan. Religious figures, gargoyles, and grotesques, she thought, looked fine on Gothic cathedrals, but she'd always spent more time looking at the murals inside the buildings than the carvings outside.

So why did this one seem to have captured all her attention?

She approached the base of the statue, the enormous hunk of slate-colored granite that served as the figure's pedestal, and wished she dared to turn on the lights. Better not to advertise her presence, but there was barely enough illumination coming in through the room's stained-glass windows to navigate through the dark. She felt like one giant stubbed toe just waiting to happen.

Her eyes had adjusted as well as they were likely to, so Fil circled the stone platform, trying to find the angle that shed the most light on the subject of her fascination. She found it mostly by accident, when she tripped over her own feet and caught herself by shooting a hand out to brace against the granite. Instinctively, her gaze flicked up, and she stared right into the figure's smooth, blank eyes.

Darkness hid the fine details from her, but she could make out the sharp angles of a square jaw and high, slanted cheekbones. The artist had posed his subject more like a classical archangel than a monstrous demon, slim hips clad in the kind of paneled kilt most often seen in gladiator movies, his body poised straight and tall with a spear held in one hand. He looked like Michael poised for battle, the way she'd seen the head of God's armies depicted in a thousand Italian masterpieces.

You know, if she ignored the claws. And the fangs. And the way his legs, jointed like a stag's, ended in giant raptor's talons. Just those few, pesky details.

Even the statue's enormous, mostly furled wings appeared more angelic than demonic. Heavily creased and carved as if to denote the presence of feathers, the top joints rose above the figure's head while the trailing ends rested on the pedestal by its heels. She imagined that if the things had been real, the way they stirred the air would have more in common with a tornado than a gentle spring breeze.

Whatever church or fortress this guy had once protected, Fil figured it had stayed safe and sound from the forces of evil. Unless, of course, evil had been really, really stupid.

The itching in her palms intensified, until it felt more like a burning than anything else. She rubbed the skin together to try to ease the sensation, but it didn't help; nothing did. Not until she reached out and laid her palm flat against the cool, smooth stone.

Fil jerked at the contact, an involuntary gasp torn from her lips. It felt like she'd just licked a nine-volt battery, the sweet shock of electricity making her pulse race. And didn't that just add to the bizarreness of this whole situation? Not only was she inexplicably drawn to an inanimate hunk of stone, but said hunk made her feel like she'd just plugged into an electrical outlet designed specifically for her. There had to be a reason for it, for all of it. She just wasn't sure she was going to like it.

You have to look. The little voice in her head sounded too much like an obnoxious younger sibling to be ignored, and Fil should know; she'd been trying for years to pretend her instincts didn't yammer at her all the live-long day. *There's only one logical explanation. You know that. This statue has to be special. Now take a look, and see.*

The tight clenching beneath her breastbone should have been enough proof of what was going on, but Fil looked anyway. Taking a deep breath, she briefly closed her eyes so that she could open her sight. When she lifted her lids, the truth shone back at her.

The sculpture glowed.

It didn't cast a single shadow, and it didn't make anything else in the room easier to see, because the only one who would be able to detect the light was Fil. At least she assumed so; she'd lived for twenty-seven years, after all, and she'd never met a single other person with a talent quite like hers.

Fil could "see" energy. She'd heard some people call it seeing auras, but she didn't like that term. The energy she saw wasn't the normal kind that surrounded every living thing in some sort of ethereal nimbus of colored light. She could see that if she wanted to, but she'd learned almost before she could read that blocking out that kind of everyday energy was the best way to stay sane.

No, what Fil saw when she lowered her barriers and *looked* was special energy, the kind that not everyone had; and she saw it in things, too, like the statue. She'd never quite decided what to call it, mostly settling on *energy* for lack of a better term, but it was the stuff that emanated from unusual people and objects—people like her friend Ella, who had always struggled so hard to hold it back.

People like herself, if she bothered to look in a mirror, or her grandmother's elderly aunt, who had always known who was coming to the door before the bell rang. The energy came from people with special abilities, and very rarely it came from an object with a special history.

She'd seen it come from objects only a couple of times in her life. Once it had clung to a blessed crucifix that her grandmother's mother had brought with her to Canada when her family had fled Lithuania. The silver necklace had shone gently, even in the pitch dark, making Fil rethink her brief foray into atheism.

The second time she had seen the energy, she'd been making her way slowly through an exhibit at the British Museum, viewing items unearthed from an ancient Saxon burial hoard. The medallion had been carved with beautiful images of horses and hounds, and the etched lines had given off a light so brightly golden that she'd nearly reached for her sunglasses before coming to her senses and closing off that inner eye of hers.

Neither of those objects had glowed like this statue.

It wasn't the volume of the blue-white light that had Fil's breath catching in her throat; it was the intensity. Somehow this light felt almost powerful. She couldn't think of the words to describe it, but despite its relative dimness, it seemed to vibrate or pulse with restrained force.

Shifting her fingers, Fil realized the tingling in her palms had faded and the buzzing drone in her ears had stopped as if it had never been there. Suddenly she could hear everything: the soft puffs of her own breath, the tapping of a tree branch against one of the far windows. The rustling of fabric against fabric near the entry door.

Realization slammed down like a hammer. She was no longer alone.

She spun into a half crouch, ready to flee in a rush of pure animal instinct. Her gaze had no trouble picking out the source of her panic, mostly because he, too, lit up against the shadows. Unlike the icy blue of the statue's light, though, the stranger glowed with a sick, muddy-red color that pulsed and throbbed like an open wound in the darkness. The color hit Fil's senses like a bad smell, making her lip curl and her throat tighten. Whoever this was, he had not a single good intention. Quite possibly, he never had.

"Well." The low hiss cut through the stillness and raised the hairs on the back of Fil's neck. "I hadn't planned on another little thief in the night here. But no matter. I'll be long gone by the time anyone finds a body in the rubble."

Fil couldn't tell if the dark figure was talking to her or to himself, but it didn't matter. She was moving before the question had time to form. Instinct pushed her forward, fast, and she ducked around the corner of the gargoyle's pedestal at a velocity she hadn't achieved since she'd gotten her last speeding ticket.

Light flashed in the shadows near where the stranger had spoken, and in the next instant the marble sill of the window just beyond where Fil had stood a second before shattered and crumbled to the ground.

Holy shit! Was the guy packing a grenade launcher?

She pressed her back against the cool stone of the pedestal and decided maybe prison didn't sound so bad after all. At least if she were in prison, she'd be alive, and out of this maniac's line of fire.

"Hmm, another surprise." The voice grated like metal on china. "I don't think I like surprises. How did you see that coming, little girl? Is there anything you'd like to tell me about yourself? Hmmm?"

The words ended on a high, sharp giggle that made Fil's stomach lurch. Seriously, this guy sounded like a certifiable psycho lunatic. Maybe she should think about calling it a night here and heading home, freaky-compelling statue be damned.

Too bad Mr. Crazypants was blocking the only doorway out. He moved farther into the room but kept himself between Fil and the exit.

"The Hierophant only told me to smash the Guardian," the stranger mused aloud. He seemed happy enough talking to himself—or maybe his imaginary friend—and Fil had no intention of making herself easier to find by engaging the nutjob in conversation. "He never mentioned I might find a prize to bring him. No, no, no. But yes! Bring the man a prize and win a prize myself! If he's pleased, he might ask the Master to reward me."

Okay, it was one thing to read about people with serious mental illnesses, and another still to see them in documentaries on television; but to have one stalking her in real life was a bit more than Fil had bargained for. This man scared her—his voice, his actions, his aura, that not-in-any-conceivable-way-right laugh, they all set her nerves on edge. In a flash of insight she understood—all the way to her toes—where the term *spine-chilling* had come from. She felt like someone had just replaced her cerebral spinal fluid with ice water.

"Little girl," the man called, his voice singsong and creepy beyond measure. "Come out, little girl. I've got a piece of candy for you."

That sent him into a fit of giggles that had Fil's stomach churning inside her.

"Candy is dandy, little girl. Or maybe—" He paused, and she could hear the faint whisper of movement.

When he spoke again, the sound was closer. "Maybe you're a little mouse, skittering through the dark looking for crumbs."

Holding her breath, Fil eased to the side and caught a glimpse of the muddy-rusty glow emanating from the stranger. He had definitely gotten closer, but he was sticking to the sides of the room, keeping the thick stone walls at his back. She realized that the faint rustling sound she heard from him came from the long, dark costume he wore, a fall of voluminous fabric like a monk's robes. It disguised his shape and, Fil realized, could have obscured any number of things in its folds. Hell, the man actually *could* be packing a grenade launcher under that thing, and she'd never be able to tell.

The madman moved again, and she ducked back behind her cover. The guy was getting closer all the time. Fat lot of good it did her, though. Insane the man might be, but he was clever enough to approach on the side closest to her hiding place. She still couldn't get to the door without passing way too close to him for comfort.

Bugger. How did she always manage to get herself into these positions?

The man giggled again. "A little church mouse. That's it. Mice don't want candy. Church mouse wants cheese! Come out, come out, little mouse, and Henry will give you a nice big chunk of cheese to nibble on. Hee hee!"

Fil shivered. This just kept getting better and better.

She gathered herself into a crouch, keeping her legs under her so she could move fast if she got the chance. Up, down, sideways, through a dimensional portal, she didn't much care which direction at the moment. The only way that mattered was away. Leaning forward, she reassessed the situation.

She could see the man lit by his aura of twisted menace standing in front of an alcove approximately twenty-five feet ahead of her and to the right. The gargoyle loomed between them, offering Fil a decent amount of cover for the moment, but she knew it wouldn't last, especially if the lunatic took another shot at her.

Part of her wanted to pretend that the man had blasted in her direction with some kind of weapon, like a pistol or a sawed-off shotgun—or a rocket-propelled grenade launcher, given the crater in the windowsill—but she knew better. A couple of quick glimpses of that nasty light swirling around him told her that the only thing the crazy man had attempted to harm her with was magic.

And wasn't that just a kick in the teeth?

Of all the special abilities Fil had glimpsed in the auras of the people she met, she'd never seen anything quite like this. She'd never seen energy used as a weapon before. She hadn't known it was possible. Ella's abilities might have been the closest to this stranger's, but whatever Ella had, she'd never discussed it with Fil, and it had always appeared to come from inside her somewhere, as if it were woven into the fabric of her being. This man's aura was rooted inside him, but like some kind of invasive plant species it grew out of control the minute it pushed past the surface. It twined around him, feeding not on the faint bits of rust-colored light that surrounded him, but on the darkness.

The wrongness of it seeped into Fil's bones and made her shudder. She had to get out of here. If the loon kept circling, she might be able to seize a second's worth of opportunity. Gathering herself into a desperate ball of fear and muscle, she prepared to make a break for it.

"Naughty, naughty, stubborn little mousy. If I can't charm you out, I suppose I'll have to harm you out. Ha!"

Instinct sent her flying, helped along by a hefty shot of adrenaline. She leapt not back under cover but forward, throwing herself out of the firing line of the man's next bolt of malevolent energy. She could almost swear she felt it singe the soles of her boots before it blasted off the corner of the gargoyle statue's enormous pedestal.

And then the world shifted, because the statue suddenly stopped being a statue. In its place stood a seven-foot-tall stone-skinned warrior with a spear in his hand and fire in his eyes. The creature spread his wings and let out a bellow that knocked Fil straight onto her ass and made the crazy stalker across from her scream like a little girl.

Hm, Fil thought hazily as the world went a little bit fuzzy, *I wonder if they'll let me have paints and canvas in the psych ward?*

Chapter Two

Danger!

His senses screamed a moment before the sleep left him, and in that instant he battled fiercely against the immobilizing chains of the magic that forced his slumber.

The helplessness tormented him and confused him. This was not the way he woke. He recalled other stirrings, remembered the gray haze of sleep, followed by the instant rush of awareness, the way he sprang into motion almost before his vision cleared. That was the way a Guardian awoke, with an explosion of power and might. This slow and agonizing slog toward awareness would kill him; and with his death the Darkness would grow even stronger.

His hearing came back first, what seemed like an eternity before the fog that clouded his vision began to dissipate. He could make out the sound of a male voice, thick with glee and evil, even while the words eluded him. He didn't need to understand to recognize the Darkness in them. It poured from the male like the thick stench of sulfur, fetid and cloying, the mark of a dedicated servant. But he could smell nothing darker, nothing like the charred rot of the truly demonic.

If none of the Seven had appeared to pose a threat to humanity, why had he awoke? The *nocturnis,* those who served the Darkness, could be dealt with by the Guild; they didn't require a Guardian to intervene. Something was not right here.

Awareness began to rush back. He began to see shadows through his hazy vision, and his hearing returned to full acuity. Now he could detect the faint stirring of breath and cloth somewhere very close to him, on the ground below his feet. He drew a breath and smelled something fresh and sweet, entirely at odds with the stench of evil that surrounded the male voice.

Spar frowned—for he was called Spar, he remembered now, fourth among his brothers—and inhaled again. It was female, he realized, female and human, and when the bite of fear came to him, he knew it was in danger.

"Naughty, naughty, stubborn little mousy." The evil one spoke, his voice screeching with a madness that drove Spar to fury. "If I can't charm you out, I suppose I'll have to harm you out. Ha!"

At once movement flashed from two directions, and Spar's vision cleared in time to see a bolt of defiled magic blast from the hands of the *nocturnis*. It grazed the edge of his pedestal and impacted the wall behind with a quaking boom. At the same time, a blur of motion, all dark clothing and moon-bright hair, dove away from the very point of impact and tumbled hard into the adjacent wall.

Without thought, Spar roared his battle cry and sprang off his perch into the air. His wings spread, muscles stretching for the first time in centuries, and he could feel their tips brushing the walls of the confined space. Spear in hand, he hovered just below the ceiling and saw the wave of terror and hatred flow across the *nocturnis*'s features.

Good. The man should tremble and cower in the face of a Guardian's rage. A single human, no matter how much power he drew from the Darkness, was no match for one of the warrior protectors in the midst of his battle frenzy.

The *nocturnis* might be outmatched, but Spar still expected him to put up a fight. He almost looked forward to dodging a few futile spells cast in his direction, but instead of going on the defensive, the corrupt human screeched something in the foul tongue of Dark magic and flung a hand out in the direction of the dazed female.

Spar bellowed in outrage, the sound nearly drowning out the shocked cry of the female human. He saw how she raised a hand to protect herself, but the *nocturnis*'s spell would not be denied. It blasted into her palm with a burst of muddy-red energy that made the woman's pale skin glow as if lit from within. Spar could see muscles and veins and the tiniest, most delicate bones he could ever have imagined for a chilling instant. Then the light went out, and the female hissed as if she'd been burned.

Rage welled within him, unexpected but undeniable. Only a worm would seek to harm a woman when a warrior stood before him in challenge. Of course,

Spar should expect no better from a minion of the enemy.

He drew back his spear, prepared to skewer the rodent where he stood. The cry stopped him.

"Is that a fucking *bomb*?"

The female had clutched her injured left hand to her chest, but her horrified gaze was fixed on the *nocturnis* and the strange bundle the man had withdrawn from beneath his robes. The item meant nothing to Spar, who saw a messy handful of colored wires, metal, and plastic, but the expression on the female's face told him she perceived it as a threat even before the word *bomb* registered. He understood this word. Even if the Guardians had never used so cowardly a weapon, he had lived centuries enough to have witnessed the destruction such things could cause.

"Hierophant wants the Guardian smashed!" The servant's cry rang with madness, and Spar could see the sick fire of it in his eyes. "Should have smashed the cold, cold stone. But the mousy made me forget!"

Hands fumbled with the misshapen bundle until an ominous click sounded and the pale green face of a digital clock began to glow.

"Holy shit!" The woman scrambled to her feet, her gaze darting between the minion's bomb and the Guardian warrior hovering above the floor. "I did not sign up to die tonight, damn it, and I refuse to wind up a feature on the morning news. I am *outta here*!"

Spar had had centuries to study the ways of humanity. He had, after all, been created to protect them from the Darkness; but in all his long existence, he had never witnessed a member of the race behave with quite so much foolish courage. Without an instant of hesitation, the small, fair-haired female tucked her head, rounded her shoulders, and launched herself straight at the cultist and his destructive device.

She might very well have gotten herself killed. Should have gotten herself killed, he reasoned even as he found himself diving after her. She reached the madman a moment before Spar's arms closed around her, and the force of her tackle knocked the *nocturnis* off his feet. The man went stumbling into the nearest window ledge, and the device in his hands tumbled free to skitter across the marble floor. It landed near the base of Spar's pedestal with a series of sharp beeps and the rapid flashing of green lights.

The female in his arms shouted an oath and attempted to free herself from his grip, but Spar was having none of it. He held tight even as her tiny hands beat frantically against his chest.

"Let me go, you giant idiot! That thing's about to blow!"

The high-pitched squeal of the cultist emphasized the truth of that prediction. Somehow the bomb's timer had been accelerated when the *nocturnis* had dropped it. Detonation was imminent.

"Hold on," he growled. There was no time for anything else.

He had no way of knowing how powerful a weapon the cultist might have devised, but he gathered it was strong enough that it had been expected to shatter his immobile form into rubble. It was a cowardly, dastardly plan to destroy an enemy in such a vulnerable state, but it might actually have worked. Locked in his sleep, a

Guardian had all the vulnerabilities of the stone form he resembled. Fortunately, something had awoken Spar before the plan could be carried out. A fully awoken Guardian was one hell of a lot harder to kill.

Before he had even finished his warning to the small human, he had drawn her hard and tight against his chest and dragged her down to the floor with him. Folding himself in around her, he shielded her with his body and wrapped them both tight in the shelter of his wings.

His feathers hadn't even settled before the explosion shook the foundations of the building.

Spar had his eyes closed against the potential debris, but he heard the deafening boom and felt the initial shock wave buffet him in a blast of scalding air. Shrapnel, some from the bomb, some from the destruction of the room around them, thudded and pinged off his wings and the bits of stony hide it managed to penetrate. He smelled the sharp tang of burned feathers, chipped stone, and blood, as well as something bitter and chalky that he assumed was the explosive itself. It filled his head and coated the back of his throat, and he rumbled his displeasure.

In his arms, the female had frozen like a startled deer. He could feel her heart pounding against her breast, could smell her shock and terror. It sparked something inside him, something fierce and protective and somehow different from his basic drive to perform his duty. This feel wasn't about protecting humans; it was about protecting *this* human, and to do that he needed to get them out of this space and away from the *nocturnis*. Quickly.

He didn't pause to think. He simply opened his eyes

to the gaping hole in the building's ruined wall and launched himself into the night. As the cool air rushed over him, rustling the tips of his feathers, he heard the wail of sirens and the hoarse cries of humans hurrying to the scene of destruction.

Whatever they decided to make of the blast site and the cultist who had devised it, Spar didn't care. He had the human in his grasp. Getting her to safety was his first priority. After that, he could start asking questions. For example, who in the name of the Light was she?

And how had she awoken him from 250 years of sleep?

They're coming to take me away, ho ho, hee hee, ha ha, to the funny farm . . .

Fil hummed the words in her head and clutched hard at the thick muscles currently holding her suspended over the streets of Montreal. Since it would be her new theme song, she supposed she might as well start practicing. Insanity, after all, was the only way to explain the events of the last thirty minutes.

Raging insanity, in the case of the final five, because that was how long ago she estimated an impossible animated work of art had swept her up into its arms and launched itself into a flight path she felt certain had not been cleared with Nav Canada. Because wouldn't that be an interesting filing?

Nav Canada, this is Gargoyle One. We are ready for takeoff from l'Abbaye Saint-Thomas l'Apôst. Please confirm.

Roger, Gargoyle One. You are third in line for departure. Begin flapping at twenty-to-twenty-five wing beats per minute.

The snort escaped without her permission, puffing against the smooth, stone-textured skin under her cheek. If she was going to lose her mind, at least she could maintain her sense of humor about it. That might help her adjust to the secure ward they'd likely place her in. She could giggle her way between her doses of medication.

Provided, of course, that this really did turn out to be a hallucination. Fil supposed she shouldn't discount the possibility that she had in actuality just been kidnapped by the statue of a monster come to life. It wouldn't be the only strange thing that had ever happened to her.

The strangest, sure, but after you grew up being able to see when a person's words didn't match the intentions in their energy, you learned to keep an open mind. So if she had landed in the clutches of the bogeyman, she might still end up as table scraps in some sort of demonic landfill. You know, after the fiend had finished sucking the marrow from her bones.

Either way, she could think of at least a dozen ways she'd rather spend the next few years of her life, and they all hinged on her being alive. As well as in full possession of all her mental faculties.

At the moment, those faculties had begun to warn her about a change in altitude. She had barely enough time to squeak and clutch harder at the one in charge of those things before she felt a gentle bump. The sensation of motion halted, and her boots touched the ground beneath her. Followed closely by her jeans-clad ass when her knees buckled, her legs refusing to hold her up in the face of systemic shock.

"Are you hurt?"

Fil looked up reflexively. Above her—way, way above her—a surprisingly human voice emerged from the face of what looked like a monster. Admittedly, the voice rumbled about an octave below bass and managed to make James Earl Jones sound like a soprano, but it spoke easily and fluently and not at all like a slavering beast. In fact, something inside her relaxed at the sound of it, releasing at least a little of the tension that had her tied in knots that should have earned some Boy Scout his merit badge.

Of course, that still left a whole boatload of tension.

Fil shook her head. "I'm not hurt. I might very well have lost my ever-loving mind, but physically I'm just peachy."

Despite the cold damp seeping into the seat of her pants, she realized she spoke the truth. She felt fine, not as if she'd been caught in the middle of a bomb blast at all. Her legs still resembled limp rubber bands, which was why she hadn't bothered trying to get to her feet yet, but she couldn't detect so much as a scratch on the rest of her. Somehow, she didn't think she could chalk all that up to the protective characteristics of worn jeans and a battered leather jacket, either. The figure that loomed above her deserved the credit.

"You protected me from the explosion," she said, frowning up at him. "I should be asking you if you're hurt, not the other way around."

The creature made an impatient gesture. "I am unharmed. Such a paltry attack caused no more than a few minor abrasions to my hide. A Guardian is designed to withstand much worse."

"A Guardian? Is that what you are? I'd have gone

with figment of my imagination, personally, but I suppose you'd be the expert."

Fil shivered, and thought vaguely that chills were one of the symptoms of shock. The fact that she might be going into it proved somehow reassuring and terrifying at the same time. On the one hand, if she could experience shock, she might not have lost her mind, which meant that everything she had just experienced was real.

On the other hand, it meant everything she had just experienced was *real*; and that in turn meant that she was currently sitting on the ground in the middle of a field having a conversation with something that should not even have existed.

Holy hell.

"I am one of the seven Guardians of the Light," the not-figment confirmed. When he hunkered down on his beast-like legs, she could see the serious expression gracing his stern, inhuman features. "What I am curious to know, however, is why you have awoken me from my slumber, little human, and in what manner you were able to accomplish it."

Fil snorted. "You're asking me? Buddy, I'm not even sure I know my own name anymore, so I am not the girl to go to for answers. You'd get more out of that tree over there."

"You are injured." The creature scowled and reached out with a surprisingly gentle claw to lift her face to the light. "Where is your wound? How badly does it pain you?"

"I told you, I'm not hurt. I'm fine."

"Are you? What about your hand?"

The reminder caught Fil off guard, and the throbbing sensation in her palm that she'd almost forgotten returned in a rush of hot discomfort. *Great*. She'd been happier when her subconscious had blocked out that feeling in favor of more immediate concerns.

Not that having a limb feel like it had been stung by five thousand angry bees was an easy thing to forget, but a lot had happened in the last couple of hours. Fil had been a little preoccupied with flying over the city sans airplane to worry about a flesh wound, until her erstwhile rescuer brought it up again.

She recalled seeing the maniac in the robe turn on her when the gargoyle confronted it. Throwing her hands up to shield her face had been pure instinct. She hadn't known what the bastard had planned, but after the havoc he'd already wreaked in the chapter house the bolt of Dark energy shouldn't have surprised her, especially when she had so many other surprises to contend with.

Looking down at her left hand, she could see no evidence of the magical blow she'd inadvertently warded off. The sensation of swelling, heat, and stabbing needles wasn't supported by outward appearances. Her skin looked unmarred, the back of her hand smooth and pale in the dim starlight. Even her palm appeared fine—at worst a little pink in the middle where she'd felt the point of impact.

She shook her head and pushed aside the concern. "My hand is fine, and it's not even the one I paint with. Right now I'm a little more worried about my mental state. Unless you can offer some sort of logical explanation for your existence, statue boy."

For the first time in her life, Fil got to see what it looked like to actually ruffle someone's feathers. The giant next to her shifted his wings in what struck her as a gesture of irritation, creating a whisper of breeze in the air.

"I am no statue," he growled, the tip of one fang flashing as his lip curled. "I told you, I am a Guardian, defender of humanity against the evil of the Darkness. My sleeping form may resemble something carved by human hands, but I can assure you my brothers and I are entirely different."

"Guardian. Darkness. Brothers," Fil repeated. "I recognize those words, but I have the feeling they do not mean what I think they mean."

She shivered hard, as if she'd been lifted by the scruff of the neck like a puppy and shaken. She was definitely suffering from shock. What she wouldn't give for an EMT with a survival blanket. Hell, at this point she doubted she'd argue too hard against a nice white coat with buckles in the back. She was freezing.

Next to her, the monster—statue, Guardian, whatever—frowned and reached toward her. Instinct had her pulling back warily, but instead of grabbing her he simply draped a layer of heavy wool over her shoulders and tucked it carefully around her. Since he wore about as much as your average Chippendales dancer, she had no idea where he'd gotten such a thing, but she just pulled it tighter and decided not to ask. When you were wondering about how huge chunks of rock managed to come to life and start talking, somehow the origins of a little blanket seemed less important.

"Thanks, Rocky," she murmured, eyeing him warily.

"Now, unless you're planning to whip out some graham crackers and marshmallows and build us a nice little campfire, how about you define those words that seem to be tripping me up."

"My name is Spar. I am neither called Rocky nor made of rock. I am a Guardian, one of those warriors who were summoned to battle against the seven demons of the Darkness and to prevent their possible return to this human plane of existence. I consider the others of my kind to be my brothers."

Above the fiery blackness of his eyes, his brows drew together, and Fil couldn't help providing the mental sound effect of stone scraping against stone. No matter what he said, he sure looked like he'd been carved straight out of a rock. A voice in the back of her head pointed out that despite the hardness of his muscles, his tough skin had felt way too warm and intriguing to be stone. She ignored it.

"The Darkness is . . ." He paused and shook his head. "It is the Darkness. It is that which devours the Light. Humans have called it evil, but that word is simple. It does not encompass the whole truth. Darkness is evil, but it is evil so pure and so deep that it creates an entire absence of good. Good cannot exist in the Darkness, not even to struggle against it. It is consumed to fuel the spread of the enemy. Nothing can exist within it. Not life itself."

Fil felt his words sink in. This time when she shivered, it had very little to do with shock. It was a visceral reaction to the total annihilation of existence she'd just heard described.

"That sounds . . . nasty," she finally said, tugging her

blanket tighter. "But, um, I'm not sure it explains how you managed to be a statue one minute and a—a—a . . . a *you* the next."

Spar didn't get the chance to respond. Under the blanket, a chime started, a ringing of bells that wouldn't have sounded out of place at the abbey they had recently left behind. Fil's phone was ringing.

Habit had her reaching into her pocket and glancing at the screen to see who was calling. When she read the name at the top of the window, she nearly laughed. Tapping the ANSWER key, she held the phone up to her ear and narrowed her eyes.

"Well, well, well," she purred, her gaze still fixed on her stony companion. "If it isn't Miss Ella Harrow, my old pal. What's new, El?"

"Fil! Thank God I got you!" Ella sounded as if she'd just discovered a tornado was coming and her friend was her only ride out of town. "I just saw the news. They said there was an explosion at the Abbey of St. Thomas. They thought it might be a bombing. Isn't that where you told me they had the gargoyle statue?"

"Yup. That's the place."

"Oh, God, Fil, please, please don't tell me the statue was destroyed! Do you know? Have you heard anything?"

Fil heard the urgency in her friend's voice and felt something click into place. All her feelings that there was something weird about the statue had obviously been right on the money, and now she had a pretty good idea that Ella had known more than she'd let on. The other woman sounded more like she was trying to find out if someone she knew had been injured in an explosion than like she was checking up on a work of art she thought might be related to one she had formerly curated.

"Have I heard anything about what, El?" she asked. "About the explosion? Well, I haven't seen the news, but that might be because I was there when the bomb went off. Or maybe I was just distracted by finding out that the statue you asked me to locate turned out not to be a statue at all."

She heard her friend gasp and managed a narrow smile.

"By the way, Spar says hello. And I say, Ella, you've got some 'splainin' to do."

Chapter Three

For a moment, the only sounds Fil could make out were the chirps of insects and the beating of her own heart. Then Ella let out a deep breath and whispered into the phone.

"He's awake, isn't he?"

Fil felt a flush of irritation. Since Ella couldn't see her, she glared at Spar instead, which was almost as good.

"Yes, Ella. He's awake. He's not logically possible, of course, but he's up and moving, his name is Spar, apparently, and a few minutes ago he grabbed me and flew me across the city to what looks like one of the islands in the Saint Lawrence. So now might be a pretty good time to tell me what the hell is going on around here."

"This is really a conversation we should have in person."

"Well, I'm not exactly in a position to fly to BC at the moment, pal, so unless you happen to be paying an impromptu visit to my fair city, 'in person' is not going to happen. Now spill."

She heard a rustling noise, then what sounded like a muffled conversation in the background. After a moment, her friend came back with, "I need to see you, and there are things you need to see on my end, too. How soon can you get to a computer with Skype?"

"It's the twenty-first century, El, and I'm using a smartphone. You want to video chat, we can do that right here."

"All right. I'll call you right back."

The call disconnected, and Fil blew out a breath of frustration. "This is not the night I signed up for," she muttered, staring at her phone and waiting for the video call to come in.

"You are taking a telephone call?"

Spar asked the question in an even tone, but Fil could feel the disapproval behind the words, even if she hadn't been able to see the faint shadings of irritation in his aura.

"It's not like I'm chatting with my sorority sister about the latest style trends," she snapped. "Ella is the one who sent me looking for you in the first place, and it's becoming pretty damned clear she knew something about you before she did. Frankly, she owes me some downright heavy-duty explanations right about now."

He folded his arms over his chest and settled farther down on his haunches. "Your friend knows of my kind. Is she a Warden?"

"A what-den?"

"A member of the Guild," he added, as if that clarified things.

Fil rolled her eyes. "Two species separated by a common language," she paraphrased under her breath.

She nearly jumped when the phone in her hand chimed again. This time, when she answered the call, Ella's familiar face filled the screen.

"Okay, El," she bit out, staring into her friend's troubled gray eyes. "Now would be a really good time to tell me what the h-e-double-hockey-sticks is going on here."

"I will, Fil, I promise. But first there's something you need to see."

Before Felicity could protest, Ella shifted out of the picture and the camera panned over to focus on someone else. Or rather, something else.

The image on the screen halted Fil's breath in her throat. An angelic male face peered back at her with eyes blacker than pitch, lit from behind with a thousand fires. They made Fil think of lava flows, molten-red in the cracks, but topped with a crust of obsidian.

The eyes were set in a face that looked as if it had been carved from granite, and if that wasn't enough for her to make the connection, the skin like stone and the horns curving back from the rugged brow would have tipped her off. The man on the screen could have been Spar's brother. In fact, Fil would have bet a year of her life that was exactly who he was.

"His name is Kees." Ella's voice came from out of frame, but Fil had no trouble making out the words. "He's a—"

"A Guardian," Fil finished, feeling grim. "Let me guess. Could he possibly be the 'statue' that was supposedly stolen from the Vancouver Museum of Art and History just a few short weeks ago?"

Ella shifted back into the picture, sharing the space with the enormous creature beside her. Something in the way the woman leaned against the Guardian's massive chest sent a stirring of something through Fil, but she ignored it. She had bigger things to worry about right now.

"He is," Ella confirmed with a nod. "But I think you know by now that Kees was never a statue. Not really. He was just sleeping."

"Yeah, it sounds like there was a lot of that going around." She sighed and shook her head. "Well, let me be the one to get the reunion started. Kees, this is Spar. Spar, I have a feeling you know Kees."

Fil handed the phone to the creature beside her. Another time, she might have laughed at the way his giant hands fumbled with the small piece of technology, but her head had begun to ache way too much to risk it. The way she felt right now, the damned thing might explode on her at the smallest chuckle.

Spar scowled down into the screen, moving the phone back and forth toward his face as if trying to zoom in the picture. "Kees? Is that you, my brother?"

"It is," the other Guardian snarled. "For the sake of the Light, will you hold still before you make us both dizzy?"

"You look so small. I can hardly see that it is you. Why do you not come closer so that I might view you more easily?"

"I am on the other side of the continent at the moment, my friend," Kees explained. "What you see is a transmission of my image. This technology is new to you, I take it. When was the last time you woke?"

"They told me the year was 1789. A great human slaughter began that fed one of the Seven too well. It began to stir, and I was summoned to send it back to its prison."

"I trust you succeeded, for I was never called to aid you. Were any of the others?"

"Of course not. I handled it myself, as I was charged to do." Fil watched as Spar's expression grew even more fierce. "What is the meaning of this, brother? Why have both of us awoken together? Why have I awoken at all? I cannot feel the presence of one of the Seven. The Darkness poses no immediate threat of escape from its shackles. So what is going on?"

"That's what I'd like to know." Fil stepped forward and laid her hand over Spar's, directing the camera until it captured both of their images. "I don't care who explains it to me, El, you or your pal there, but I definitely want to know what's going on and why my new reality has to stretch to include talking statues and terms like *the Darkness,* with a capital *D.*"

"It's a really long story."

Fil glanced at the clock on her phone and raised an eyebrow. "Well, El, it's two twenty-seven in the morning, and I seem to be sitting the middle of a provincial park with a creature out of a book of fairy tales, so quite frankly I can't think of anyplace else I need to be at the moment. Start talking."

Spar watched the human female—Fil, her friend had called her, though he found the masculine name ridiculous—as she listened to her friend relate the story of his kind. He found her face fascinating. Each of her thoughts passed over it in succession. Perhaps it was the purity of her features that made them so easy to read, for she had the finely drawn look of a Madonna: small, straight nose, clear brow, rounded cheeks, and a mouth like Cupid's bow. Her skin could pass for porcelain in the faint illumination of her mobile phone, and her wide green eyes bore a fringe of lashes a hundred shades darker than her pale-blond hair. She looked like walking innocence. Of course, Spar acknowledged to himself, when she opened her mouth she sounded like something entirely different.

He studied her while the one called Ella repeated a familiar tale. Thousands of years ago in the face of great evil, a group of powerful magic users—mages—banded together to summon forth a power capable of defeating the demons who formed the Darkness. Seven immortal warriors were called, one for each of the demons they would combat, and the mages named them the Guardians, because their purpose was to guard humanity from the servants of evil.

The mages quickly learned, however, that the Seven demons of the Darkness could not be entirely destroyed. They were formed from the Dark itself, and so would exist forever in the same way that the Light would exist forever. In order to contain them, they were separated from one another to prevent them from feeding on one another's power, and each was banished to a desolate plane where they were imprisoned.

Knowing of the potential for the Seven to return, the mages made the decision to remain united and form the Guild of Wardens in order to monitor the ongoing threat from the Darkness. They gathered and shared knowledge of the enemy, assisted the Guardians with tools and support needed to battle, and monitored the activities of humans seduced or enslaved by Dark powers. The Wardens bore the ultimate responsibility for alerting the Guardians when they needed to rise and face a renewed threat, and they also acted to send the warriors back to sleep when the threat was vanquished. Even during those periods of slumber, the Guild remained vigilant against the forces of the Darkness.

"That's the way it's supposed to work," Ella concluded, "but Kees and I have discovered a problem. A big one."

"We believe the *nocturnis* have developed a new strategy," Kees explained. "Ella and I discovered that over a year ago, a fire destroyed the headquarters of the Guild of Wardens in Paris. Twenty-three of the members, including most of the inner council, died in the blaze."

Shock tore Spar's attention from the intriguing human to his brother's image on the small screen. "Impossible. You are mistaken, brother. Fire could never destroy those who can shape it to their will."

Kees set his jaw. "It can if Dark magic fans the flames. The human authorities were eager to label the fire accidental, the fault of antiquated wiring in a historic building, but you and I know that such accidents do not befall the Wardens. We know the *nocturnis* must have been behind it. But that is not the end of the story.

"When I awoke in this time, I tried to seek out my own Warden," Kees continued, "the descendant of the family that served at my side for more than a thousand years. Ella and I found that he, too, had been murdered."

A chill of foreboding and the heat of rage clashed in

Spar's chest. "You believe the *nocturnis* are hunting the members of the Guild."

"We know they are." Ella's voice sounded grim and touched with pain. "We managed to track down one remaining Warden in the northwestern United States, and he confirmed our suspicions. For at least the past five years, the Guild has been aware of an increase in the activity of minor fiends all over the world. It was clear that the Order was behind it all."

Fil interrupted with a frown. "The Order?"

"The Order of Eternal Darkness," Ella said. "It's the formal name for the group we refer to as the *nocturnis*. The Guild discovered that the Order had been making a vast push to expand, not just inducting members into its established sects, but founding new ones as well. Dozens of them. Maybe more. They monitored the situation, of course, but they waited too long to act, because that's when the Wardens began dying."

Spar uttered an oath in a language that had been dead more than a thousand years. It didn't help.

"Go on," he bit out. Hearing the story stabbed at him like a poisoned blade, but he needed to hear it. He needed to know the extent of the threat he faced, because this, he reasoned, must be the summons that had awoken him.

"The first few to die looked like accidents." Kees picked up the thread and continued. "Even though the casualties always seemed to be Wardens without immediate successors in place, the need to replace them never seemed quite urgent enough to worry anyone. Until Gregory Lascaux."

The bite of fury underlying his brother's tone provided the key to Spar's memory. Names could change over the centuries, but in this case he didn't think coincidence played a part.

"The Lascaux family once belonged to you," he said, watching Kees's expression in the phone. The mixture of anger and grief confirmed his suspicions.

"They did. Gregory was my personal Warden, though we met few times during his tenure. I thought things were too peaceful to need my attention. Instead I woke to find that the *nocturnis* had developed a new strategy to defeat us, one that involved dismantling our support network in order to weaken us."

Spar growled, long and low. It took concentration to keep his rage in check, especially when each new revelation landed like fuel on a blazing fire. "A cowardly plan that suits the craven nature of the corrupt ones. But they must realize even if destroying the Guild weakens us, we will still wake if the Seven stir. Not if every Warden on the earth were to die could a Guardian sleep through that."

"Maybe that's what made them decide to try to blow you up tonight while you were asleep."

Fil's words rang out like a bell in the silence. They cut through the thick blanket of anger and speculation and jabbed at Spar like an icy shard of truth.

He and Kees both turned to fix their gazes on her face, and he heard Ella curse softly in the background.

"Damn it, I was really hoping we were wrong about that," the woman said. "Fil, are you sure? Was there a bomb? Is that what happened tonight? Did someone deliberately try to blow up Spar? You have to tell us everything."

"Oh, there was a bomb all right. In fact, I think I might still have pieces of it in my hair."

Fil—oh, how Spar hated that name—reached up and ran a palm over her hair, then tugged at the long tail in which it was bound. He ignored the way his own fingers itched to follow the same path.

"I saw it as well," he said, at least partly to distract himself. "I am not well versed in such incendiary devices, but from the information I have absorbed from my Wardens through the years, I believe it was indeed a bomb."

"A pipe bomb, but a pretty damned powerful one."

"And the human who carried it was without a doubt a member of the Order. A fully inducted one. He wore one of their robes."

Kees cursed, and Fil eyed him curiously.

"There are levels of membership in evil?" she asked.

"The *nocturnis* go through training and indoctrination much as those who join the Guild would do," Spar said. "Their members might be evil inherently, but they are not born knowing how to channel the Darkness. It must be taught."

"Fair enough."

"Fil, you saw the guy, too, right? Are you certain he was targeting Spar?"

"He said he was. I mean, the guy was a stone cold babbling nutcase, El. He had diarrhea of the psychosis, or something. I think he was mostly talking to himself, but he said someone had told him to 'smash the Guard-
Of course, I had no idea what he meant, and my
must have distracted him. He obviously
there, and once he spotted me he

seemed more concerned with coming after me than setting the bomb."

"Did he say who gave him his instructions?"

Fil shook her head. "No, not that I remember. Not a name anyway. I think he called him by a title, though. Um . . . 'the Hierophant,' maybe?"

Ella frowned. "I don't know what that means."

Spar heard his fellow warrior hiss and knew Kees understood exactly what that meant, just as he did. Their eyes met in the video screen, and neither one looked pleased.

"*Hierophant* is a title," Kees confirmed. "It is given to the highest-ranking priest in the Order. In other words, if this cultist was sent by the Hierophant, it means he was ordered to destroy Spar by the head of the entire *nocturnis*."

"Why do you look worried by that?" Fil asked. "I thought you said you guys were immortal, and since Spar not only flew away from the blast in tip-top shape, but carried me with him while he did it, clearly a little bomb is not the way to get rid of one of you. Right?"

Kees shook his head. "Immortal does not mean invulnerable. We can be destroyed, though to do so is not easy. The problem is that we are at our most vulnerable while locked in our sleeping forms. That is one of the reasons why each Guardian was appointed a personal Warden, so that he would have someone watching his back during his slumber. While we sleep, our bodies react much like the stone we resemble. If that stone is broken to pieces, our essence is released from this plane and we cease to exist in this world."

"That's why knowing the *nocturnis* have been

bumping off the Wardens has us so freaked out," Ella said. "Not only is losing them a blow to our knowledge base, but with the Guild destroyed the Guardians become more and more vulnerable. At first, the destruction of the headquarters helped us—by burning out the library there, the *nocturnis* also destroyed any records of the last known locations of the seven Guardians. Still, they can't stay hidden forever. We've been trying to locate the other six—well, the other five now—in the hope that we can wake them up before the Order gets to them. Awake, a Guardian is next to impossible to kill, at least for anything less powerful than one of the Seven. While they're asleep, though, it's a whole different ball game."

Spar watched while understanding tightened Fil's features. She looked fierce when she grasped the gravity of the situation.

"So the fact that this Hierophant dude sent one of his evil minions to the abbey to off Spar means that the Order knew where he was." She nodded and fixed her friend with a sharp gaze. "Do you think they know where to find the others?"

"We have no real way of knowing," Ella said. "I hope not, because we're having a heck of a time finding them ourselves. Kees and I have made that our top priority, but without records it's slow going. We've been following leads to a few surviving Guild members in the hope that some of them will have information, but most of them have gone into hiding. They don't want the *nocturnis* to find them, and we're paying for that right alongside the bad guys."

Fil's eyes narrowed, and Spar noticed her knuckles turning white where she continued to grip the blanket around her shoulders. He could detect no real anger in her expression, but he could see a hint of suspicion and something else that tugged at him down in his gut. Something like vulnerability.

"You say 'we' pretty easily there, El." He had noticed the way she used her friend's shortened name when she expected a displeasing response. "How exactly did you say you got mixed up in all this anyway? You didn't forget to mention someone tried to blow you up, too, did you?"

The camera showed the other couple exchanging a meaningful look before Ella turned back to answer. Spar did not miss the way his brother laid his hand over the human's shoulder, as if offering his strength, and he had a feeling Fil didn't, either.

"No, no bombs on this end, but it's kind of a long story. Let's just say that I accidentally managed to wake up Kees, which confused him almost as much as it confused me. I offered to help him locate his Warden, and by the time we found out Gregory was dead . . . Well." The woman shrugged. "By then, I was already in it up to my eyeballs, so it seemed a little late to try to bury my head in the sand."

Spar could practically see the gears turning in his little human's head as she connected the dots between what Ella had just revealed and the rest of the information her friend had recently dumped on her. The question she asked then was one Spar, too, wanted to hear answered.

"Wait a minute. You woke up Kees?" Fil demanded. "What happened to that neat little story you just told me about how the Wardens were the ones in charge of waking up the Guardians and then tucking them back in for nap time?"

Ella hesitated. "We have a theory about that, but it's just a working assumption at the moment. You see, it turns out that I kind of am a Warden."

She must have noticed Fil's baffled expression, because she rushed to clarify. "Only kind of, because I haven't had any formal training of course. With the Guild scattered to the four winds, it's not like I have a mentor guiding me through a series of lesson plans. I'm studying a few materials we've been able to dig up, and Kees is helping as much as he can, but we think that if the Guild had been operating normally I would have been recruited years ago and done the whole apprenticeship thing, the way it's supposed to happen."

The news took Spar by surprise, and—judging by her expression—that word barely scratched the surface of what Fil was feeling about it. He watched confusion, understanding, shock, and bafflement play across her features before she uttered a ragged half laugh.

"For that to have been the cause, I would have to be some kind of magic user, too, right?" Fil shook her head. "El, come on. I don't even own a rabbit, let alone a top hat to pull one out of."

"Magic, Fil, not illusion. Trust me, I've learned a lot over the past couple of weeks, and one of the most important lessons for me was that *magic* is just another word for 'energy,' and a magic user is nothing more than a person who can work with that energy on a level above the average human being." Ella gave her a level look. "Are you honestly going to try to deny that you're one of those people? To me? After you saw some of the things that happened with me?"

Spar saw the quick denial rise to Fil's lips, and saw her just as quickly push it down. She looked less than happy to have such an admission pulled from her lips.

"Fine. I can't deny that I can see things most people can't," Fil bit out, clutching her blanket tighter, "but I have never in my life 'worked with' it, or however you want to phrase it. Seeing auras and being able to identify people with special abilities is a hell of a lot different from casting spells and battling the forces of evil, El. In case you hadn't noticed."

On the screen, Ella's face went hard for a moment, the expression ill suiting her appearance of soft sweetness. "Believe me when I tell you, Felicity Jane, that I know more about evil forces at the moment than I hope you will ever have to find out, but neither one of us gets to make that choice. If you've awoken a Guardian, you're in this war now, and your place is as a Warden. Like it or not."

"Um, not."

Felicity. Was that the human's actual name? It suited her far better than that masculine nickname he so disliked, Spar decided. At the moment, however, a name that translated as "happiness" sat poorly on her small shoulders. She looked as pleased with the news of her involvement in the battle against the Darkness as he felt. A longing to protect her surged within him, and he fought back the urge to snarl his displeasure.

He leaned down and peered into the phone, seeking out his brother's gaze, hoping to convey his feelings without stating them so abruptly. "I like this idea no more than she does, Kees. Even if you are correct about Felicity being an unnamed Warden, the very fact that she has no training makes bringing her into a situation like this untenable. She cannot be expected to face *nocturnis* untrained. We must find what is left of the Guild and deliver her to them. They can protect her while you and I confront this danger."

" 'Deliver' me? Am I a bloody package now?"

Both warriors ignored her.

"Were you not listening, Spar? The Guild no longer exists, not as we knew it. Even if we could locate a member who would agree to train her, it would do us no good. The Wardens have all they can handle protecting themselves at the moment. We cannot place on them another burden."

"And now I'm a burden. This just keeps getting better and better."

Spar felt a tiny thud on the back of his shin, as if a moth had butted against him on its flight through the night air. Wait, had that been the small human? Had she *kicked* him? He could not tell by glancing at her face. She had worn the same belligerent expression for at least half an hour.

"Yet more reason to think she must be placed somewhere out of harm's way." He turned back to Kees, determined to impress upon him the importance of keeping Felicity safe. "She has already been injured once. It is too much to ask that she risk such danger a second time."

Ella butted back into the center of the frame. "Fil, is that true? Were you hurt? You sounded fine, so I just assumed Spar got you out without a problem."

Felicity shot Spar a glare, which he ignored. If she

expected that he would not mention the *nocturnis*'s spell, she was mistaken. Kees and Ella needed to realize what sort of risk they courted by asking her to join this crusade.

"I'm not hurt," she repeated, irritation filling her voice. "Like I told rocks-for-brains over here half a dozen times, I'm fine. The lunatic at the abbey tried to blast me with something, but I don't think it took." She held her hand up to the phone's camera and showed them her palm, where only a patch of reddened skin indicated the spot where the magical blow had landed. "A little sunburn is all. Magicburn. Whatever. I'm fine."

Kees peered at the screen and scowled. "The vermin cast a spell at you? And it touched you? What was it? What did he say?"

Fil raised an eyebrow and pursed her lips like she'd tasted something sour. "Um, yeah, sorry, but I was too busy trying to get the hell out of there to take notes on the ravings of a certifiable basket case. I'll do better next time."

"As you can see, it is too dangerous to involve her," Spar cut in before the other warrior could respond to that sarcastic taunt. Now was not the time for squabbling. "I will leave Felicity and come to you, Kees. We will make a plan to deal with this threat together."

The other Guardian jerked his head. "I understand your reaction, Spar, but you must pause and think. What if the minion the Hierophant sent survived the explosion? You know there are spells that can shield a human from such things. If the *nocturnis* lives, he will undoubtedly report back to his sect that a human woman witnessed the attack, as well as your awakening."

"And," Ella cut in, "if they even suspect that Fil has powers of her own, they'll come after her, Spar. Believe me when I tell you, the Order isn't kidding around about destroying the Guild. Whether Fil is a member or not, they'll want her dead. They don't want new recruits replacing the members they've already destroyed. They want to salt the proverbial earth the Guild stands on."

Kees sighed. "I am afraid she is already at risk, my friend, whether we draw her deeper into our confidence or not."

"Then I will send her to you. If she is not safe here, she must go elsewhere," Spar insisted. "You will guard her while I determine if the *nocturnis* still lives. If he does, it will not be for long."

"Spar, you are reacting without logic. You must stop and think. Vancouver is no safer for Felicity than Montreal. In fact, the Order has more reason to be wary of Ella and me, since we already destroyed several of their number here. It is only a matter of time before they come after us again. We must concentrate on more important matters. Our first priority is to locate the rest of our brethren. We must all be awoken and warned of the enemy's plans."

A shrill beeping sound punctuated the statement Spar had not wanted to hear. With a sigh, Felicity reached past him and tapped the phone's screen.

"Um, not that I'm disagreeing about the world needing saving, and all," she said, "but my phone is about to run out of battery. Could we maybe continue our kaffee-klatsch later? Like, near an outlet?"

Ella forced a smile that dragged with weariness. Spar

could read it in the dark circles under her eyes and the drooping of her shoulders.

"Of course," the other woman said. "We've thrown an entire encyclopedia of information at you—"

"Felt more like you dropped an Acme anvil on my head," Felicity muttered.

"—and it's already getting close to morning. You need to get some rest. And, you know, wash some of the gravel and stuff out of your hair." Ella smiled and gestured to her face. "Maybe wipe off the smears of charcoal."

"We can meet again tomorrow to discuss what must be done." Kees's nod was all masculine meaning and aimed squarely at Spar. "I will admit that while I would not have wished another human female to be dragged into this war, I will be glad to have you stand at my shoulder, brother. I fear it will require the strength of all our brethren to cast the Darkness back into the abyss this time."

His gaze flickered to Felicity, and Spar nodded grimly. "Whatever must be done, we will do," he vowed. "By my honor as a Guardian, I swear this. The Light will lead us to triumph."

"Yeah, that's just great," his small human said beside him, her tone dry and acid. "But since you flew us here without so much as letting me pick up my bike first, and since I'm not entirely sure exactly where 'here' is anyway, Mr. Tall, Gray, and Invincible, the real question is: Is the Light going to lead me back to my apartment? Because I would kill for a shower right about now."

Chapter Four

The question had been rhetorical, but Fil had meant the bit about the shower. Her skin felt dirty and gritty, coated with a layer of gray silt made up of the debris from the bomb, Spar's pedestal, and probably a good bit of the abbey's four-hundred-year-old stone walls. She wanted hot water and the largest shower pouf known to man or God, and she wanted them stat.

Unfortunately, she may have expressed her urgency a little too strongly to her winged companion, because she found herself whisked back up into the sky before she could do more than squeak in protest. This led to the discovery—on her part, at least—that arguing with a stubborn male while suspended several hundred feet in the air by no more than said male's goodwill affected her blood pressure in a way her physician would never have approved of.

By the time she managed to convince him to set her back down on solid ground, Spar had returned them to within a half-mile of the scene of the crime. When she managed to open her eyes and pry her fingers from around his neck, she was able to read the street sign on the nearby corner and determine that the spot where she'd parked her bike for her illegal excursion onto the abbey grounds—and didn't that feel like about eight or nine lifetimes ago—was less than two blocks away. Thankfully, they were just beyond the area already cordoned off by the authorities. Yay for preplanning and paranoia.

As soon as her legs stopped trembling, Fil straightened her spine and turned on her heels. She began marching toward her parking spot without sparing her companion so much as a word of parting. Frankly, she couldn't be sure that if she opened her mouth, she wouldn't start screaming again. Flying without an airplane around her was for the birds.

Or the gargoyles.

She could feel Spar's presence lurking behind her as she cut through a narrow alley to save herself some time. It occurred to her that he might not exactly blend in this neighborhood, but at just before four in the morning, the chances of anyone being out on the street and getting past the police to see him were slim. She decided dealing with freaked-out bystanders was his problem. As was the potential for getting his enormous ass wedged between the centuries-old buildings that pressed close on either side.

A vindictive thought, perhaps, but one Fil found quite satisfying in the moment.

Spotting her bike parked just where she'd left it, Fil fumbled in her pockets for her keys, grateful they'd been buttoned safe inside. The last thing she needed right now was to discover that her keys had tumbled out and landed at the bottom of the St. Lawrence at some point during her little adventure. Not that it would have surprised her. Not after tonight.

"Come on," she said, slinging her leg over the motorcycle and settling into the worn leather seat. "I'm not quite sure you're actually going to fit on here with me, but I've given up hope that I get to go home alone after all this. Right?"

"You are correct. I believe Kees spoke the truth when he said that there is too great a chance the Order will seek you out after the events of this evening. You require protection, and as a Guardian it is my duty to provide it."

"Oh, goody." Fil sighed. "Okay, then. Climb on, if you can manage it."

When Spar didn't move, she glanced over to see him frowning down at her with his brawny arms crossed over his massive chest. Now that she thought about it, she could have skipped inviting him to ride with her. She doubted he could fit so much as one foot on the pillion of her restored Triumph Tiger.

"Ooookay, so that's not gonna work, then." She shrugged. "If you can't squeeze onto the back there, you'll have to fly, I guess. Just keep an eye on me, and I'll lead you back to my place."

Spar shook his head and refused to budge. "To be separated from you by the necessary distance required to remain unseen as I fly puts you at too great a risk. You could be attacked before I was able to reach you."

Exasperation made Fil snap, though she supposed the exhaustion didn't help either. Damn it, she wasn't wild about overbearing males at this best of times, and this damned sure didn't qualify for that distinction.

"Look, Rocky, if you won't fly, your only other choice is to get on the damned bike. You got a shrink ray in your pocket so we can move this along, maybe?"

"A shrink ray?" Spar shook his head, his expression indicating that maybe he was considering lumping her mental state in with that of the exploding cultist earlier. "I do not even wish to know what such a thing might be, so I feel certain that I do not have one in my possession. However, if this is indeed our only mode of transportation to your living space, perhaps this might help?"

A waspish demand fizzled on the tip of Fil's tongue as she watched yet another impossibility occur before her very eyes. For an instant the air around Spar seemed to shimmer, but before she could focus on the strange phenomenon, her eyes were too busy focusing on the drop-dead-gorgeous specimen of apparently human man candy that stood in the gargoyle's place.

"Wha-huh?" she stuttered.

Who could blame her? Fil might have found something compelling about the gargoyle statue that had drawn her back to the abbey that evening. It had possessed a kind of inhuman beauty in its ferocious strength and unwavering stance. This, though, this man who stared back at her from Spar's bright black eyes . . . this man's beauty was entirely human.

"Spar?"

Her voice wavered, and she felt ridiculous asking, but she had to be sure she wasn't hallucinating. Or, you know, having a stroke. The man nodded, a short, proud dip of his chin, and the gesture solidified her first impression—that this was a gargoyle in human's clothing.

He still towered over her, but at six foot and three or four inches, he no longer loomed high enough to draw immediate attention. His hair was cropped close to his scalp, dark and barely too long to be called a buzz. The style appeared vaguely gladiatorial, the way his clothing had been in his other form, but it suited him and his almost military bearing.

The wings were gone, of course—where, she couldn't even hazard a guess—and his legs, clad in ordinary, faded blue jeans, appeared jointed in the normal human manner. She could only assume the feet in his heavy, battered boots no longer sported the kind of talons that could disembowel a bison with one swipe, because his hands looked claw-free, strong, and entirely normal.

His features, she realized, appeared almost the same, maybe a little less severe, softened even more by the shadow of stubble that covered his jaw, but recognizable from his statue form. His eyes still shone as if lit from within, but that could be a trick of the light. Spar the Guardian now looked like Spar the perfectly ordinary human man.

Only about fifty times hotter.

"Is this acceptable?" he asked, his voice still low enough to rumble through her, but not as booming now. "Have I erred with my appearance in some manner?"

Yeah, you made yourself so sexy, I want to lick my way from your forehead to your heels, you big hunk of man, you.

Quickly, Fil shook her head and cleared her throat.

"Um, no. Not at all. You look, uh, you look fine." She had to tear her gaze away, something that took more willpower than she wanted to admit, and she covered her discomfort by starting the bike's engine and lifting the kickstand.

"Come on," she said, desperately hoping her voice didn't sound as husky to Spar as it did to her own ears. "I'd like to get home before sunrise, if you don't mind."

"Of course."

Fil stared straight ahead and gritted her teeth while her newly gorgeous companion moved to straddle the motorcycle behind her. She just hoped he wouldn't notice her fingers curled so tightly around the handlebars that her knuckles had turned white.

The Triumph had been a gift from her grandfather, a project the two of them had worked together to restore before his death, and it was her most prized possession. For the first time in her life, she wished she hadn't driven the damned thing. If she'd taken the van she used mostly for business and in driving rainstorms, she could have put some distance between the two of them.

Instead she found herself holding her breath and praying for strength while the most attractive man she'd met in at least a year pressed himself tight against her back and wrapped his thick, muscular arms around her waist. His thighs nestled along the back of hers, and she swore there wasn't room between them for so much as an impure thought.

Which was fine, because every single one of those that had ever been invented had just taken up residence inside Fil's head.

Oh, but she felt like a dirty, dirty girl.

"I have never ridden on a machine like this." The saddle of the motorcycle might have been built for two passengers in theory, but apparently the Brits had never accounted for one of those two being the size of Spar, because it forced them closer than Siamese twins. "I believe I must hold on to you in order to maintain my seat, correct?"

"Correct."

Resorting to cursing under her breath in Lithuanian— *Pisam rugsti is cia!*—was a sure sign Fil had reached the end of her rope, so she revved the engine and put actions to words.

It was so past time to get the fuck out of here.

Fil opened her eyes and blinked up at the ceiling above her bed. Bright sunlight reflected off the smooth white paint and bounced around the room in cheerful beams. Clearly, the sun had better sense than to spend the night sneaking into museums, getting attacked by mad cultists, and arguing with men whose skulls were literally hard as a rock.

Because that's what Fil remembered doing before she crawled into bed, and her mood upon waking definitely did not count as cheerful.

"I have been thinking."

Aaaanndd . . . there went any hope that her memories of last night had been nothing more than the remnant of a very bad dream. She recognized that voice, damn it, but what was it doing coming from inside her bedroom?

No. You know what? She didn't care. Grabbing a spare pillow from the other side of the mattress, Fil thumped the feathery softness over her face to stifle her aggravated scream.

"Aaarrrrggghhh!"

"I cannot understand your words," the voice continued. "Perhaps if you uncovered your face, we might speak more clearly."

The pillow went flying toward the voice, making the second scream much more audible. Fil sat up in a tangle of sheets and blankets and glared at the man sitting in the corner chair.

"I wasn't using words, stone face," she snapped. "I was expressing my frustration using nonverbal articulation."

Spar, still looking human and gorgeous and oh-so-annoying, caught the cushiony projectile in one hand and frowned at her. "What have you to be frustrated over, Felicity? You have only just awoken."

"What are you doing in my bedroom, Spar?" she asked instead of even attempting an explanation that would adequately sum up her current state of mind. "Didn't we have this conversation last night? I agreed you could stay to 'protect' me, but you were supposed to sleep on the sofa. In the living room."

"I did. I am finished sleeping." He shrugged and set the pillow aside. "Guardians need very little of it during our waking periods. I could have gone without easily, but I thought it best to try to adapt to human customs while we are working together. Did you have an adequate rest period?"

"Peachy, but if you've going to adapt to my customs while you're here, you might want to remember that my 'custom' is not to wake up with uninvited guests in my bedroom, okay?"

He looked genuinely puzzled. "But I could not observe you from the other room, so how I was I know when you awoke without entering this room?"

"You could preserve your little granite soul in patience and wait until I got up and came out to tell you I was awake, Einstein."

"That seems much less efficient than my way, but while we are speaking, I would like to address the issue of these names you keep giving me. I told you, I am called Spar, not Rocky, not stone face, and not Einstein. You will cease to refer to me in this manner."

Fil rolled her eyes and threw back the covers. "Haven't you ever had a nickname, Spar? It's something we humans give to people we spend time with. Why don't you accustom yourself to that, too? I'm going to go take a shower."

When he rose as if to follow her, she shot him a look of disbelief. "Alone, boulder boy. You can wait out here. Sheesh."

Spar didn't look happy, but he obeyed her. At least for the time being.

Fil stomped into the bathroom and closed the door with a snap, or about two decibels short of a slam. Damned overbearing gargoyle. She seriously wondered if English was the guy's first language; he had that much trouble listening. If Ella had faced half this much aggravation when she'd met Kees, Fil was prepared to feel some genuine pity.

Her reflection in the bathroom mirror only served to remind her that having the Guardian's hulking presence in her apartment had completely thrown her off schedule. The dark circles under her eyes and the tangled mess of hair she hadn't remembered to braid before falling into bed just went to show that no woman should ever be forced to gaze at her own reflection before at least one cup of coffee.

Grabbing her toothbrush, Fil slathered on the paste and went to work scrubbing the last of the gritty residue of the night before out of her mouth. There really had been a moment, just before she'd fully woken up, when her poor, confused little mind had her half convinced that the events of the previous evening must have been a dream. A vivid, confusing, disturbing, and surreal sort of dream, but a dream nonetheless. Catching sight of Spar, however, had put the kibosh on that feeble hope. He wasn't the sort of sight a girl could explain away easily, or forget. He tended to stick with you.

She spat into the sink and groaned. Why, oh why, had she not listened to her brain instead of her gut and stayed away from that damned statue? If she'd just dug in her heels and ignored the strange compulsion the thing exerted over her, she wouldn't be here in this mess—and more important, Spar wouldn't be here in her home.

Which meant she wouldn't have to stand here and admit to herself that the fascination she'd felt for the inanimate hunk of stone couldn't compare with the draw she felt toward the flesh-and-blood man.

Gargoyle.

Guardian.

Whatever.

Fil rinsed her mouth and reached into the shower to turn on the water. She wished to hell she could figure out why she had this ridiculous reaction every time she got within ten feet of the man. When she'd thought him nothing more than a sculpture, the compulsion had still confused her, but she'd been able to rationalize it. It had, after all, appeared to be an impressive work of art, not just well made but rather remarkably preserved, too, given its estimated age. As both an artist and an art restorer, she'd could admire another artist's creation, along with its ability to withstand the ravages of time and the elements.

Now, though, when she was faced not with a statue but with a breathtaking example of male physical beauty, chalking up her reaction to professional admiration had started to ring a little false. What Fil experienced when she looked at Spar's stubbled jaw and chiseled muscles had less to do with her trained eye and more to do with her uncontrollable hormones.

The man just turned her on. Hard.

Wasn't that a hell of a pill to try to choke down, Fil reflected as she stepped behind the shower curtain and turned her face up to the warm spray. Like she didn't have enough on her plate in her everyday life without now discovering she might be the target of a mad cult, her old college pal wanted to recruit her to help save the world, and she needed a supernatural, immortal bodyguard to protect her from magical attacks? Now her body had started screaming that she ought to end her long sexual dry spell by climbing said inhuman Guardian like the Swiss Alps and planting her flag right in his tight, bitable backside.

Oh, she so didn't need this.

Didn't need and wouldn't worry about, she decided, sleeking her hair back from her face. She saw no point in getting tied up in knots over things she couldn't control. She'd be much better off if she just focused on the things she could actually accomplish, like finding out how big a threat this Order of Eternal Darkness cult was actually likely to be.

She had a few ideas about that, beginning with finding out whether the bomber from last night had survived the blast. After all, if the guy never made it out of the abbey, chances were he hadn't gone blabbing about her to any of his demon-worshipping buddies. That would mean the risk to Fil was relatively small, and she might just be able to get out from under the protection of Spar and back to her life.

Let him and his buddy Kees worry about saving the world. She just wanted to save her own sanity.

Keeping that hope firmly in the forefront of her mind, Fil flipped open the cap to her shampoo bottle and squirted a dollop into her palm. Then she yelped, and the bottle slipped from her suddenly limp fingers and thudded against the fiberglass floor of the tub. What the hell was going on?

A question she repeated when the door burst open and Spar flung the shower curtain aside to glare down at her, wings and stony skin very much in evidence.

"What is wrong?" he demanded, his gaze searching the small room as if he expected crazed cultists to start jumping out of the steam around them. "I heard you cry out. Are you hurt? Was someone here? What happened?"

The unheralded interruption had been bad enough, but when the gargoyle reached for her with a huge, clawed hand, she slapped it hard and backed away, tugging the corner of the shower curtain with her.

"Hey, naked here!" she snapped, trying to cover herself with white fabric that rapidly began to lose its opacity as it soaked the water up off her skin. "What did I tell you about barging in on me in private rooms, huh? Get the hell out of here and go wait in the living room, *žioplys!*"

He ignored her, except to continue glowering. "I heard you scream, and there was a banging noise. I believed you to be in danger. Tell me what disturbed you."

"You're disturbing me right now." But she glanced down at her hand and felt a fresh jolt of shock at what she saw there.

On her left palm, the one she'd instinctively thrown up to block the lunatic's magical attack the night before, something disturbing had begun to take shape. Last night, the skin had just looked a little red, like she'd incurred a mild burn, so she'd figured whatever the jerk had tried to do to her had failed. It hadn't pained her, after all, so how serious could it be?

Now she began to wonder.

Spar followed her gaze to the source of her distraction and gently seized her hand, lifting and angling it into the light from the bathroom window. He studied the faint pink pattern for a moment, then cursed. From the sound of it, Fil was willing to bet it beat the Lithuanian version of "fucker" she'd called him a few seconds ago by a nautical mile.

"What is it?" she asked. Anxiety clawed at her belly, but she needed to know. How much more trouble did this mean she was in?

"I am not certain, because it appears not to have fully formed," he told her, "but it seems that the spell the *nocturnis* cast upon you may still be affecting you. This pattern is faint, but it looks to be the symbol of Uhlthor."

"A symbol of what? Was that supposed to be a word, or were you just clearing your throat?"

Spar traced the strange lines and curves with the tip of one claw, the sharp point barely grazing her skin, and Fil had to work to suppress the shiver that passed through her.

"Uhlthor," he repeated, enunciating through gritted teeth, which tipped her off that this news wasn't making him very happy. "The Defiler. It is the name given to one of the Seven, the demons worshipped by the *nocturnis.*"

Fil jerked her head back. "You mean—what, like that psycho at the abbey branded some demon's name on me? Are you kidding me? What the hell is that supposed to mean?"

"I am unsure, but I do not believe it can lead to any good."

"Oh, ya think?" Shaken, Fil snatched her hand back and pulled the shower curtain closer. "Well, if you don't know, we'll have to find someone who does. Until then, you still need to get back on the other side of the damned door. And the next time you decide you want to come into the room where I am, you can fucking knock. Act like a normal person already."

She knew she sounded like a bitch, but she couldn't keep the words from tumbling out of her mouth. Once again, her day had gone from normal to nightmarish before she'd had time to blink. If this kept up much longer, she was going to end up with whiplash.

On top of everything else.

Wisely, Spar retreated, leaving Fil alone in the steamy shower. Damned convenient, she thought, bending to retrieve the fallen shampoo bottle. The way she felt knowing she had some evil symbol branded into her flesh, this was going to wind up being the longest shower in the history of Canada.

She might never feel clean again.

Chapter Five

Spar followed his small female to the eating establishment and tried to look human. After snapping back to his natural form when he had feared Felicity might be under attack in her bathroom, it had taken him an unexpectedly long time to calm himself enough that he could resume his human appearance.

He found his lack of control baffling. Never, in all of his long existence, had he encountered such a challenge in maintaining his temper. He had not even realized that he had a temper, given that Guardians did not suffer from the weakness of human emotions. Other than the hatred he felt for the Darkness and its minions, he had never known fear or anxiety or protectiveness.

Or lust.

It shamed him to know the small human in his care could inspire every one of those feelings within him. When he had thought she was in danger behind the closed door of her small bathing room, he had felt the shock of the first three, and seeing her wet and bare and vulnerable had brought the last crashing down upon him.

Spar had looked upon Felicity, and he had lusted.

Even now, he had to struggle to force the images from his mind, the expanse of pale, silky-looking skin, the full curves and intriguing hollows. Every time he let his concentration slip, his thoughts went straight back to that moment before she had shielded herself with the fabric curtain. Every time, his fingers ached to seize her, to feel her softness and press it up against him.

Perhaps he was the one suffering under some malevolent spell.

The scents of frying meats and toasted bread managed to grab Spar's wandering attention as he stepped into the café close on Felicity's heels. She had informed him that this was where they would find the acquaintance she believed they needed to see.

"I've thought about this a lot," she had told him, after emerging dry and fully clothed into the living room of her home. "The way I see it, the most important thing we can do right now is figure out if anyone else in this Order group knows I even exist. Because, if not, I'm perfectly happy saying I can take care of myself and showing you the door."

He had tried to protest, but she had cut him off.

"However, I'm not stupid enough to send you packing if there might really be some magical mystery freaks looking to feed me to their demon overlord or something. So, first things first. We need to find out if our mad bomber friend made it out of the building last night. If he didn't, well, that's that; but if he did, then we can start figuring out how much trouble I'm really in."

Spar had assumed they would simply return to the abbey and look for the *nocturnis*'s remains, but Felicity had disabused him of the notion.

"The explosion was big enough news that they aired it on the station Ella and Kees were watching in Vancouver. That means the police will have the scene locked down tight. We'd never get near it, and if we called the authorities or started poking around, they'd think we could have had something to do with it. No, we need to talk to someone they expect to be asking questions about it, because that's who just might have the answers."

Following someone else's lead didn't sit well with Spar; he'd had to remind himself a thousand times on the short walk to the restaurant to refrain from ordering Felicity about. He wanted to order her to walk close behind him, that he might protect her from attack, and to remember to allow him to pass first through any doors so he could assess the safety of each new environment. One hard kick to his shin when he'd tried to yank her back into her apartment so that he could exit first had assured him that she would ill appreciate any such chivalry on his part.

She might be small, but he thought her boots must be lined with steel.

Felicity paused inside the crowded room to unzip her coat and scan the sea of faces. Spar watched her closely enough to note when her gaze settled on a lone human male in a corner booth near the window. He followed closely as she waded through the tables and chairs to her target.

"Hey, there, Ricky," she greeted, sliding into the

seat opposite the human without waiting for an invitation. "Fancy meeting you here. Buy you a *café*?"

Spar squeezed into the booth beside her, noticing the way the man she spoke to eyed him coolly before his gaze dropped to Felicity's chest.

"Morning, *chère*," the man drawled, finally lifting his eyes to her face. "To what do I owe this pleasure today?"

"Coffee first." Felicity reached around Spar to grab the attention of a passing waitress. "A refill for my friend," she said, accepting a menu and handing a second to Spar. "*Café au lait* for me and, uh, *noir* for him."

The woman nodded and bustled off before Spar could comment or wonder what it meant. He spoke French—and English, Latin, Greek, all the Romance languages, as well as Russian, Sanskrit, and Arabic—so he recognized the work for "black," but how did that translate to a foodstuff?

"Not that I'm minding the company, Fil, but aren't you going to introduce me to your friend?" The human called Ricky drained the liquid from his thick white cup and gave Spar an assessing glance.

"Ricky, this is Spar. Spar, this is Ricky Racleaux. He's a reporter for the *Gazette*."

The human snorted. "Spar? Don't tell me. Did you finally pick up an old man to decorate the back of that bike of yours, *chère*? Find him down at the Maison Grande?"

"Yeah, right between the knife fight and the heroin deal."

Spar tensed for a moment before the sarcasm in Felicity's voice registered. Apparently, she was not in the habit of frequenting places where people routinely engaged in armed combat or traded in illicit substances. She was simply doing what a former Warden of his had referred to as "giving the other guy some shit."

"Hey, we haven't talked much lately. How do I know what you do for fun these days?" Ricky gave a Gallic shrug, but his expression denoted humor. "I was starting to think you'd forgotten about me."

"As if."

Felicity paused to thank the waitress, who had returned with a tray of hot beverages and to take their order. She requested a savory crepe for herself and chose something for Spar without pausing to ask his permission. He would be more inclined to argue had his breakfast not prominently featured the word *steak*. He enjoyed beef, so he would reserve his judgment for the moment.

Calmly, he sipped his *"noir,"* which turned out to be a large mug of black coffee. He had heard of the beverage, but had not previously had much occasion to sample it. He found the bitter, earthy flavor unusual, but pleasing. Catching the other man watching him, Spar simply raised a brow and waited.

"Doesn't he talk?" Ricky asked, directing the question at Felicity but keeping his eyes on Spar. "Frankly, it's starting to creep me out a little."

Spar glanced at Felicity, who just rolled her eyes and gulped down her own drink, before answering. "I speak when I have something to say. I don't know you, therefore I can think of nothing I believe you must hear."

For a moment there was silence, then Ricky threw back his head and laughed. "Well, damn me twice, Fil, but I think you may have actually found someone in this world with an even worse temperament than your own. I'm not sure which one of you deserves my pity more."

"You can save the pity and just answer some questions," Felicity said.

Ricky leaned back and let the waitress deposit Spar's and Felicity's plates, then whisk away his own. He curled his fingers around his newly refilled mug and nodded at them. "Fire away, *mon amie. Je suis à ton service.*"

"So, tell me what happened last night. At the abbey."

Spar speared a forkful of steak and eggs and chewed while he watched Ricky's face. Judging by the man's expression, he had not been expecting Felicity's line of questioning.

"The abbey? Why do you want to know about a bombing at the abbey? Did you do some work for them or something?"

Felicity shrugged and cut into tender crepes layered with ham and Gruyère. "I'm interested. I mean, how often does a semi-decommissioned Catholic monastery get blown up, right?"

"Not very often."

"What are they saying about it?"

"The authorities? Not a lot. There was an explosion. It occurred sometime shortly after one in the morning. The type of explosive, the identity of the perpetrator, and any possible motive are still to be determined."

"And what about the damage? Was anyone injured?"

The man's eyes narrowed and he tilted his head to the side, as if he was attempting to see something beyond Felicity's calmly phrased questions. "Why do you want to know?" he demanded.

"Why does it matter?" she countered.

Spar tightened his grip on his utensil until he felt the metal begin to soften and bend. He did not appreciate the change in Ricky's tone, but Felicity appeared unperturbed. Instead of looking threatened, she met the other human's gaze head-on and drew her shoulders back with determination. The tension stretched for a long, brittle moment.

"Look, Fil," Ricky said on a sigh, finally giving an inch of ground, "I know you, and I've known you for a long time, so I know that you're not the kind of girl who would have planted a bomb in an abbey. If only because the idea of destroying the artistry of the architecture and the windows would offend your sensibilities too much to even contemplate it.

"But," he continued, lifting a hand to point across the table at her, "you ask questions like this of the wrong person, and someone else might think you're checking up on your own handiwork, *hein*?"

Felicity nodded calmly. "Which is why I'm not asking anyone else, Ricky. I'm asking you. Do you know what was damaged? I heard the explosion went off in an area they used for storage, so I'm assuming no one was in there at the time."

She had a talent for deception, Spar acknowledged. Neither her expression nor her tone betrayed the slightest hint that her leading question was full of misinformation.

"They're still adding up the damage." The reporter finished his coffee and set aside the mug. "The bomb went off in the chapter house, which was unoccupied. They'd been using it to store a few of the abbey museum's newly acquired works, including at least one pretty big statue they were planning to display out in the gardens. It looks like that was a total loss, since it sounds like the thing would be hard to miss if it hadn't been blown to bits."

"That's it?" Felicity prompted. Spar noticed the way her fingers gripped tightly around her mug, but her voice gave no indication of her tension.

"That's the part I'm not going to ask you about, Fil, because the police haven't released it, and no one outside the department is supposed to know." He grinned roguishly. "Well, outside the department and those of us with really good sources." He sobered. "The chapter house was unoccupied, but the emergency responders did find a person in the rubble. A man. They think it's possible he was the bomber, and something went wrong while he was setting up the detonation. The blast went off before he could get out."

Felicity nodded, but her expression didn't shift. "Wow. Was he dead? Or did he live through that?"

Ricky watched her for a moment before sliding out of the booth. "He was alive at four this morning. That's when they managed to dig him out and transport him to Montreal General." He shrugged into his coat and gave Felicity a hard stare. "I don't know why you wanted to know that, Fil, and I don't think I want you to tell me. But it's costing you more than a cup of coffee. You're buying my breakfast."

The reporter turned and left without another word.

Spar looked back at Felicity, expecting to see the tension in her body ease now that she had the answer to her questions. Even though they had learned the *noc-*

turnis had survived the explosion last night, if he had been taken to a hospital he must be sufficiently injured to pose no immediate threat. So why did she still appear so upset? Should he haul Ricky back here and make him apologize?

With a start, Spar realized that Felicity's state of mind affected his. For some reason, her feelings stirred answering sensations in him. Emotions. Because of her unhappiness, he himself felt unhappy as well. Unhappy enough to glare at the café's exit and contemplate following the recently departed reporter. With his fists.

Catching his gaze, Felicity shook her head and tapped the table. "Finish your food. Montreal General is the local trauma center, so chances are our little lunatic is too messed up to have gone blabbing to his goat-sacrificing pals about me, but I want to make certain. When we're done here, we'll head up to Mount Royal to check."

Spar reluctantly turned back to his breakfast. The steak really was quite tasty.

"I do not believe the ritual slaughter of livestock is a defining characteristic of the Order," he pointed out, hoping to distract her from her thoughts. "Blood magic is certainly one way to raise demons, but I was under the impression that large animals can be difficult to come by in modern cities."

The look she shot him wasn't what Spar would call lighthearted—she appeared to believe he also might have lost touch with sanity—but at least her grip on her cup loosened perceptibly.

"It was a figure of speech, Rocky," she said as she lifted her cup. "I just mean that if we're really lucky, I might be able to slip under the *nocturnis* radar while you go off and fight the good fight. I, for one, would like to forget any of this ever happened."

Spar knew of no spell cast by the Light or by the Darkness that would ever make him forget Felicity Shaltis. He would carry her memory with him for his next thousand years.

It was a thought that had him shifting in his seat. She was only a human, he reminded himself as he cleaned his plate. Humans barely lived long enough to register in a Guardian's consciousness. Why should he feel this one would be any different?

She would not, he told himself sternly. He must remember that whatever strange sensations she stirred within him, Felicity was simply another fragile human in need of his protection from the Darkness. He would answer the threat to her, aid his brothers in ensuring the Seven never escaped their prisons, and then return to his rest until the next time evil threatened.

It was all very straightforward.

Really.

Chapter Six

Montreal General Hospital—l'Hôpital général de Montréal—occupied a sprawling complex atop Mount Royal itself, between Cedar Avenue and Côtes-des-Neiges. Fil herself had only ever been there a couple of times in her life, to visit a friend who'd been involved in a bad car wreck. She did, however, remember how to get to the emergency room, and where to ask for information.

She headed there with a determined stride, her stone-faced bodyguard looming behind her like a determined shadow. She'd felt his gaze on her since before they left the café. You'd think he'd be sick of looking at her by now, but no. He just kept watching, like he expected her to do a trick or something. She felt like she ought to be wearing tap shoes, just in case.

No, that wasn't fair, she admitted silently. He watched her because he figured she might snap at any moment, and frankly Fil couldn't blame him. She could feel how tense she was; she practically vibrated with it. Until she'd gotten the news about the cultist surviving the explosion, she hadn't realized just how heavily she'd been counting on that not happening.

Oh, she'd rationalized the possibilities. After all, a guy who could throw spells at strangers like softballs might have a trick or two up his sleeve to protect himself from a little dynamite, or whatever he had used, but it had seemed so far-fetched. According to all the laws of physics that Fil understood, people standing directly in the paths of bombs didn't live to tell the tale. Period. They ended up as grave-faced stories on the evening news, not continuing threats to the safety of others.

She had so badly wanted all of this to be over. If the cultist was dead, the secret of her identity would logically have died with him. Spar would have no reason to hang around and protect her, and she could wave him away before going on with the life she'd always known.

So what if Ella wanted her to join their little Justice League? Nothing obligated Fil to do it. Just because she could see things about people that others couldn't didn't mean she had abilities like Ella. She'd never been able to affect others the way her friend could. The way she saw auras qualified her for reconnaissance at best, not full-fledged battle with the forces of Darkness.

And by the way, could she please just take a moment or twelve to get over the fact that there were in this world things that actually, literally qualified as the Forces of Darkness?

Šūdas.

The familiar curse word failed to make her feel any better, and thanks to modern conveniences she couldn't even slam open the doors to the emergency room with excessive force. What did a girl have to do to do a little venting around here?

She blew out a frustrated breath and slowed briefly to allow Spar to draw abreast. Reaching out, she pinched the sleeve of his shirt and tugged to get his attention.

"Listen," she murmured. She'd have whispered, but unless the man knelt beside her, the sound would never have reached his ear. "Let me do the talking. I doubt anyone will buy that we're family, so chances are we won't be able to get in to see him, but I might be able to worm out an update on his condition. If he's conscious and talking, we'll come up with another plan to get to him."

Spar gazed down at her with his dark, dark eyes and nodded briefly. "Fine. You talk. I will plan."

Okay, not what she had meant, but she'd worry about that later. "Wait right here. You can keep an eye on me, but I work better alone."

Assuming the air of a slightly harried and possibly distracted professional, Fil strode up to the information desk and offered the middle-aged woman in the wheelie chair a polite, offhand smile. "Hi, I'm Mr. Racleaux's assistant. Have you got an update for him? I'm sorry I'm late, but traffic up the mountain was a bear."

All she got in response was a blank stare, followed by a confused frown. "I'm sorry, was there something I can help you with?"

Fil absorbed the slightly testy tone of voice and adjusted her approach. She glanced quickly at the woman's name tag and straightened her spine. When dealing with a secretary general, best to stand at attention.

"Marie-Luce, *excusez-moi*," she said in a tone that

conveyed sheepishness, competence, and francophone camaraderie in equal measures. "Let me apologize. My name is Philomena Schultz, and I work for Richard Racleaux at the *Gazette*. He's working on an update for the paper's website to his story about last night's explosion at the abbey. He asked me to get in touch with his contact here, and I thought that was you. I'm assuming you'd be the one to let me know the current status of the casualty who was brought here."

Fil watched and opened her other senses. She saw the woman's basal aura color of pale peach flash with irritation, curiosity, pride, and hesitation. It looked like the woman wanted to help her, but was remembering the rules of her position.

"I'm sorry," Marie-Luce finally said, shaking her head with a regretful smile. "I'm not at liberty to give out information on a patient's condition to anyone other than next of kin. If the *Gazette* would like, I can give you the number of our media liaison. He may be of more help."

Fil fought back a wave of impatience and shared a look of sympathy. "Trust me, I understand. I wouldn't want you to get in trouble, but if I don't get Mr. Racleaux this info ten minutes ago, I'll be doing nothing but fetching beignets for the next year. Let me just do this. We have his condition so far listed as critical. If that hasn't changed, all I have to do is put a little checkmark on my report. Can you help me out that much?"

Indecision stained the woman's aura a dark magenta for a moment before compassion won out. She turned to her computer screen and typed in a command. A second later her eyes scanned something, and Fil didn't need a read her aura to know what she'd learned. The way all the color washed out of her told her what she needed to know.

"I'm sorry, miss," the woman stammered, "but I really would be in trouble if I told you anything. Please give Mr. Charbonneau in our media office a call. His number is right here."

Fil accepted the card Marie-Luce handed her with a smile. "Understood. And thanks for your help. I'll call him right away. *Au revoir.*"

She turned away and rejoined Spar, already tucking the card into her pocket to be forgotten. She didn't need to call anyone, and the spring in her step as she led the way out of the hospital and into the bright sunshine should have told her bodyguard all he needed to know. With the cultist dead—and therefore clearly unable to talk—she would no longer be in need of his services.

When Fil returned his inquiring glance with a broad smile, she could read the confusion in his furrowed brow. Didn't matter. For all intents and purposes, she was as good as free, and didn't that feel better than an hour-long massage?

As clichéd as it felt, Fil couldn't stop herself from clasping her hands together in glee.

"Ding-dong the witch is dead," she half said, half sang. "Our crazy bomb-making friend failed to survive, despite medical intervention. He's gone, which means that even if he wanted to tell the Order about me, he'll never get the chance. I can finally—"

A stabbing pain in her left palm cut her off, making her hiss and glance down in confusion. Before she could even focus on her own skin, the pain shot up her arm into her chest, squeezing as if she were having a sudden, massive heart attack. At the same time she felt as if the point of a white-hot dagger had been thrust with brutal force into her brain just behind her eyes.

The agony sent her crumbling to the pavement. Vaguely she heard Spar's voice calling to her, demanding an answer, but she was incapable of speech.

Then the world went black, and she became incapable of anything else.

The cold—so cold—penetrated her clothing, her skin, her muscles. It settled in her bones, gnawing them from the inside like a cancer. Like a cancer, she knew, it could be deadly, but she knew as well there was no escape. The cold had consumed her. She lived in it as much as it lived in her.

In the cold, there was darkness. Darkness. Deep and thick, it wrapped around her, blinded her, seized and carried her until she felt as if she floated in an endless ocean of black. Nothing existed but the Darkness, and she began to panic.

She needed to escape, to break free of the void. At least she needed to find something there, something other than the nothingness, something to cling to that could reassure her that she herself still existed.

She began to fight the grip of the Darkness. It surrounded her and clung to her like a forest of kelp, slimy tendrils always grasping and grabbing, twining around a wrist, an ankle. It tugged and slithered, trying to pull her down deeper, down to where she couldn't see. Couldn't move. Couldn't breathe.

Couldn't escape.

Terrified and determined, she poured every ounce of strength into the struggle until she felt the tendril imprisoning her snap. A pinprick of light, weak and red but still discernible, appeared in the distance. The flash of hope energized her, and she threw herself toward the faint promise of illumination.

She felt herself buffeted, tumbling, lifted on a wave of blackness until the Dark disgorged her like a sickness onto a hard, unforgiving surface. She landed heavily. The ground felt like stone, rough and bruising. In fact, her entire body felt like one big bruise, as if she'd been battered and discarded, and she held herself very still for a moment, trying to catch her breath.

She opened her eyes and let them adjust to the light. There was little enough of it, but compared with the void she had just escaped, the small amount was enough to briefly blind her.

After a moment, she blinked and surveyed her surroundings. She half lay, half sat on a dirty concrete floor, her back and side pressed tight against cinderblock walls. The room looked like a basement of some sort, and a brief inhalation confirmed the impression. It stank of damp and soil, an odor of dry decay overlaid with hints of heavy incense and the whiff of sulfur.

She could see no windows; the only light came from an open flame snapping amid a circle of stones. It appeared in the center of the cavernous space, barely enough to illuminate a small circle around it. The other walls remained hidden in shadow.

Silhouetted against the light, a tall figure in heavy robes stood motionless, his attention centered on the flames at his feet. He made no sound, no gesture, but somehow his very presence made her skin crawl. Opening her senses, she attempted to sight his aura, but all she could see was darkness, an absence of the nimbus that normally surrounded every living being. In this man, she saw only a lack of light, as if his being absorbed instead of emitted.

Unwilling to draw attention to herself, she stayed frozen in place and simply watched.

For long moments there was no sound but the hiss and snap of the fire, no movement but the flicker of flames. The being before it appeared as if in a trance, head bowed and eyes fixed on the glowing light. The longer she remained in his presence, the more she began to feel the urge to leave, to flee. She tried peering into the darkness, searching for an escape, but there was nothing. She felt trapped, and the pressure inside her continued to build.

Go. Now. Run. Quickly.

Her muscles tensed as she began to gather herself. Where she would go, she had no idea, but everything inside her commanded she could not stay here. She could wait no longer.

Just as she poised herself on the edge of flight, there was . . . not a sound, but a sensation, like the rush of air into a vacuum, followed by a thunderous pop and a sudden flash. The small fire flickered and then roared, the circle of flames leaping from one foot to fifteen feet off the ground in a single rush. As the column of fire reached high, she could smell wood charring, the tips of the flames teasing across the beams that spanned the ceiling.

She heard a word, foreign and guttural and full of

rage, just before the Darkness rushed back in on her, and the world disappeared.

She had hoped it would reappear with the streets of Montreal leading the way, but no such luck. Instead she found herself looking down on a bed in a room full of beeps and chirps and soft whirring buzzes. It was a hospital, but instead of standing against the wall, as she had in the basement, this time she felt as if she floated in a corner, up near the ceiling, with a bird's-eye view of the still figure lying on crisp white sheets.

Despite the heavy swathing of bandages and the array of lines and tubes leading from machines to the motionless body, she recognized him immediately. Henry. The mad bomber cultist.

He had survived the blast, but not unscathed. Burns marred his skin where she could see patches left unbandaged, and cuts and bruises had turned his face a rainbow of ugly hues from black to red to sickly yellow-green. He was a mess and hooked up to so many monitors, she was unsure if he slept or simply remained unconscious.

She watched for what seemed like hours, unable to move, unable to leave, simply floating and watching while the machines beeped along with his heart. A light shone from a shallow alcove behind the head of the bed, but otherwise the room remained in shadow, and she remained waiting.

She didn't know why she was there, let alone why she floated in the corner, but after a long time something in the corner caught her eye. A patch of darkness seemed to draw in on itself, to grow denser and blacker until it looked almost solid. Somehow she knew that if she reached out, it would feel that way under her fingers, but just the idea of touching it made her stomach churn. When it moved, she understood why.

Out of the darkness—the Darkness—stepped the figure from the basement. Still clad in robes and nothingness, it stepped forward to the side of the bed and laid a pale, narrow palm against Henry's forehead. With a desperate gasp, the body in the bed convulsed and arched as if shocked with an electric current, and his eyes flew open to gaze up at the visitor.

"Mercy . . ." His voice gasped and choked, barely audible, as if it were being torn from him by some violent force. "Hierophant . . . Guardian . . ."

"Yes," the robed figure hissed, and from her vantage point she could see his mouth twist in the cruel parody of a smile. "The Guardian survives, and you have failed, Henry. The Master does not accept failure, and neither do I."

"Girl. Hierophant . . . ," Henry managed, the sound more a groan than a word. "Magic . . . Warden . . ."

The figure in black stiffened, his eyes narrowing. "A Warden here? One I have not seen? Show me."

A second hand pressed against Henry's temple. Again, it looked as if a seizure grabbed him and shook him hard. The visitor threw his head back and she could see his eyes fixed toward the ceiling, blind and unseeing. Whatever Henry showed him, it appeared to no one else.

A moment later the visitor shuddered, and his gaze dropped back to the figure in the bed. "A girl with magic is an interesting development indeed, but whether you marked her with the intent to gift her to the Master or to win her to his service is unimportant. Your brothers will *deal with her. The fact of the matter is . . . you still failed, Henry. And failure must always be punished."*

The man smiled again, and bile rose in her throat at the sight. It was evil, she knew, pure and undiluted, and it rejoiced in knowing that it was about to feed.

He lifted one hand, leaving the first pressed to Henry's forehead. The second he laid over the wounded man's chest, and when he spoke, the filthy sounds cut at her ears like daggers thrust deep into her brain.

There was a flash of blackness, if you could call it that, where the nothing she had felt before waking in the basement seemed to well up out of Henry. It hovered for a moment before diving back in on itself, like a pack of starving hounds falling on fresh meat. Henry screamed, high and shrill and piercing. The sound rattled her bones for a long moment before it went abruptly dead, only for the call to be taken up by the monitors that began to whine and buzz and scream out warnings of their own.

It wouldn't do any good. Henry was dead, she realized, just before the figure of the visitor dissolved back into the shadows and Fil rushed back into herself with a painful, jolting thud.

"Felicity!" Spar roared in her ear.

Directly in her ear, she realized as it began to ring at the volume of the bellow. She tried to yell back for him to shut up, but the only sound that emerged was a weak whine.

She frowned. That was hardly like her.

The bright sun seared her eyelids, and she lifted them to squint up at the glowering face of a gargoyle who had begun to go gray at the edges. Judging by the feel of the

hard pavement beneath her and the buzzing sound of human witnesses in the area, she figured having him shift
back to his natural form would be a very bad idea just
then. She reached deep to find her voice and tried again.

"Calm down," she croaked. "I'm fine. You can stop
yelling at me."

"Fine? How can you be fine! You swooned! Right in
front of me. One moment you walked calmly out of the
hospital, and the next you collapsed at my feet as if
felled by an enemy's blow. You cannot be fine."

"Miss?" she heard, and reluctantly peered over Spar's
shoulder to see a concerned security guard frowning
down at her. "Miss, are you hurt? Do we need to get you
back inside to see someone?"

By which the well-intentioned stranger meant to ask
if she needed to see a doctor. As if being poked and
prodded and pronounced physically healthy but marked
by a demon and newly prone to psychic visions would
make this day any better.

"No, thanks, I really am perfectly fine." She forced a
smile and pushed herself into a sitting position, smacking Spar's arms when they tried to pin her in place. "I,
uh, I just forgot to eat breakfast, that's all. I'm, um, I'm
hypoglycemic, so I guess my blood sugar just took a
nosedive. That will teach me to oversleep, right?"

Her light laugh, as lame as it sounded to her, seemed
to convince the security guard. His worried frown eased
into a cautious smile. "Ah, I see. Okay, then. Maybe we
should still get you inside. The nurses can at least get you
a glass of juice or something."

Fil pinched Spar hard when it looked like the big
idiot intended to agree with the stranger. He glared

down at her, but she ignored his displeasure and used his bulk to slowly lever herself to her feet. He followed her up, hovering all the way. His arms loosely circled her, not touching, but braced as if waiting to catch her in case of another tumble. Chivalrous, maybe, but unnecessary. She needed him to stop acting like she was really sick, so they could get the hell out of here and discuss what she'd just seen.

"Thanks, but my boyfriend will take care of me. We keep emergency snacks in the car. I'll get something in my stomach quick, and then we'll head home for some real food. Right, honey?"

Plastering on a glowing smile, Fil wrapped one arm around Spar's waist and leaned against his broad chest. She snuggled against him like a lover and willed him to play along.

She saw confusion and hesitation flicker behind his dark gaze before she felt him relax against her. He pulled her closer with an arm around her shoulders and nodded, turning to smile at the hospital guard.

"Indeed, I will take very good care of my . . . girl-friend, sir," he rumbled, and even though he wasn't look-ing at her, Fil thought she caught a glimpse of mischief glinting in his eyes. "In fact, after I feed her, I will make certain to keep her off her feet for the rest of the day."

The guard chuckled and relaxed completely, raising a hand to wave in farewell. "Glad to hear it. Just be care-ful, you hear. Next time, you make sure she eats before you leave the house."

He turned to stride back to his post, and Fil made to pull away from Spar's embrace. Instead of letting her go, though, his arm tightened around her, and when he looked down at her the hint of mischief in his gaze looked more like a spark of attraction.

Her stomach dropped before she could warn herself against letting her attraction to this man slip back into her consciousness. She'd been blocking out the way Spar set all her senses on high alert for most of the day, and damn it, she'd been doing a pretty good job, too. But now all he had to do was look down at her with the faintest bit of interest and her hard work went down the drain.

When his gaze dropped to her lips, she had to bite back a groan. Of course, Spar noticed, because she saw his own lips curve before the rumble of his voice raised gooseflesh on her arms.

"If we are to convince the guard that we are . . . what did you say? 'Boyfriend' and 'girlfriend,'" he murmured, "we should indulge in the typical human display of affection, no?"

Oh, that so wasn't necessary, she wanted to tell him. In fact, she had a feeling it would be a really, really bad idea, but he never gave her a chance to protest.

Shifting his grip on her, Spar turned Fil until she fully faced him and gently drew her against him. She had an instant to marvel at the way he made her feel like a midget in comparison with his massive size before he bent his head. His kiss blanked her mind faster than the vision and just as thoroughly.

This time, Fil knew exactly where she was. Spar's heat surrounded her. His broad chest pressed against her, his arms surrounded her, his legs parted just enough to made her feel cradled by his presence. Every inch of his body was covered in muscle as solid and hard as rock, so she'd almost expected his mouth to feel the same.

Wow, had she been wrong.

His lips skimmed across hers, soft and fleeting, like a butterfly testing for nectar. Once, twice, he brushed their mouths together before adjusting the angle and diving in for the kill.

It felt almost like a blow to the solar plexus, forcing the air out of her lungs in a heavy gust only to replace it with the feel and scent and taste of his kiss. He drank from her deeply, his mouth surprisingly clever and infinitely mobile. His tongue stroked, teeth nibbled. He consumed her, drawing forth an answering hunger that had her fingers curling in the fabric of his shirt, clutching desperately at an anchor in the maelstrom of sensation.

For an eternity, he possessed her with nothing more than the touch of lips on lips, and Fil could almost believe the world had ground to a stop. Until a shrill wolf whistle pierced the air.

She wrenched herself from his arms, stepping away and fisting her hands. It was the only way to keep her fingers from lifting to her mouth, to test the tingling of the swollen flesh. Damn him. She was not a way for him to distract himself during his waking hours. If he wanted a girl in this time-port, he could find someone else.

Shoving her hands in her jacket pockets, Fil dug out the keys to her bike and shot him a glare. "I think just leaving together would have been plenty convincing, Romeo, so next time keep your lips to yourself. Now let's go. We'll head back to my place, and I'll fill you in on where I went during my little nap a minute ago."

She turned and headed toward the hospital parking lot, knowing Spar would be hard on her heels. Of course, his legs were so damned long that with one stride he'd overstepped her heels and drawn up beside her.

"What do you mean, where you went?" he demanded. "You traveled nowhere, small human. I caught you when you fell and held you for almost five full minutes while you lay unconscious on the ground."

"Yeah, well, I wasn't unconscious." Fil climbed on the bike and turned the ignition, waiting while Spar settled behind her. "I was having a vision?"

She felt him stiffen before she heard his growl. "A vision?"

"Yeah. I saw Henry die, and it wasn't from his injuries. I think someone from the Order killed him, but not before they found out about me."

"This is very serious news, Felicity. This confirms that you are in grave danger. If the *nocturnis* know of your existence, they will not stop until they have found you."

"My name is Fil, but yeah, I'm beginning to figure that out. The thing is, that wasn't all I saw."

"Tell me."

"I think I saw the Hierophant."

Chapter Seven

Spar had no intention of letting Felicity out of his sight. Not for an instant. Hearing the story of her vision only made his determination stronger. He had no doubt that what she had seen had been real events. He knew how the Order worked, and he knew that having learned of Felicity, her powers, and her connection to a Guardian, the *nocturnis* would not stop until they destroyed her.

He worried they had already made a beginning.

His human had been very quiet since returning from the hospital and sharing her story. Once she'd related the vision, she'd spoken barely a handful of words. She seemed upset, which he knew to be reasonable, given what she had seen and what they had both witnessed upon returning to her home.

The mark on her hand had darkened.

Immediately after the bombing, Felicity had shown her hand to Spar and her friends, and all anyone had seen was a faint blush of pink across the pale skin. Then the next morning, in the bathroom, they had seen where the mark had appeared in shiny reddened areas, almost like a burn. This evening after the vision, there was no longer any doubt that her hand bore the mark of Uhl-thor. The lines of the symbol had darkened to a rusty-brown color, like a henna tattoo, and Spar saw the way she rubbed at it unconsciously when she was distracted.

Felicity claimed the mark did not pain her, but Spar knew pain came in many forms, not all of them physical. He had intimate acquaintance with the Darkness, and he knew that even a sliver of it could weigh on a human soul like an anchor chaining one to the depths. Especially a soul as pure and sweet as Felicity's.

The thought brought a smile to Spar's face, almost made him chuckle. He had known his little female for barely a full day, yet he knew there were few of her acquaintance who would describe her as sweet. She prickled like a thistle on the outside, all sharp tongue and wary distance. Already he had seen the way she used humor as a shield against fear, and how she snarled when she felt unsure or off balance.

She seemed to snarl at him a great deal.

What surprised him was how she made him feel off balance in turn. The sensation fit him ill. Duty urged him to believe what he felt for her was no more than the protective instinct any Guardian naturally felt for humanity, a race he had been summoned to defend, but that did not explain the way in which his feelings shifted from protective to possessive every time she drew near.

He had not thought himself capable of such emotion. Guardians had been created as warriors with a single purpose. Not only did their commitment to battling the Darkness supersede all other concerns, but their very natures as fighters, hardened and vicious, made them disinclined to softer emotions. They needed devotion to their cause, loyalty to their brethren, and an intense hatred of evil in order to do their jobs, but nothing said they had to be able to care, especially not for one individual human.

It was the survival of the human species that mattered in the balance between Light and Dark, not each separate entity. Losses were inevitable, as any soldier knew, so to become attached to a human was to court pain.

After all, what good would it do to care for a human female? Even if the Guardians prevailed, the Order was cut down, and the Seven remained forever imprisoned, the absence of the threat would mean Spar and his brothers would return to their slumber. He and his heart would be turned to stone until the next threat from the Darkness, and a human like Felicity would live and age and die, lost to him forever.

Logic dictated a Guardian must not feel. It was the only way to ensure he performed his duty as the Light intended.

Knowing that did not make Felicity any easier to resist, especially not now, when he knew the flavor of her. He had relived their kiss a thousand times in the hours since. The gesture had been an impulse, a small revenge on the woman who had frightened him so deeply when she collapsed at his feet. He had wanted to rattle her, perhaps cause her embarrassment at being pawed by a man in public, in full view of any strangers passing by the busy hospital. The moment he touched her, however, his intentions dissolved, melted away by the deep, rich taste of Felicity.

Sweet like honey and spiced like thick, mulled wine, she had destroyed his senses with a single touch, and he knew himself for the architect of his own downfall. He had tasted her shock and then the heat of her surrender as he feasted on her tender mouth. Her body had fit against his like a fantasy, and her response had sent fire coursing through his veins. Before she had pulled away, he had been poised to ignore their audience and dive even deeper into her warmth.

Her withdrawal had likely saved them a great deal of trouble, including a likely arrest for indecent behavior in a public place. Spar had lost his mind, too far gone to care, willing to take to the skies with her if it would have meant continuing their embrace. It had enthralled him that completely.

So why had it not done the same for her?

Spar scowled and shifted on his perch in the corner of the storefront. The object of his musings moved around the space as if he weren't even there, appearing oblivious to his presence, and he could admit to himself that her attitude irked him. He understood that her vision had disturbed her, shaking her out of the determination he suspected she had made to push him through her door and out of her life. He knew she tolerated his continued presence because she felt the threat of the *nocturnis* keenly. After witnessing it firsthand, how could she not? She did not, however, pretend to be happy about it.

For the first hour following their return from the hospital, Felicity had been absorbed with relating her vision, answering Spar's questions, and discussing the need to share the information with Ella and Kees. Having seen the Hierophant, Felicity was in a unique position of having insight to offer into the highest ranks of the Order, no matter how little what she'd seen could actually tell them. They had agreed calling the other Guardian and his Warden had been necessary, but had been forced to leave a message when neither answered the phone.

Spar had seen her unease in the way she stiffened on the edge of her chair, even before she had risen to pace the floor of her apartment. Discovering the development of the mark on her hand had only added to her tension until he had asked if there was any activity she might pursue to take her mind off the troubles at hand.

Anything involving leaving the safety of her home had been immediately vetoed. Spar might prefer to have a well-made stone fortress to house them, but failing that, at least remaining in her home gave them a defensible position. He had thoroughly explored the two floors of the apartment and knew all the entrances and exits. There were far too many for his liking, but in knowing where they were, he could secure them to the best of his abilities and judge from which direction an attack was most likely.

He could have predicted Felicity's reaction. It involved a tremendous increase in the volume of her speech, several violent hand gestures, and a number of curses, many of them in a language he only vaguely recognized. He was learning to, though, since she seemed to favor it whenever she lost her temper.

They had argued for quite a few minutes before she had threatened to escape his guard the very minute he turned his back. Not that he doubted his ability to stop her, since she would require sleep long before he did, but the threat impressed him with her seriousness. She meant it when she said she would not tolerate being held a prisoner in her own home. In the end, Spar had been forced to learn a very human skill—compromise.

Their agreement ended with Felicity promising not to leave the premises so long as Spar widened the area of her confinement to include the first floor of the building. It turned out that the apartment in which she lived sat above a storefront that had belonged to the grandparents who had raised Felicity from her childhood. She had inherited the building upon their deaths and converted the downstairs from her grandfather's sign-painting shop into her own art studio.

Spar disliked the tall plate-glass windows that faced the street, but at least he could place himself between them and his charge. He had done so the instant they entered and now watched as his small female bustled around, turning on lights, arranging supplies, and setting a large canvas atop a stained and battered easel.

"You are an artist?"

The room was Spartan, filled with little more than finished and half-done works of art, supplies he could not have identified under torture, and a few pieces of furniture built more for utility than for comfort. His low voice nearly echoed off the bare surfaces.

"Yes and no," she answered, her attention on the brushes she was cleaning with a stained rag and a solution that stank to the heavens. "I paint, but it's not how I make my living. I restore artworks for museums and private collectors. Occasionally, I take a commercial commission like my papa used to. My grandfather. He had a sign-painting business, and it's not my thing, but I still do the odd favor for old friends of the family."

Felicity had changed out of the clothing she wore to the café and the hospital and now wore a pair of battered trousers that looked like the bottom half of a military uniform. Paint and other things stained them from waist to ankles, and Spar could see why when she began to stuff the multitude of pockets with tubes, bottles, cloths, and tools. Over the pants, she had pulled an equally stained tank top that might once have been black but now more closely resembled the color of aging asphalt.

She kept the temperature in the room warm, obviously for comfort, but Spar felt the rise in his temperature had more to do with the sight of her slender arms bared by the sleeveless top. The way the fabric had hitched up at her waist around the rag she had tucked there didn't help. Every time she shifted, he caught a glimpse of the pale, soft skin of her belly and his mouth watered with the desire to see if her taste there matched the one in her mouth.

Dragging his eyes back to her face, he saw her frown at him and quickly cleared his throat. He required a distraction.

"You said before that your grandfather raised you," he said, thinking perhaps conversation would help. "Why did your parents not do so?"

"Grandparents. Both my grandfather and grandmother." She shrugged and began to squeeze pigments onto an oval palette. "My parents weren't in the picture. I never knew my father. He was just a guy my mom fooled around with, and she wasn't capable of taking care of herself, let alone of me. She had a drug problem.

Leaving me with her parents was probably the best thing she could have done."

Her tone held no bitterness, which surprised Spar. He had always believed that humans harbored intense feelings of attachment to their parents.

"Grandma and Papa were amazing. They raised me without a question. I belonged to them, and as far as I was concerned they belonged to me right back. I had the best childhood I could have asked for."

"Did your grandfather teach you to paint?"

Her mouth curved in a smile. "Among other things. He taught me to paint, how to run a business, how to fix cars, anything with a motor really. The summer before my sixteenth birthday, he brought the Tiger home from a junkyard for me. We spent four months rebuilding it so he could teach me to ride in time to get my driver's license."

Her voice glowed with affection. Spar found himself envying her grandfather for holding so much of her heart.

"And Grandma taught me how to cook, cheat at cards, and swear in Lithuanian."

"Lithuanian?" Spar shook his head. "I had wondered at the words you use. I speak Russian, and I did not understand why you made no sense to me."

Felicity smiled as she feathered dark paint onto the blank canvas. "Lithuanian. Both Grandma and Papa were born in Canada, but their parents all emigrated from there back in the 1920s."

"Your grandparents sound like fine people."

"They were." She dropped her brush in a jar half filled with solution and reached for another. "What about your family? Do Guardians have families?"

She cast him a brief glance, but her attention was focused on her painting. Already the tension in her shoulders had eased, and Spar realized how much her art soothed her. He would be sure to bring her here regularly until the danger passed. The outlet would help her cope with the situation into which she had been thrust.

"The other Guardians are my brothers," he told her, pleased that she wanted to know more about him. "I have no mother or father because we are not born, but summoned."

"What does that mean?"

"I was never born, never a child. I was summoned into this realm as I am now."

"Summoned by the Guild, right?"

He hummed a yes. "Indeed. Each of us was called when the need was great, so we had to be ready to go immediately into battle."

"I suppose that's why you carry that ginormous spear, huh?"

"It is a useful weapon, though not all of us use weapons. Our teeth and claws do damage enough to vanquish many foes."

Felicity made a face. "Yeah, nice image." She layered more color on the canvas according to some pattern Spar could not determine. "So, when were you all summoned that first time? I mean, exactly how old are you guys?"

"The first summoning took place more than seven thousand years ago, according to human reckoning."

Her head snapped around and she stared at him, mouth agape, until he realized her thoughts and smiled. "I, however am not quite so ancient. None of my brethren has lived all those years unbroken. Three have lived since before the birth of your Christ, and they stand as the most ancient among us. Four of us were summoned later at different times in order to replace those who fell in battle."

Felicity's brows drew together, and her expression turned serious as she looked back at her painting. "You can be killed in ways other than just destroying your statues, then."

Did she ask because she feared him coming to harm? He felt a warm rush of pleasure at the thought.

"As Kees told you, our immortality simply means that we do not die of natural causes. Like any other creature, we can be killed. Destroying our sleeping form is the easiest way, because we cannot defend against such a cowardly attack, but we have fallen in battle over the years. The wounds that fell us must be grievous, though. We can fight on almost until our heart is destroyed. And of course, there is no creature who can survive for long if its head is removed."

She grimaced, and Spar had to remind himself that she seemed not to enjoy vivid descriptions of battle or bloodshed. He would need to remember to choose his words carefully.

"Suffice it to say, we are a hearty bunch," he hurried to assure her. "As Guardians we need to be. The enemy we fight is powerful, not to be taken lightly. You should remember that, Felicity. The foulest deeds of the *nocturnis* are like the games of a child compared with the destruction one of the Seven could cause with the smallest of gestures."

"I told you, don't call me Felicity." She pursed her lips and shot him a glance that tried to be sourer than she could manage. He could see the humor under the surface. "No one uses that name. Everyone calls me Fil."

Spar found he enjoyed the chance to tease her, just to watch her eyes light with mirth and temper. "Everyone must be too dim-witted to understand what is clear to my eyes. Fil is a name for a man. I could not mistake you for a man, Felicity, not if the Darkness struck me blind and stupid."

"I think someone already beat them to that second one," she shot back, but he heard no heat in the words. In fact, he thought he detected a certain amount of pleasure. Did she like the idea that he needed her to see him as separate from any others? Or did she like the knowledge that he saw her first as a woman, someone to be desired?

Tearing her gaze from his, she dropped another brush into her jar and set aside her palette. "I need some more linseed oil. I think I have a new jug in the back. Be right back."

He wanted to seize her, to grasp her and force her to meet his gaze, to see the feelings she stirred in him, but he held himself back. His female was skittish. He sensed the attraction in her, the way she was drawn to him, just as he felt the way she fought against it. She wanted to reject the magnetic force that pulled them together, but he could have told her it was futile. Never in his life had he felt an energy as strong as the one that drew him to her.

Clenching his hands into fists, he watched her step

through the half-open door into the stockroom at the back of the shop that she now used for storage. She disappeared from his sight for only a moment before he found himself leaping to his feet and charging after her.

She had screamed violent, bloody murder.

Chapter Eight

Fil drew in a deep breath as she headed toward the stockroom. She had to fight back the urge to run, to put as much distance between herself and Spar as quickly as she was able. The electricity that flared between them had reached the kind of voltage she knew could stop her heart with one careless touch.

She had no intention of getting burned.

When she thought about the strange fascination she'd felt for the gargoyle statue just twenty-four hours earlier, Fil wanted to throw back her head and laugh. As scarily intense as that feeling had been, it was like a drop in the ocean of what she felt for Spar every moment she spent in his company. It was as if there was some strange physical force that wanted to draw them together, some potent pheromone that turned normally rational art restorers into raging nymphomaniacs the minute they came into range of a living, breathing gargoyle.

Or maybe, Fil winced, it was just her.

She really wished she had been able to convince Spar

to let her out of his sight for even ten lousy minutes. A brisk walk around the block, just a few minutes of peace out of range of his brooding, sexy presence would have done her a world of good. With luck, it might even have given her panties a few minutes to dry out.

But no. The stone-skulled lummox had been adamant. She would not stray from his line of sight for so much as a minute longer than it took her to pee, and even then he had insisted that she leave the bathroom door open a crack so he could hear if someone tried to accost her. At this point, Fil could have told him that the only one in any immediate danger was Spar himself, and that was because she was about ten seconds away from wrapping her hands around his neck and squeezing for all she was worth.

Either her hands, or her thighs.

Groaning, Fil pushed open the storage room door and stepped inside. Convincing him to let her come down to her studio had seemed like a major victory an hour ago. It had certainly taken a hell of an argument and three of her favorite curses learned from her grandma to win him over. She'd thought that immersing herself in her painting might prove enough of a distraction that she could be in the same room with him for an entire hour without fantasizing about licking him somewhere inappropriate.

By her calculations, she'd lasted approximately seven and a half minutes.

It didn't help that the man had started a conversation with her. Why did he have to ask about her life? And why the hell did he have to sound so sincere when he told her that her grandparents sounded like fine people?

Her life had been hard enough when she'd just lusted after his delectable body. Why did he have to go about making her like what was on the inside, too?

Maybe coming to the studio hadn't been the best idea. Fil was starting to think that the paint fumes in the air could not be helping her struggle for rational thought and hormonal control. After she grabbed the oil, she'd ask if Spar would let her open a window or two. She could definitely use a breath of fresh air.

Fil didn't bother flipping on the light in the storage room. She'd been mucking around back here since the time she could walk, and she'd arranged every one of her supplies with her own two hands. The linseed oil, she knew, sat on the second shelf from the floor against the back wall. In her mind, she was already reaching for it when something shifted in the shadows.

She screamed before she could think.

The thing snarled at her. At least, she thought it did. It was hard to tell since she wasn't even certain it had a face. Could something without a face really snarl?

Okay, having this conversation with herself was probably the first sign of hysteria, but what the hell with this day?

The thing leapt at her, and Fil dove to the side. Instinct sent her in the direction of the exit door to the alley behind the building, but it didn't protect her from slamming her shoulder against the wooden frame hard enough to make her cry out. It also didn't stop the thing from catching her side with the tip of a wickedly sharp claw. It slashed through fabric and skin and muscle like paper, leaving behind a gash that felt bathed in acid and lit on fire.

Pain and fury welled within her, and her vision went dark. Not black, like when she had lost consciousness, but darkened, as if she looked out through a thin veil of black tissue. She could still move, still think, could still hear the thunderous roar of Spar's battle cry as he launched himself through the door to rescue her. She could even see perfectly clearly, as if her special sight had activated without her even trying. Both Spar and the creature crouched on the floor between them glowed with energy, Spar's a brilliant blue-white, the thing's a sickly yellow-green.

Her Guardian had come prepared to save her. Gone was the gorgeous human form with the dark stubble and the snug, worn jeans. In its place stood the seven-foot warrior with claws and spear and vengeance in his eyes. Even as he shouted and raised his spear, Fil knew he intended to destroy the creature that had threatened her, and she felt a stirring of warmth.

Too bad her left hand felt as if it had been encased in ice.

Without conscious thought, Fil raised it, she thought to check if it had turned blue with the cold, but instead she turned it outward, pointing her palm at the slimy, furry, faceless thing in the center of the storage room.

Seriously, how could something be slimy and furry at the same time? she wondered vaguely.

She knew she opened her mouth, but she could have sworn that the word that came out was nothing she had ever heard before in her life. It felt thick and heavy on her tongue, and it left a bitter taste behind. Almost before the last foul syllable had passed her lips, her palm turned from frozen to incendiary, and a ball of red-black energy flashed from her to the nasty little creature that had attacked her.

It exploded.

In an overwhelmingly creepy, messy, entrails-on-the-ceiling kind of way.

Fil screamed, and the veil over her eyes lifted, just in time to see black sticky *thing*'s guts drip off the tip of Spar's wing. Turning, she took one frantic step and vomited violently into the trash can.

She heaved for what felt like forever, but there wasn't enough in her stomach to sustain the episode for long. The dry heaves hurt enough that by the time she was finished, she fell to her knees on the concrete floor and was just grateful for the strength to keep her from landing face-first in a pile of putrid black goo.

Her eyes drifted shut, whether to block out the sight of the mess all around her or because her body had just expended enough energy to fuel a nuclear reactor for three days, she wasn't certain. Either way, her lids simply felt too heavy to hold up. She kept them closed when Spar's arms closed around her and scooped her off the floor in a single smooth movement.

Something in her wanted to protest that he shouldn't touch her, but somehow she found herself leaning into his hard chest. "Put me down. I'm disgusting."

He grunted. "I have emerged from battle with far worse than a bit of *hhissih* blood on me. You're fine."

Fil hadn't been talking about the blood, but she kept quiet.

She felt him shoulder through the door to the enclosed stairway to the second floor. Carrying her seemed not even to register as an effort for him. He whisked her up the stairs and through her apartment without his breathing even changing, providing her with the clearest possible evidence that yes, he was exactly as strong as he looked.

When her feet touched the floor, she opened her eyes and found herself standing inside her bathroom being crowded toward the tub. Spar reached around her to turn on the shower and then frowned down at her.

"The smell of the blood will make you nauseated again if you don't wash it off. Get under the water."

Fil had no argument with that. He was right about the smell. Sulfur and rusty iron and rotten meat made for one hell of a stench, and her skin crawled when she realized it was coming from her. Well, to be fair, from both of them.

She waited for him to leave so she could strip, but Spar had other ideas. He reached for the hem of her tank top, clearly intending to whisk it off over her head. Fil squeaked in protest and slapped at his hands.

"Watch it, buddy! I can take care of that myself."

"You are not in the water yet," he grunted, ignoring her ineffectual blows and taking the expedient way into her panties. He flexed his talons and ripped straight through both the tank top and her battered BDU trousers. Her thin cotton panties never stood a chance.

By the time she had blinked past the shock and on to the outrage, he had lifted her over the edge of the tub and whisked the curtain closed around her. Fil stared at the expanse of white cloth and bounced between outrage and gratitude. The gargoyle might have the manners of a wild pig, but he was taking care of her, in his own brusque, domineering way. It was almost sweet.

That thought lasted all of five seconds, which was how long it took for the curtain to open again and a very human-looking and very naked Spar to step into the tub with her. Fil sputtered in outrage.

"What the hell is wrong with you?" she shouted.

The man shrugged and reached for her bottle of shampoo. "My true form would not fit in such a confined space, so I shifted."

Belatedly, Fil wrapped an arm over her breasts and pressed the other hand to the juncture of her thighs. God, she felt like a bloody cliché, but shock and the feeling of being really, really exposed could apparently do that to a girl.

"I mean, what the hell are you thinking, climbing into this shower with me?" she said, shooting him a glare that would have knocked his stony head right off his shoulders if he'd still been sleeping. "Get out! Now!"

Spar ignored her and spread a ridiculous amount of shampoo over the top of her head before beginning to work up a lather. "You are injured and in shock. I am tending to you. Now be quiet and let me tend."

"No! I'm naked and wet, and I've known you for less than twenty-four hours. Get out. I can bathe myself, for chrissakes."

Spar lifted his hands from her hair and raised an eyebrow. Very gently he touched one finger to the cut in her side. The contact made her hiss, and it wasn't because he'd gotten soap in the gash. It hurt, burned and throbbed and stung badly enough to bring tears to her eyes. She'd almost forgotten it until he pointed it out. Maybe she was in a little bit of shock.

Then he lifted that same finger and grazed it along

the side of her jaw. Abruptly Fil realized her teeth were chattering as if she'd been standing naked in a February blizzard, instead of directly under the spray of her steaming-hot shower. The fight drained out of her, and she dropped her forehead to his shoulder.

But she kept her hands over her important bits.

Spar said nothing, not even the mildest of I-told-you-soes. He just lifted his hands back to her hair and finished washing the silky strands. She obeyed the gentle pressure that urged her to tilt back under the spray for a rinse. When he was satisfied that the water ran clean, she let him turn her to face the tile while he reached for a bottle of body wash.

When his gentle fingertips brushed the bare skin of her rib cage just below her right breast, Fil gasped and stiffened.

"Your wound," he murmured, and his fingers stilled but didn't retreat. "The creature's claws can carry poison. Let me cleanse it, and I will leave you to do the rest."

Her head jerked in a shaken nod.

His hands were tender as they traced the length of the cut from a few inches below the lower curve of her breast, around her side, to a few inches above the dip of her waist. At least six inches long, she guessed, but judging by his probing not worrisomely deep.

Keeping her left arm over her breasts, she had to raise the right over her head to give him access, which also allowed her to see the cut. The edges looked clean and straight, as if they'd parted beneath the sharp edge of a razor, but the skin on either side looked almost bruised, mottled a nasty blackish-purple. The highlights of putrid green really gave it a certain *je ne sais quoi,* she reflected sourly.

Spar patiently soaped and scrubbed the wound, easing back every time she hissed in discomfort but never stopping. When he stepped back and angled her into the spray to let the water rinse the slice clean, she sighed in relief.

"Finish cleaning yourself," he said gruffly. "When you are through, I will bandage the wound."

"Will it need stitches?" she asked. At the moment, going back to the hospital sounded about as appealing as running a full marathon. Uphill.

He shook his head. "Sewing the cut would do more harm than good. I washed it as well as possible, but any remaining poison will need to drain. A bandage will protect it while you heal."

"Okay." She nodded, and he vanished behind the curtain.

Fil hurried through the rest of her shower. Well, as much as she could, given the pain and stiffness in her side. She wished for a second that Spar had left the injury alone, since it hadn't started to hurt until she remembered it was there, but somehow the idea of the huge Guardian ignoring anything that harmed her made her snort. She didn't think he had the gene for that. The man was a natural-born caretaker, like her grandmother had been.

Not that the feelings that overwhelmed her whenever she got close to him had anything to do with grandmothers. Even in her current state, weakened, injured, and traumatized, with the remnants of shock clinging to her like icicles, she couldn't make herself stop wanting him. Oddly enough, the nudity of their shared shower hadn't been what fed her desire. Instead it had been the tender way he had tended her wound, the care he had taken to examine and clean the gash that had brought her attraction to him welling back to the surface.

That had to be a sign of some kind of sickness, right? First, that she could even think about sex after having been sliced up by some kind of demonic creature lurking in her storage room; and second, that it was the man who had signaled the transformation of her life into the surreal nightmare it had become. There had to be something wrong with her.

The thought unsettled her, but it didn't stop her from finishing up as quickly as she could so she could get back to Spar. Whether it was healthy or not, she felt comforted by his presence. He had already proven he would do whatever it took to protect her, and these days it looked like she could use the help.

When she pushed back the curtain and stepped from the tub, she found him waiting on the other side, a snug pair of jeans his only covering and half the contents of her medicine cabinet spread on the counter behind him. He moved so silently that she hadn't even realized he'd stayed in the room. Of course, preoccupied with her own thoughts, she hadn't exactly been listening.

Spar said not a word, simply handed her a towel and waited while she dried herself. When she began to wrap the cloth around her, he shook his head.

"I still need to bandage your wound. I brought this to protect you from the chill."

He handed her the white spa robe she kept in her closet. Fil slipped it on, grateful for the covering, not just because she felt chilled after the warmth of the shower, but because standing naked in front of him set her nerves to rioting. Her skin pebbled with gooseflesh, and her nipples followed suit. No need to flash him with the evidence of her clamoring hormones.

"Come. Stand here." After a glance to make sure his supplies remained in easy reach, Spar shifted to sit on the lid of the commode. Spreading his knees wide, he urged her to stand between them and brushed open the sides of her robe.

In this position, her breasts were almost level with his head, but instead of staring at them the way most men would have, Spar immediately ran his gaze down to the cut on her side. He frowned when her robe threatened to fall closed and block his view.

"Hold this," he told her, pinning the fabric against the back of her hip with her own hand.

Reaching for a gauze pad and a bottle of hydrogen peroxide, he wet the material and began to wipe carefully at the wound. Fil hissed at the first touch of cold, then relaxed. The solution caused minor stinging, but the sensation dissipated quickly. As sore as the gash felt, Spar took obvious care to be gentle.

"How does it look?" she asked, her voice sounding husky in her own ears.

"Offensive," Spar rumbled. "I should not have let you out of my sight. The *hhissih* should never have gotten near you."

"*Hhissih*? Is that what that thing was called? I'm still trying to figure out what the hell it was."

"They are creatures of the Darkness, minor, unintelligent beings that are drawn to black magic. The Order often uses them as a distraction in battle or as a sort of guard dog. We are fortunate there was only one. Often, they travel in packs. They are not difficult to kill, but they are vicious and in numbers are capable of inflicting great harm."

Fil shuddered. "Yeah, meeting one was enough."

"It appears you caught only a glancing blow. The wound is not deep, and I do not think the creature had time to inject much of its poison into the wound. It should heal well."

"Good."

She watched while Spar finished cleaning the wound, letting it dry briefly before spreading it with a thin layer of antibiotic cream. His expression remained grim while he positioned a layer of gauze over the top and began to secure it with white medical tape.

"Spar, my getting hurt wasn't your fault," she told him after a minute of uncomfortable silence. "You realize that, right? I mean, you can't keep your eyes on me twenty-four seven, no matter what you feel your duty is. I just went into another room. You were only a few steps away, and when I got hurt, you were right there to keep it from being any worse. You didn't do anything wrong."

He grunted and reached for her left hand. "I have done nothing right from the moment I awoke. If I had, this would not be here."

He traced a finger over her palm, following the lines of the demon's mark. Fil followed his gaze and choked on a gasp. The reddened henna-like lines of the mark had darkened again, now appearing a dark, dark brown, almost black, with a charred look on the outer edges. It no longer pained her, she realized, but it was starting to freak her the hell out.

"What's going on, Spar?" she demanded in a whisper that threatened to break into jagged pieces. "It's getting worse. Why is it doing that?"

"It is the way of the mark. I had hoped I was wrong, that it hadn't fully settled on you." He looked up at her, pinning her with his gaze. "The mark is attempting to claim you."

"Claim me?" She choked on the words, and a sense of foreboding swept through her. "What the hell does that mean?"

Spar grasped her other hand and tugged her closer. His knees closed around her, but instead of making her feel trapped the pressure comforted her on a visceral level. Without Fil realizing it, in the past twenty-four hours this man had become a safe haven for her. Somehow that frightened her almost more than everything else put together.

"Listen to me," he said, squeezing her hands to focus her attention back on him. He waited for her to take a shaky breath before he continued. "I want you to understand that I will protect you from this moment forward. I will allow no other enemy to touch you, no other harm to come your way, and we will find a way to remove the mark. I swear this to you."

"Okay, I know you're trying to reassure me, Spar, but you're just kinda freaking me out even worse. What the hell is up with this mark thing? Why is it changing?"

"The mark was placed on you to try to claim you in the name of Uhlthor, one of the Seven. By placing his symbol in your skin, the *nocturnis* hoped for one of two outcomes: either you would become an offering for the demon to feast upon, or you would surrender yourself to his power and become another in his army of minions."

A hysterical laugh bubbled out of her chest. "Uh, neither of those options really works for me, you know?"

"And neither will come to pass. I swear to you." He squeezed her hands again, then dropped her unmarked palm to wrap his free arm around her hips. "You have two advantages for which the *nocturnis* failed to account, Felicity. The first is that you have a Guardian sworn to protect you. The Defiler will never touch you so long as I survive, and were I to fall, Kees or one of the others would step into my place and a new Guardian would be summoned. You will never be left to face the evil alone."

"Yeah, um, could you just not be destroyed, please? That would be great. In fact, if you could just not even talk about destruction unless it's in relation to something evil, I'd really appreciate that."

"Hush. I am going nowhere." His arm tightened in a comforting hug. "And you need to know this, Felicity. The second advantage you possess, which the *nocturnis* could never have conceived of, is your own goodness. Had your will been weaker or your soul darker, the mark placed upon you would already have consumed you and turned you to the Darkness. But it hasn't. That is due entirely to your own character. Continue to be the woman you have always been, and the mark will have to fight for every ounce of ground it gains."

Fil shuddered out a sigh and raised her free hand to Spar's shoulder. The feel of warm skin and hard muscle steadied her, grounded her. She needed something solid to hang on to, and she could think of nothing more solid than him.

"It is getting darker, though," she managed.

Spar's jaw tightened. "I have thought on that, and I believe I have seen something of interest. From what I can recall, the look of the mark darkened slightly from the initial impact until this morning when we first checked it, but then it seemed to remain steadily of the same color for several hours."

Fil nodded.

"The next time it darkened was after we went to the hospital. Specifically, after your vision."

"So?"

"So I believe there must be a connection. Even after the vision, nothing darkened again until you destroyed the *hhissih*. The energy you channeled then was Dark, and I believe that might be what caused the change in the mark."

Fil jerked back, or tried to, but Spar tightened his grip and held fast. "Wait, what? I channeled Dark energy? What are you talking about?"

Even as the words tumbled out, the churning in her stomach told Fil she already knew the answer to her own question. She flashed back to the moments of the attack, to the dark veil that had clouded her vision and the bolt of red-black energy that had flown from her hand, almost against her own will. The foul bitter taste that had coated her tongue came back to her, and she grimaced.

"I spoke poorly. That was not you, Felicity. It was not your doing. The energy funneled itself through the mark, and it destroyed the *hhissih* because it threatened you. You did nothing wrong."

The hand she had pressed against his shoulder trembled, but she still tried to use it to push away from him. It was like trying to push back a mountain. "Nothing wrong? I used black magic, didn't I? That's what I did to get rid of that . . . that thing. And it was like a reflex. I didn't even realize I was doing it until it was too late. What if I use it to hurt someone else? Someone innocent. How could that not be wrong?"

"Because you would never do it," Spar insisted. "You are not evil, so evil can take only so much a hold over you."

"Wait," she continued as if he hadn't even spoken. "You said that the *hhissih* is drawn to Dark energy. That's why it came after me to begin with, isn't it? It was drawn to me because of the mark."

His expression hardened. "It is possible. The fact that the Order knows of your existence means they could have sent it, but their way is more typically to deploy the creatures in packs. If they had sent it, they would almost certainly have sent more than one."

Fil clenched her teeth. "Then I brought it on myself. It was my fault."

"No, it was not." Spar surged to his feet, but he kept Fil trapped in his embrace, her body now pressed against his in the small space of her bathroom. "You brought nothing on yourself, Felicity Shaltis. You have had this thrust upon you, and you have handled it better than most humans could ever dream of. I meant it when I told you that it is you—your character, the goodness in your soul—that has beaten the Darkness back thus far, and I know it will continue to triumph. You are a warrior in your own right, little human. Small and soft though you may appear on the outside, the weapons you possess could save the world if it asked you."

She heard the ring of sincerity in his voice and knew he meant what he said. Fil was having a harder time with it. Suddenly she felt dirty all over again, as if she hadn't just stepped from the shower, and exhaustion threatened to fell her.

"I wish I could believe that so easily," she murmured, "but I feel tainted. Knowing this is here, that it's trying to work its way inside me . . ." She shook her head and tried to tug her marked hand from his grasp. "It scares me."

"Do not let it. I will see you safe." He raised her fingers to his lips and pressed a kiss to her palm, right in the center of the mark. "I vow it. The Defiler will not have you, Felicity. I have claimed you for myself."

The rumble of those words, soft and dark, sent shivers racing through her. Her imagination supplied all sorts of images of ways she could be claimed by him, and none of them had anything to do with evil.

Heat flooded her cheek, then wormed its way lower. It built in the pit of her belly until she couldn't bear it anymore. Her hand shifted from his shoulder to his cheek, and she lifted herself up on her toes.

"Show me," she whispered, just before she pressed her lips to his.

Chapter Nine

He froze. Shock and uneasiness warred within him, until hunger swept forward on a fiery steed and took the battle with a single blow.

Spar felt it down to the soles of his feet. In all his thousand and more years, he had never experienced anything of its like. It threatened to knock him to his knees, to offer him the sort of defeat with which he had never been threatened. He had not lied when he had told Felicity her weapons were potent, but he had never expected her to wield any against him.

Her lips alone packed a greater punch than any mace or flail ever swung. The force of them made his head spin with the gentlest of touches, but she did not remain gentle for long.

She huffed a soft breath into his mouth, pushing on him the taste of cinnamon and clove and dark, sweet treacle. He drank it in and felt a groan well in his chest. His skin itched and pulled, feeling too tight to contain him, and he fought back against the urge to shift back to his natural form. Something inside him wanted to use fang and claw to mark her, to show the whole world she was his, but he feared hurting her. She felt so small and fragile in his arms that he knew his true self could rip her to pieces, and he would rather throw himself on his own spear than cause her the slightest harm.

Conscious of his own strength, he pressed her closer. Her lithe form, wrapped only in her unbelted robe, fit against him as if it had been carved in mirror image. Curve and valley nestled perfectly against angle and plane, but where the material around her gaped open, he could swear his skin had turned to lava. The heat generated by the feel of soft, silky skin pressed to his thicker, rougher hide could have melted mountains.

He needed more.

The hand still grasping hers lifted and guided her fingers to his shoulder so that he could be free to wrap her entirely in his embrace. She never hesitated. Sliding both hands up, she linked them behind his neck and used her grip to haul herself higher against him. One of his arms hooked under her bottom to support her, and in an instant she had her legs up and twined around his hips. The position pressed the hot core of her directly against his groin. He broke the kiss with a low snarl.

"Be certain you do not resent my claim, little human," he panted, desire digging like talons in his gut. "If you give yourself to me, I will not be able to let you go."

Her green eyes had darkened to the color of ancient moss, the lids heavy and languorous. "I can't think about it, Spar. I can't think. Just don't let me be taken. Unless you do it yourself."

He growled and bent his head back to hers. "They

shall not touch you, baby. I swear it. None shall touch you but me."

"Then touch more of me."

If he had his wish, there would not be an inch of her he would not touch. Every part of her would wear his scent, his primitive claim on her. No one would doubt that she belonged to him, not even her.

With long strides he carried her from the bath and into the next room, laying her carefully across the bed. She clung to him, arms and legs refusing to let him go, so he followed her down and pinned her to the soft mattress. The sound she made reminded him of the purr of a cat, all warm pleasure and approval. He wanted to pet her like a cat, with long, slow strokes, and gentle pressure, but desire and possessiveness rode him hard. He didn't think he could make this easy.

She didn't help matters by arching beneath him, crushing her breasts against his chest and her soft belly against his painfully hard erection. He let his breath out in a hiss. The touch both soothed and inflamed him. He needed to be as close to her as possible, but with every passing second the need for "close" turned more and more to a need for "in."

His hand nearly trembled as he curled his fingers around the smooth silk of her leg just above her knee. Her skin felt warm and tender, softer than the softest thing he had ever touched. The contrast between the feel of her and his rough, callused hands fascinated him, as did the sound of her breathing catching in her throat as he stroked higher.

The tips of his fingers dipped beneath the edge of her short robe and found the lingering dampness of her skin in the crease where leg met hip. He traced the line down and in, feeling her tremble. When he brushed his knuckles over curls wet with more than bathwater, he couldn't hold back his growl of satisfaction. She desired him.

"Spar."

His name quivered on her lips, and he kissed it away. He didn't want her speaking, or thinking, or doing anything but letting him discover her.

Her taste, he already knew, offered a rare pleasure. He explored further, discovering the depths of her mouth while his hands pushed and tugged and freed her arms from the sleeves of her robe. Her flavor went to his head faster than any alcohol ever brewed by man, and he knew that if he were ever to find himself drunk, it would be on her.

His tongue demanded a response from her, initiating a game of hide-and-seek that had them both breathing in labored gasps. She moaned when he pulled free and teased her lips with nibbles both soft and sharp. The edge of his teeth grazed the line of her jaw, following the smooth curve up to the shell of her ear. She shivered at the first touch of his lips and moaned when he tugged gently at the lobe.

Her hands helped him press the side of her robe open, spreading it on the bed beneath her to expose her fully to his heat. She seemed to relish the freedom, arching and squirming and rubbing her skin against his as if begging to be touched everywhere. Spar was happy to oblige her.

While his lips trailed a path from her ear along the side of her throat, his hands traveled the opposite direction, skimming over her hips and up her sides. Every soft inch of skin made him want to stop and linger and simultaneously see if the next could possibly feel as gorgeous. It always did.

He dragged his mouth across the faint ridge of her collarbone, letting her feel just the edge of his teeth, then soothing the scrape with the gentle lap of his tongue. The urge to consume her rose within him, and he felt his jaw ache where his fangs should have been. He offered up a quick thank-you to the Light for his dull human teeth that couldn't cause any serious damage. He wanted to cause her no pain, only pleasure.

"Stop teasing," she moaned and tugged hard at his shoulders. "I want you."

"And I want more of you," he rumbled. "You will have to be patient, little one, for I intend to take my fill of you."

Her breath shuddered out, then drew back in with stuttering steps. His lips coasted down to her breastbone before beginning the climb up a pale slope toward her turgid nipple. He felt her anticipation gathering, her fingers curling into his flesh as she tensed in anticipation. He considered prolonging the agony, but he'd only be torturing himself. He craved the taste of her, needed to feel that little bud hardening against his tongue. He would be willing to bet it would be delicious.

He was not disappointed, not by the experience and not by the way she cried out helplessly and offered herself up to him, urging him to take more. One hand lifted to grip the back of his head, her fingers sifting through the painfully short strands and failing to find anything to which she could cling. Spar didn't want her to cling; he wanted her at the mercy of the heat that rose between them, as helpless against it as he felt.

Reaching up, he closed his hands around her wrists and pinned them to the bed beside her. She moaned again and struggled weakly, but he ignored it, switching his attention to her other breast and devouring it in turn. Every time he drew on her nipple, her body quivered beneath him, and when he brought his teeth into play, nibbling carefully at the sensitive peak, she cried out her pleasure.

"God, you're killing me." Her voice sounded thin and choked, and it still made him hard enough to pound nails. "Spar, please."

"Sh. Let me know you."

Felicity gasped, but he felt the way she forced her muscles to relax. Her willingness to give herself to him made him want to throw his head back and roar like a beast, announcing to every living thing within the sound of his voice that she was his. He had to have her. Soon.

Keeping her hands pinned at her sides, he slid his body down the mattress on a train of kisses. He tasted the concentrated flavor of her skin just beneath the curve of her breast, the hidden crevice of her belly button, the quivering curve of her stomach. All the way, he found himself lured by the sweetness of her scent, its intensity increasing with every inch he drew closer to her center.

He filled his head with her perfume, rich spice, warmed honey, and her own intoxicating femininity. Too earthy for a flower, too sweet for a musk, it reminded him of the heady smoke of frankincense, something even the gods themselves would find pleasing. Not that Spar was willing to share her, not even with them.

She breathed in ragged pants punctuated by tiny whimpers that went straight to his cock. Knowing she might desire him even half as strongly as he did her was the most powerful aphrodisiac in the universe. He needed to show her how much she pleased him, but more than that, he needed to taste her.

When his lips brushed the soft curls of her mound, her body jerked. She attempted to tug her wrists free of his grasp, but Spar had no intention of letting her go. Instead he angled his shoulders and insinuated himself between her thighs, forcing them to spread around him. He created a place for himself he would have slain a thousand demons to defend, and he intended to make the most of it.

With an appreciative hum, he let his tongue press against her soft fold, and savored the first taste of her. Sweet and wild and incredibly hot, it only fed his hunger. He licked again, this time parting her to delve deeper; she spilled across his tongue like honey from a comb, awakening a sweet tooth only the taste of her could assuage.

"Oh!"

Her cry was short and sharp, breathless with surprise and pleasure, and it only spurred him on. He feasted on her, on her delectable cream, her breathless cries, on the strong, beautiful essence of her. The way she melted against his tongue, growing softer and wetter on every pass, fascinated him. He felt her thighs trembling and straining against his shoulders and wanted to feel them clasped around his hips, clinging while he eased himself inside all this welling heat.

Lifting his head, he let his gaze run up over all her

glorious curves to see her throw her head back and gasp for air. Her skin glistened with a fine sheen of perspiration brought on by the heat they generated together, and Spar knew he had never seen anything more beautiful.

Sensing his gaze on her, she forced her eyes open and met his, her own hazy and unfocused. A tiny crease appeared between her eyes. Her hands began to twist and pull in his grasp, demanding to be set free. When he released his grip, she lifted one small hand and cupped his cheek with tender intensity.

"Now," she urged him in a hoarse whisper full of need. "Come to me."

For a long, breathless moment he continued to watch her, his dark eyes gone black and glittering like his gargoyle's. Fil felt not a twinge of unease. This was her Guardian, her protector, and he would die before he allowed her to be harmed.

Her hands shifted, tugged, urging him over her. He had stirred a need inside her that part of her feared would never be satisfied. Her pussy literally ached, empty and wanting, clenching around nothing. She had to have him, now.

"Please," she begged, and like her own guardian angel, he answered.

With his gaze still locked with hers, Spar nudged her legs wider and settled his hips between them. She felt the head of his erection slide against her crease, a heavenly sensation made slick by her moisture and his. She arched helplessly into him, her body urging the joining she craved, and she heard his rough whisper tell her to relax, to be calm, that he would take care of her.

She knew that, trusted that more than she trusted herself at the moment, but it didn't fill the aching emptiness. For that, he needed to take her.

Her nails dug into the smooth skin of his shoulders as she gasped out her plea. "Inside me, Spar. Please."

He groaned as if the sound were ripped from his very soul, and in one powerful thrust he joined them.

Fil cried out, breathless and overwhelmed. She felt her body stretch to accommodate him and reveled in the flash of discomfort, in the way it melted into pleasure so great she wanted to weep for joy. Nothing in her life had ever felt like this, had ever shaken her so deeply it felt like dying and being reborn. She might as well have been a phoenix, consumed by flame and simultaneously created by it.

Spar was her flame, and she wanted more than anything to feel him burn along with her.

With hands, voice, and body she drove him on, rising into every thrust, clinging through every withdrawal. She wrapped her legs around his hips to pull him closer and savored the shift and flex of his muscles as he moved within her. She felt surrounded by him, encompassed, overtaken, and at the same time full of feminine power. By taking him inside her she had conquered him, and now she let him conquer her in return.

They moved together in heat and hunger. Passion might have lit the spark, but something else lived in the blaze, something new and tender. Fil could sense the tendrils growing inside her to curl around her heart, not to squeeze or crush, but to support and protect. It fed on the heat of their desire, growing stronger as their pleasure built.

The tension within her ratcheted higher. Her thighs quivered where they clung to his hips; her fingers trembled where her nails bit into his skin. She could feel the tremors begin deep in her womb and knew she was close. She could almost feel the edge of the cliff beneath her toes and needed only the tiniest little shove to send her flying over.

She found it in him, in the thousand pinpricks of blazing fire that burned behind his night-dark eyes, in the intense focus in his expression as if nothing in the world existed but her, in the shifting angle of his hips that dragged the head of his cock over the most sensitive spot in her passage again and again with relentless determination.

Mostly, she found it in the curling of his lip, in the way he bared his teeth and dropped his chin and pressed his forehead against hers.

"Mine," he growled, and the sound rumbled through her like a shock wave, setting off a chain reaction that had her clenching hard around his shaft. Her entire body shook and her vision went not dark but bright, like a star bursting behind her eyes.

Vaguely, she heard herself cry out, but the noise meant nothing. All Fil could hear was the echo of that possessive statement, and the hoarse roar that followed it as he joined her in oblivion.

Chapter Ten

Fil woke to the chill of an empty bed. Stretching out a hand, she touched the cool crispness of cotton and nothing else. Spar was gone.

Disoriented, she pushed herself into a sitting position and felt the blankets slither down to her waist, leaving her bare to the cool night air. Never one to wake easily, it took her a minute to get her bearings, to realize it was night, that she had fallen asleep after the most amazing sex of her life and obviously napped for at least a couple of hours. A glance at the bedside clock told her it was getting close to eleven, which boded ill for getting a good night's sleep in an hour or two.

Unless maybe Spar was willing to tire her out again.

Heat rose to her cheeks. The man made love to her one time, and already she couldn't wait to touch him again. He should be labeled a controlled substance to keep potential addicts like her safe from his influence.

Pushing back the blankets, Fil reached down to snag

the robe that had fallen to the floor hours earlier. At least, she assumed that was what had happened. Once the darned thing had opened under Spar's touch, everything else had ceased to exist. Nothing had mattered but him. Touching him.

When she stilled, she could hear the gravelly rumble of his voice coming from the living room. Who could he be talking to? Did he forget to mention he had a sister and a couple of nephews living in Montreal he wanted to ask over for dinner?

Curious, she opened the door and padded down the short hall to the living room. Spar sat in the middle of her sofa frowning down into her cell phone. Fil recognized the voice on the other end immediately.

"I really wish you'd wake her up so I can talk to her," Ella argued, worry threading through her voice. "I'm sure you took very good care of her, but I won't feel entirely comfortable until I can talk to her myself."

"You will do as my mate asks, Spar. Otherwise she will worry. I dislike it when she worries."

"I will not," Spar growled, and Fil assumed the thunder in his expression was for Kees's benefit. "She is injured and exhausted. She needs to rest. I will not wake her simply to satisfy your human's curiosity."

Fill stepped forward and laid a hand on his shoulder. "You don't need to wake me. I'm up."

Spar turned to her, but he didn't look any happier. "Why are you awake? You need to sleep."

"I did sleep, and I'm pretty sure I'll sleep again at some point, but for the moment I'm fine. Ella, did you hear that?"

"I did. Spar, move the phone so I can see her."

"Hold on." Fil circled the sofa and took the seat next to Spar. "Is this better?"

He grunted and shifted her onto his lap. "This is."

"I wasn't talking to you."

"I do not care."

Fil rolled her eyes and turned to gaze into the phone. "Sorry, El. I dozed off. I had kind of a rough day."

Her friend stared back at her with wide eyes, an expression of surprise and delight suffusing her features for a moment before she seemed to catch herself. She cleared her throat. "So Spar was telling us. I'm so sorry, sweetie. How's your side feeling?"

"Tender," she answered honestly. "It pulls a little when I try to move around too fast, but mostly it's fine. Spar said it could have been worse. I should be fine in a week or so. Did he call you to tell you what happened?"

"No, I called you. Kees and I just got in a little while ago and got your message. The battery on my phone had died while we were out. I'm sorry it took so long to get back to you."

"It's okay. You guys have more than enough of your own stuff to worry about."

"At the moment I'm mostly worried about you." Ella frowned. "Let me see the mark."

Reluctantly, Fil raised her hand and held it palm-out to the phone's camera. "Pretty, right?"

"I would not call it so," Kees said, shifting into the frame. "Spar told you what it means?"

"That I'm right on the top of Uhlthor the Defiler's most wanted list? Yeah. Great name, by the way. Sounds like a real charmer."

"Fil, I am so sorry," Ella said, worrying her lower lip between her teeth. "I should have known something was wrong after you told me about what happened at the abbey. I mean, I figured the *nocturnis* had tried to cast some sort of spell on you. I should have dug around more and found out what he did."

"It's not your fault, Ella. Even if you had figured it out, the damage was already done by the time I talked to you. There's nothing could have done to change it. Unless the Guild has some kind of snazzy time-travel mojo you've managed to uncover."

"Not so much. Or if they do, it's one of the billion secrets that disappeared when the headquarters was bombed."

"Then don't worry about it," Fil said firmly. "It's done. At this point, I'd rather forget how it happened and focus our attention on what can be done to get rid of it. I mean, a spell is like a curse, right? So aren't there supposed to be antidotes to those? Counter-curses, or something like that?"

Ella sighed. "Theoretically, yes. The problem is that we would need to know exactly what curse was used in order to find the correct counter-spell. If we picked the wrong one, we could end up doing more harm than good. Besides which, you need some pretty serious skill to manage stuff like that. It's delicate work. I might have a decent amount of power, but as far as Wardens go I'm still basically untrained."

"I thought you were studying like a third-year law student."

"I am, every chance I get, but at the moment I have to settle for learning the spells I have access to, and even then it's kind of on a need-to-know basis. So far, I've had to know more about wards and bindings and portals than I have about curses. Sorry."

"Again, not your fault. I really would like to get rid of this, though. There's got to be something else we can do."

"I'm going to push hard on the leads we have to another Warden," Ella said. "An actual fully trained member of the Guild is going to know a lot more about this than either of us, so if I can locate him, he may be able to help."

Fil made a face. "Great. Provided he's still alive when you find him, right?"

Ella looked away.

"Wardens are not the only individuals with power," Kees said, laying his hand on Ella's shoulder in a clear gesture of comfort. "The magic they wield is the purest expression of such power, but for centuries there have been humans with the ability to channel the energy of the earth or to manifest simple blessings into the mortal realm."

It took a moment for Fil to piece that together. "What? Are you talking about witches and priests? Do I need an exorcism?"

Spar snorted. "Exorcism is nothing more than sending the weakest form of Dark spirit to its room for a punishment. The mark of one of the Seven cannot be removed so easily, and especially not by the holy man of a human church waving a crucifix and chanting a simple prayer."

"Well, if there are demons, then there must be a God, right? So why shouldn't a priest be able to help?"

"God is such a human concept." Spar shook his head. "There is the Light and there is the Dark. What you humans call gods are facets of the Light that you have built stories around to aid your understanding of the unknowable. A priest of one facet cannot hope to counter the corruption inherent in one of the Seven."

"But a witch would do better?" Fil snapped.

"A witch's treatment might be more direct." Kees stepped in before Spar could reply. "Their kind can channel the energy of the earth and also apply the remedies it provides. It is unlikely to remove the mark, but it might help to slow its progression."

"At this point, I'll take that."

"But how is she supposed to find a witch?" Ella demanded, frowning at her Guardian. "She's human, Kees, like me, remember? I doubt she's hanging out with the local coven, or whatever it's called."

Fil laughed. "You're right, I'm not. But I might know someone who can point me toward one."

"Who?"

"Tim Massello. He's a professor at McGill, a sociologist or an anthropologist, something like that, but his real hobby is the supernatural. About a year ago, he hired me to restore a page from an illuminated manuscript. He'd come across it while doing research for a book he was writing on the evolution of witchcraft from historical persecution to modern paganism. He said he'd spent a lot of time talking to present-day witches for his project. I wonder if he'd be willing to put me in touch with one."

"It can't hurt to try, right?" Ella sounded almost enthusiastic about the idea. "You've got to give it a shot,

Fil. I hate to think about that thing on your hand getting any worse. Or, God forbid, spreading."

Fil shuddered. "Yeah, thanks for putting that thought in my head, because it's not like I had anything to worry about."

Her friend winced. "Sorry."

"We will contact this professor tomorrow," Spar said, reaching out to take her hand in his. "And if he cannot help us, we will find someone who can."

"In the meantime, Ella and I will search for the Warden. We have hopes not only that can we find him alive, but that he might have information on the location of one of our brothers. We must assume that the danger to them is greater than ever."

"Agreed. We should stay in contact every few days at the very least. We will need to pool our knowledge and resources in order to remain ahead of the *nocturnis*."

"This method of communication seems adequate and efficient."

Ella shot Fil a grin. "That's big, coming from Kees. Modern technology has yet to win him over. At least, anything that doesn't have wheels and a really big engine."

Spar met his brother's gaze in the screen, and his lips curved at one corner. "My human has a motorcycle. I quite enjoy riding on it, but I hope to persuade her to allow me to drive it."

"Just as soon as I'm cold in my grave," Fil growled, frowning at him.

Ella laughed. "Good luck with that, and with your professor. Send me a text or an e-mail and let me know how that goes, okay? And call if there's anything you need."

"I will, El. Thanks."

"No problem. Talk to you later, sweetie."

"Bye."

Fil took the phone from Spar's grasp and ended the call. She leaned forward to set it on the coffee table, only to have him tug her right back against his chest.

"You should have remained asleep."

She leaned into him and let her head rest against his shoulder. "If you didn't want me to wake up, you should have stayed in bed."

"I feared the sound coming from your device would disturb you."

"No, I was disturbed when I got cold."

His hand slipped between the sides of her robe and traced over the top of her bandage. "I worry that I might have been too rough with you. Your wound needs time to heal."

"I'm fine." She laid her hand over his chest and felt his heart beat against her palm. "Physically anyway. I can't deny that I'd feel better without this thing on my hand. Getting rid of that would certainly brighten my day."

She felt the press of his lips, warm and tender against her forehead. "Tomorrow we will contact this man at the university and demand that he find us a witch."

Fil chuckled and angled her head to give him a wry glance. "We might want to try asking nicely first. He was pretty stoked about the work I did on his manuscript page. I think he'll help if he can."

"Good."

He held her in silence for several minutes, and for the first time since her break-in at the abbey she felt completely safe and nearly at peace. Of course, with his hard thighs pressing against her bottom and his large hand absently stroking her hip, it wasn't long before she began to feel another, more urgent sensation.

Tilting her head back, she pressed her lips against the scratchy underside of his jaw. She felt him tense and let her tongue dart out to tease his skin.

"You should rest," he said, his voice the familiar low rumble that went straight to her libido. He made as if to ease her off his lap, but she could tell his fingers had tightened around her, reluctant to let go.

"You know where's a really good place to rest?" she purred, wiggling her bottom and feeling his erection beginning to swell beneath her. "In bed. Why don't we go there, hm? Together."

Spar groaned like a man tormented, but that didn't stop him from surging to his feet with her still cradled protectively in his arms. "You will rest," he ordered, heading toward the hallway with a determined stride and eyes that glinted with want. "You must promise."

"Absolutely, babe. I promise I'll rest." She twined her arms around his neck and lifted her mouth to his. "After."

Professor Massello turned out to be a man of average height, average weight, and keen intelligence. In his late thirties or early forties, he looked more like an older version of one of his students than the stodgy, serious academics Spar mentioned encountering in his previous years. Of course, having not awoken for the last two hundred of them might have colored his view just a bit.

Tim, as he encouraged them to call him, waved them into his office with a warm smile and closed the door on the throng of students milling in the hall.

"Sorry to interrupt your office hours, but I figured it was my best chance to actually find you in your office." Fil smiled.

"Don't worry about it. You caught me on the tail end. I was actually just about to lock the door against the teeming vermin and get some grading done." He waited for them to sit in the uncomfortable chairs facing his desk before he hitched a hip onto the edge of the piece and raised an eyebrow. "So what can I do for you, Fil? I suspect you haven't dropped by to take me up on that cup of coffee I keep offering to buy you."

Fil heard Spar grunt and shot him a warning glance. "First, I guess I should introduce you two. Spar, this is Professor Timothy Massello of McGill University, Quebec. Tim, this is my friend Spar—"

"Livingston," the man in question broke in, offering the other a brisk nod.

Living stone? Fil nearly pulled a muscle trying not to roll her eyes at that one.

"Nice to meet you."

Tim sounded a little wary, but friendly enough. Maybe he'd picked up on the way Spar had entered the office and immediately scanned every inch as if searching for threats, or maybe he'd simply noticed the protective way the Guardian nearly hovered over Fil. Either way, he kept his expression relaxed and made no move to continue the flirtation he'd previously begun with her. She could only be grateful for that. More complications were not what she needed at the moment. She needed help and answers, and for Tim not to assume she had lost her ever-loving mind when she told him her story.

Taking a deep breath, she decided to just get it out. "Okay, so this might sound a little bit crazy—"

"Oh, all the best stories start that way." Tim grinned and waved at her to excuse his interruption.

"But I was hoping that your more, um, esoteric research might mean you can help me with a problem I'm having."

Fil had spent half the night and all of the morning debating how much to tell the professor, and in the end she'd decided to stick with the minimum amount possible. He really didn't need to know about Guardians, the Order of Eternal Darkness, or the ongoing war between the forces of good and evil. Better to keep things simple and just focus on the mark and the help she needed to treat it.

"Hm, I take it you're not talking about my papers on the spiritual dimension of rites of passage in the sub-Saharan tribes of Africa."

Fil blew out a chuckle. "Not so much. I'm thinking more along the lines of your book, specifically the more modern section."

Tim's brows darted toward his hairline. "You're interested in neo-paganism? I thought you told me you were Catholic. Are you looking to explore alternative spiritualties?"

"I'm more interested in getting your take on the people who practice them on a practical as well as a religious level." When he frowned at her, Fil sighed. "I was hoping you could put me in touch with a witch."

Tim huffed in amused confusion and shook his head. "What, don't tell me you're looking for someone to sell you a love spell, Fil. I don't think my imagination bends that way."

She forced a smile. "No, no love spells. I don't suppose you met anyone during your research with any expertise in practicing magic? Or, um, curses?"

There was a moment of silence while Tim simply stared at her. "I have a hard time believing you're trying to find someone who can help you put a curse on something, but it's even harder to wrap my mind around why else you might be asking me this."

"Tim, when we talked about your research before, while you were still out there in the field, you told me you had seen some pretty remarkable things, right? Things you wouldn't have believed if you hadn't witnessed them with your own eyes."

"Yeah, I did, but—"

"Well, at first, I thought you were a little bit off your rocker, or at least maybe too naïve to realize when some of the people you were observing were playing tricks on you. You know, using smoke and mirrors to put on a good show so that you'd write about what you thought they could do as if it were really magic."

When he just stared at her as if she'd lapsed into Lithuanian without realizing it, she sighed. She pulled her left hand out from where she'd tucked it between her leg and her chair.

"Today, I don't think you're naïve and I don't think you're crazy. I think that if you really saw some people practicing magic during your research, I might need their help."

Holding up her palm, she watched as his gaze fell to her skin.

His eyes widened. "Holy crap, Fil. What the hell is that?"

"We think it's a kind of curse, and we'd really, really like to find somebody who might be able to help us get rid of it."

Tim reached for her hand, but froze when Spar growled a warning. Fil shot him a quelling glance, then nodded at the professor.

"Go ahead, take a closer look. It's pretty messed up, I know."

Carefully, he cupped the back of her hand in his palm and angled her skin to the light shining in though the multipaned window. At first, he seemed to keep one wary eye on Spar, but within seconds all his attention was focused on the mark covering Fil's palm.

"This is amazing. How did this happen?"

"That is a really long, really weird, and really not-the-time-or-place-for-it story. Suffice it to say, someone got mad at me, ridiculous and unbelievable things happened, and this thing just kind of showed up."

"It looks almost like a burn or a brand of some sort, but the mark isn't raised off the skin the way keloid scarring usually is. In that way, I suppose it resembles something more like a tattoo. It's fascinating."

Fil made a face. "That's because it isn't on your hand."

Tim glanced up, looking guilty. "I'm sorry. Does it hurt?"

"No, it's not painful, just . . . disturbing. Which is why I'm asking you if you've ever met anyone who might know about things like this and how to counter them."

Spar reached out and tugged Fil's hand down, clasping it firmly in his. Tim looked from one to the other and shook his head.

"That's a huge question," he said. "I met plenty of witches and people who called themselves that during my interviews, but for, like, ninety-nine percent of them, what they call magic is what an academic like me would call accessorized prayer. They decide what it is they want to accomplish, and they use symbols and ritualized actions to focus their intent on making it happen."

"Remember that we are not academics," Spar said, his voice deep and sharp enough that Tim's Adam's apple bobbed as he swallowed hard.

"Right," he hurried to say. "What I mean is, say one of these witches thinks a neighbor is spying on her. You know, looking in her window while she's getting changed or something. She might get a small mirror and hang it on a string like a sun catcher. She'll cast a spell over it, which is really like saying a prayer, and envision the mirror reflecting back the energy of the person who's facing it. Then she'll hang the mirror in the window and close her curtains. When the neighbor stops spying and she finds out he lost his job when his company caught him using the Internet at work to look at porn, she tells herself her spell worked. Really, the guy stopped watching her because she kept her curtains closed, so he had nothing to look at anymore, and his company monitors all of its employees' computer usage."

Spar snorted. "That is not magic; it is self-delusion."

"That's my point. People believe in it because they have faith, the same way Catholics have faith that when they eat that little wafer the priest hands them at Mass, they're partaking in the body of Christ. It has meaning not because of what it accomplishes, but because of what they think it will accomplish."

That was not what Fil wanted to hear. She needed actual help, not futile prayers. Those she could handle herself.

"You said ninety-nine percent," she pointed out. "Doesn't that mean that there's one percent that isn't that way?"

"I did meet one woman," Tim said, looking thoughtful. "I met her by accident, really. She wasn't one of the people I sent my letter of inquiry to when I was initially looking for subjects. I ran into her when I was in an occult store talking to the people who worked there. She'd come in to sell some herbs she had grown in her garden."

"She's an herbalist?"

"Among other things. She grows herbs, makes teas and lotions and bath products from them. She's also a licensed massage therapist and a basket weaver." Tim grinned. "When I first saw her, I took her for any other hippie, new-age Wiccan type."

Spar narrowed his eyes. "What made her different?"

"At first, nothing. She went about her business with the shop manager while I talked to the owner behind the counter and left, but when I finished my initial interview and left the store, she was waiting for me outside. She warned me that some of the information the store owner had given me about plants and herbology was just plain wrong. She advised me to speak with a woman at a different store out in Anjou. After we chatted for a couple of minutes, I asked if she'd be willing to do a formal interview for my research. She turned me down flat."

"So how did you find out she was different from the other people you talked to?"

"That already was different. Most of the people I approached couldn't wait to talk my ear off." Tim shook his head. "It took me six months of dogged persistence to get her to even consider going on record about what she does."

"And what does she do?" Spar demanded.

"I once saw her bury an apple seed in a plain garden pot and place her hand over the soil. Within five minutes, I watched while a green shoot pushed out of the dirt and budded a new leaf. I dropped my digital voice recorder and nearly lost the entire morning's interview."

"That's it? She grew a plant?"

"Hush." Fil scolded Spar and turned back to Tim. "There's more, right?"

"Too much to list, most of it little stuff, but all of it like nothing else I'd ever seen. Everyone else would tell me these elaborate stories of rituals they'd done to make something or other happen, but all I heard was *post hoc, ergo propter hoc.* After it, therefore because of it," Tim explained. "Back in the Middle Ages, people thought maggots grew out of meat, because if they left out a piece of meat, eventually maggots would appear on it. They saw the first thing, then the second thing, so they assumed the first caused the second."

"I'm amazed all people weren't vegetarians," Fil muttered.

"They largely were, but that's the subject of a lecture for the history department. What's important is that none of what W—what she did," Tim caught himself, "was like that. She never made any claims. She just did things and left the interpretation to me."

Fil pursed her lips. "Do you think she could help me?"

"I think she's the only person I've met who might have an honest idea of how to try."

"Will you give me her phone number?"

Tim made a face. "I can't. I promised I'd keep her identity strictly confidential. It was the only way to get her to talk to me."

Spar's lip curled back in a snarl. "Then why do you taunt us by letting us believe she could help Felicity?"

"I wasn't taunting you, I swear," the man hurried to assure them. "I can't put you in contact with her, but I can do the reverse. I'll call her myself and tell her your story. She believes that her abilities come with a responsibility to use them to help others. I'm certain that if I tell her what's happened to you, she'll reach out to you yourself."

Fil pulled her hand out of Spar's grasp and held her palm up again. "This is important, Tim. I really need to talk to her."

"I know. And I promise she will call."

She sighed. "Then I suppose that's the best I can ask for."

"I'm sorry. Trust me, if I could help you myself, I would, but with all the stuff I know, I'm afraid it's all— forgive the pun—academic knowledge. I've seen and recorded a lot of things happening, but I have absolutely no clue how to do them myself."

Tim pushed up from his desk and walked around to the back to rummage in one of the deep bottom drawers. A moment later he was back, holding out a miniature glass vial.

"Here. I figure this can't hurt." He passed it to Fil with a shrug and stuffed his hands into his pockets. "Holy water. From the Vatican. It was a souvenir. I know it's kind of a cliché, but you are Catholic, right? I really do think that there's a lot of power in faith."

Fil let out a half laugh. "I was Catholic. My grandparents raised me that way. But after the past few days?" She shook her head. "I'm not sure what I believe anymore."

"Well, consider that in the mold of a rabbit's foot." His mouth curved at one corner. "Carrying it won't make anything bad happen, and if something good comes of it . . . *post hoc, ergo propter hoc,* right?"

Fil rose and tucked the vial into the pocket of her jacket. "Thanks, Tim. I'd appreciate it if you'd make that call as soon as possible. Like I said, it's been a rough few days for me."

"As soon as I shut the door behind you." He held up a hand with the three middle fingers extended. "Scout's honor."

"Thanks."

Slipping her hand into Spar's, Fil said her good-byes. Together they stepped out of the cool brick building and into the bright sunshine.

Chapter Eleven

Squinting against the glare, Fil blew out a breath. "That didn't go quite the way I'd hoped."

Spar rubbed his thumb across the lines that marked her palm and frowned. "No, it did not. I had rather higher expectations of the human."

"He's doing what he could. We both knew it was a long shot."

He grunted and led the way across the lawn to where they had parked the motorcycle. "I do not like this sensation of waiting for others to address a concern. I prefer to take action."

"Yeah, I kinda had that figured out. I'm not wild about the helpless shtick, either, but right now I'm not sure what else we can do." Spar growled something under his breath and slung his leg over the bike. She shot him a look. "Getting grumpy about it isn't going to help, you know."

He opened his mouth to retort, but shut it to glare at her hip. Ella Fitzgerald's "Oh, Lady Be Good" played from her jeans pocket.

Digging out her cell phone, she checked the screen out of habit. She already recognized her friend's ringtone.

"What's up?" she answered.

"I. Have got. News!"

Fil's heart sped up as she caught on to Ella's excitement. "Oh, my God. Please tell me you talked to the Warden and he's alive and an expert at removing demonic curses."

"No, sheesh, Fil. Now anything I have to say is just going to disappoint you. Did you really have to set the bar that high?"

She sighed. "Just tell me it's something more significant than finding that perfect pair of nude pumps you've been searching for."

"I have an address."

"For a shoe store?"

"For the last known location of Jeffrey Michael Onslow, antiques dealer and member of the Guild of Wardens."

Fil nearly dropped the phone. "Why the hell aren't you calling me from his living room?"

"Because," Ella said with exaggerated patience, "I just got my hot little hands on the info like twenty-seven seconds ago."

"That's no—"

"And," she continued, "because the address is in Ottawa."

"That's only a couple hours' drive from here."

"I know. That's why I just texted it to you."

"You're the best."

Fil ended the call and unstrapped her helmet and

spare from the back of the bike. "Put that on." She handed the extra to Spar. "We're going for a ride."

She broke every speed limit in Canada on the way to Ottawa. As the kilometers flew by them, Spar's warm presence behind her only urged her on. He hoped for a cure as desperately as she did.

The GPS function on her phone had her slowing off the highway east of Ottawa city. The signs reported their location in Clarence-Rockland, then Rockland itself as Fil began to navigate the local roads. By the time the directions brought her to the edges of the town and sent her turning down a rural lane, it was the middle of the afternoon. Her heart pounded in her chest, and her hands had begun to sweat around the grips on the handlebars.

A long drive brought them to what looked to have once been a farmhouse set before the remains of a small apple orchard. The white clapboards gleamed in the sunshine, with crisp green trim edging the windows and picked out on the gingerbread detailing of the eaves. It looked like the kind of home an antiques dealer would live in, and she could practically picture the interior crowded with Victorian settees and Arts and Crafts dining tables.

Fil cut the engine and sat back on the bike for a moment just taking stock. She was having a hard time at the moment distinguishing the voice of her fears from that of her intuition, but her feeling just then couldn't really be called positive.

Spar swung off the bike and glanced down at her. "What is the matter?"

She nodded to the house. "I don't think anyone's home."

"Let's go see."

Fil took the hand he held out and followed him up the wide front porch to knock on the wood-framed screen door. When no one answered after a minute or two, she pulled it open and plied the brass knocker on the inner door. Still, no one answered.

Before she could stop him, Spar reached out and turned the knob to find the door unlocked. He pushed it open and stepped inside while Fil dug her heels in at the threshold and yanked at the back of his shirt.

"You can't just walk into someone else's house," she hissed. "No one is home! We could get in trouble for this!"

"Who will give us trouble? There is no one here," he reasoned as he stepped through the foyer.

"The police, as soon as one of his neighbors gives them a call!"

He shrugged and passed through an open doorway.

Behind him Fil groaned and squeezed her eyes shut. "The last time I committed breaking and entering, it did not go well for me. Please, please do not let this end up the same way. I can only carry so many demon marks at one time."

Fingering the vial of holy water in her pocket—and fervently hoping Tim was right about it bringing her luck—she stepped reluctantly into the house and hurried to catch up to Spar.

The front parlor looked pretty much like she'd pictured it. Dark, original wood trim framed the door and windows and matched the heavy fireplace mantel with its intricate carving of leaves and acorns. An antique camelback sofa upholstered in green velvet sat facing the fire, flanked by leather wingback chairs. Hand-crocheted doilies topped the tea table, and she would have bet twenty bucks that the beautifully inlaid cabinet in the corner housed an antique Victrola. She'd have added a twoonie that it worked, too.

Spar had already crossed through the pocket doors that separated the parlor from what looked to her like a study. An enormous partners' desk held pride of place in the center of the room, its tooled, spiraling legs wider around than her arms. Looking at the top, she had the immediate impression of controlled chaos. Nearly every surface was covered, with stacks of papers, boxes, pens, cups, a clock, at least three different antique desk sets that she could identify, and books.

There were books everywhere, stacks of them, shelves of them, and volumes lying open on almost every available surface. Either Jeffrey Onslow was a voracious reader with the attention span of an ADHD gnat, or he was in the middle of some kind of research. Fil wasn't sure she'd prefer either of those answers.

Spar pushed aside the wooden clerk's chair behind the desk and flipped through the papers laid out in the center of the blotter. "You were right. He is not here."

"I suppose he could be upstairs, but no, I don't think he's in the house. It feels too empty in here. Do you think we should go back to the front porch and wait for him? He could be at work, or at the grocery store or something."

"No, I mean he is gone. He fled from the Order."

Spar looked up and caught her gaze. "But he left us a note."

"What?"

"Come and look."

He waved her around to stand beside him and pushed a piece of paper toward her. The sheet of stationery was the color of fresh cream, thick, expensive, and ridiculously old-fashioned. It suited the house to a tee. On it, someone had used a wide-nibbed pen to scribble a hasty note.

"To the Guardian," she read aloud. "I could see you coming, but not soon enough. Having run out of time, I have concluded that my best course of action is to leave now and hope to draw our enemies after me. If I have succeeded, you will find an envelope in my favorite book of poetry. I hope its contents will aid you and your female in what you must do. I fear there is One who sleeps no longer."

She flipped the page over, but saw nothing else. "That's it. Nicely cryptic, no? I hope you know what it means, because I'm really not up for guessing games right now."

Spar had already moved to the bookshelves lining the room's back wall. "It means that we must find this envelope, first of all."

"Really? Did you know Jeffrey Michael Onslow, Spar? Were you guys buddies?" she asked, the sarcasm all but dripping down her chin. "Close enough to chat about your favorite poets, I hope."

"I have never heard of him before." He grunted and pulled a heavy volume from a middle shelf. It was the size of a photo album only thicker and bound in worn leather. "But his clue was an old and familiar one used by the Guild. Every Warden for several centuries has kept a copy of this book in his library."

Fil let him set the book on the desk and flipped open to the frontispiece. "*Paradise Lost*? Seriously? Are you trying to tell me that the Guild has a sense of humor?"

"You find the poem humorous?"

"The poem, no. The Guild calling it their favorite book of poetry, yes. I mean, come on. It's all about the fall of Satan and the war between the angels and the fallen." He continued to look at her blankly, and she rolled her eyes. "You really don't think that hits just a little close to home?"

Spar shook his head. "Again, religion is merely a language used to understand the incomprehensible. I can assure you that none of the Seven is a creation of a God who cast it out for the crime of arrogance. Each is a piece of the Darkness itself, torn apart to weaken them all and kept imprisoned for the sake of the living universe. This story is nothing but a bedtime tale."

"Okay, so the Guild has a sense of humor, but you don't."

He ignored her and began flipping through the pages of the book. He grunted when several fell back and exposed a cavity cut into the paper. Inside was a seven-by-nine brown manila envelope.

Fil huffed out a breath. "Wow. After that note sounded like something out of a low-budget spy movie, I had myself half convinced this guy was a lunatic, but at least that much of what he wrote was true. How on earth could he have seen us coming?"

"I suspect he employed some manner of scrying, unless he had the ability to foresee the future naturally."

"Like precognition? Are there really people who can do that?"

He shot her a sideways glance. "Are there really those who can look at a person and know his character and ability to channel magic at a glance?"

She stuck her tongue out at him. It just seemed called for.

"Don't be a jerk. I mean, my grandma's aunt always knew when someone was coming to visit before the doorbell rang, but that's like five minutes of foresight. Judging by the looks of this place, Onslow had to have left at least several hours ago. It could have been days, for all we know."

"It is possible. I have seen oracles predict wars a hundred years in the future. I believe that after your recent experiences, you might want to rethink your definition of what is and is not possible, little human."

He flicked a fingertip down her cheek. Fil grabbed his hand and squeezed.

"Not a bad point, I guess." She plucked the envelope from his grasp and reached for a letter opener that lay amid the clutter. "Let's see what Mr. Onslow thought we ought to know."

Slitting open the edge, she pulled a thick sheaf of papers from the envelope. They had been folded inward on themselves inside a sheet of standard computer paper, but she could see a mix of materials and sizes, including photocopies, lined notebook pages, and newspaper clippings. Her curiosity stirred.

A thumping sound registered in the distance, and

Fil's head shot up. "Please tell me that was not a car door. Like the car door of the RCMP coming to arrest us for breaking into the house." She tried peering out the window, but this side of the house gave onto the orchard, not the front yard.

"We broke nothing. The door was open." Spar's voice remained as even as ever, but she noticed he had already moved toward the door. "Plus, we were obviously expected. I will explain this to the authorities."

"Yeah, you do that. I'm still getting ready to get the heck out of here. We can go through all this at home."

She found herself speaking to thin air and heard the screen door at the front of the house thump closed behind the disappearing gargoyle.

"I'm telling you," she muttered to herself, refolding the stack of papers and trying to stuff them back into the envelope. "Breaking and entering never turns out well for me."

The words had barely cleared her teeth when the sound of glass shattering directly behind her ripped a scream from Fil's throat.

Spinning like a top, she clutched the envelope in front of her like a particularly pathetic shield and watched in horror as a fist the color of mud reached in through the broken window and grabbed at her. She caught a glimpse of the thick, dark arm attached to a muscular shoulder that stooped down to allow a craggy face to peer in through the window. Considering that the set of steps to the front porch put the floor of the house an estimated five feet about ground level, the fact that whatever stood outside trying to get in had to bend down to look inside did not set Fil's mind at ease.

Yelling Spar's name, she threw herself backward onto the desk and tried to scramble out of the thing's reach. Globs of soil seemed to drop from its skin as it swiped at her again, and she realized the entire thing wasn't just the color of dirt; it looked like it was made out of dirt. In fact, the red, unearthly glow of its eyes appeared to be the only thing that didn't look like clay, soil, or tiny plant roots that had been ripped violently from the land.

And, oh, ew, was that an earthworm wriggling along its wrist?

Fil heard the ominous crack of the wooden window frame as more glass tinkled to the floor. With a sudden lunge, the creature shoved its arm through the window up to its shoulder and just managed to catch Fil's ankle in its filthy paw. Frantic, she grabbed on to the edge of the desk, but it felt like a skeleton of iron lurked beneath the crumbling topsoil. The creature pulled, and she screamed, but inevitably she felt her grip slipping until she lost hold of the desk and went flying backward out the window.

The thing managed to get her legs outside and grabbed her other ankle for a more solid grip. Fil jack-knifed her body at the hips, trying to keep at least her upper torso in the room. Plastering her chest against the wall beneath the window, she scrambled for something to hold on to. Her fingertips caught the arm of the desk chair and brought it rolling straight at her head. With a curse, she batted it away and sent it crashing into the bookshelves. The only thing left in her reach was the edge of the tasseled rug. Curling her fingers around it, she clung like a barnacle with separation anxiety and tried desperately to kick the thing holding her into next week.

The creature roared its frustration. The sound shook the window frame until Fil felt the vibrations deep in her gut. Poor baby, she thought, not getting to kill her so easily. As far as she was concerned, tall, dark, and dirty could go screw a gopher hole.

When the door to the library crashed back against the wall, Fil nearly wept with relief. Well, until the gargoyle took one look at her and disappeared back the way he'd come.

"Spar!" she screamed. "Get back here, you under-protective son of a bitch! I could use a little help here!"

The monster holding her gave an almighty yank on her ankles, forcing an entirely different scream from her throat. It felt like her hips were about to pop right out of their sockets. Either that, or he'd just about ripped the limbs off completely. Pain combined with the pressure on her abdomen to send a wave of intense nausea crashing through her. Goddamn it, she was not going to vomit again. She'd already met her quota for the week. Hell, for the bloody year.

A new roar shattered the silence, and this one Fil recognized. Somewhere outside, a Guardian had morphed into full battle mode.

"About frickin' time, Rocky."

All at once the grip on her ankles released and her knee crashed into the clapboard siding hard enough to make her see stars. She yelped and gripped the rug hard while gravity pulled her legs down and threatened to send her the rest of the way out the window.

Behind her, she could hear the sounds of outright

war, but all she could see was the inside of the library and the underside of Onslow's desk. She believed in Spar's ability to protect her, but was the thing that had attacked her hurting him? And what the hell was it, anyway? Somehow she doubted *dirt demon* counted as the technical term.

Her uncomfortable position was not helping Fil's state of mind. Quickly weighing the pros and cons of her choices, she realized finishing the trip outside would be a heck of a lot easier than attempting to drag her butt back in through the window. She just had to count on Spar to keep the monster distracted while she went out and then hauled ass for cover.

Saying a quick prayer, she released her hold on the rug and pushed off against the floorboards, sending herself backward onto the hard ground. The impact jarred already aching muscles, but she ignored the discomfort. As fast as she could she rolled to her feet and glanced around. Less than twenty feet away, Spar hovered in the air above what she could now see clearly looked like the Incredible Hulk. You know, if a little kid had molded him out of dirt, like a beach-free sand castle.

Dirt Hulk swatted at Spar, but the gargoyle just beat his wings and lifted up out of reach. Darting around, Spar came at the thing from another angle, aiming for its chest. The creature spun and grabbed again, but Fil could see it was slow and clumsy. Strong, yes, she could testify to that, but in reality it was no match for a Guardian.

Spar attacked like a raptor harassing its prey. He would dart in, tear off a chunk of earthy flesh, then retreat too fast for the creature to catch hold of him.

The thing began to dance in circles in response to the gargoyle's constant movement. It was awkward and graceless; she predicted no future for it in music videos. The sight might have been enough to make Fil laugh if the monster hadn't been trying to kill her five minutes ago.

She tended to hold grudges over things like that.

Hulk circled again until he faced the house once more. Catching sight of Fil, he seemed to forget all about the Guardian currently attempting to kill him and lurched in her direction. Spar bellowed in outrage and dove in for the kill, wrapping his hands around the creature's lump of a head and ripping it clean off the shoulders.

The thing just kept coming.

Fil blinked and yelped, scrambling backward until she came up hard against the house's clapboard siding. Even without a head, the creature lumbered unerringly in her direction. Apparently it didn't need to see her to attack her. It reached out to grab her way too early, so maybe its sense of depth perception had been thrown off at least.

The movement flexed the mass of its chest, and something strange caught her eye. Right where she assumed its breastbone would have been, the clean, well-defined shape of a medallion appeared to have been embedded in the soily flesh. It had some kind of symbol carved into it, but frankly, Fil was too busy looking for an escape route to try to identify it.

She calculated that if she timed it right, she could duck under the creature's arm when it got close enough to grab her. She'd seen how slowly it moved, and despite her aching, bruised muscles and joints, she figured she was still faster. After she ducked past it, she intended to keep running all the way to the motorcycle. Once on the Tiger, she could keep out of range until Spar dealt with the damned thing.

Luckily, she didn't have to wait.

With a furious roar, the gargoyle landed on the thing's shoulders. Unable to make a sound without its head, the creature still made its displeasure known by reaching up to grab the Guardian around the waist. Before he could flip his attacker to the ground, Spar grabbed for the strange medallion and tore it from the brute's chest. Immediately it collapsed to the ground like a mudslide, leaving nothing but a pile of rich, dark soil in its wake.

"Holy shit." Breathing the words seemed to drain the last of the strength from Fil's legs, because the moment they passed her lips her knees buckled. She slid down the side of the house to land on her butt beneath the ruined window. "What the hell was that?"

"Golem," Spar spat, closing his fist and crushing the medallion into dust.

Shocked, Fill heard a piercing shriek and watched as a cloud of sickly green mist shot into the air above them. It writhed for a moment, and she swore she could see the image of a familiar face in the vapor.

"Oh, my God! Did you see that?"

Spar watched as the mist dissipated and the scream faded to an echo and died. "Who was it?"

"It looked like the Hierophant. That's who I saw in my vision, anyway."

Spar simply growled and reached for her hand. "Come. We will collect the envelope and leave this place. You need to be home where I can defend you properly."

Without waiting for a reply, he hauled her to her feet and began dragging her around to the front of the house.

"Wait a second," she protested, pulling back. "What just happened? Where did that mist come from, and why did it form an image of the Hierophant? Spar, you have to tell me what's going on."

He ignored her attempts to slow him down, but at least he answered her questions. "The golem is a creature made of earth and animated by the power of its creator. It has no mind, no will of its own, but it makes for a relentless and unquestioning servant. The medallion on its chest contained the magic that gave it life, and when I destroyed it, you saw the essence of the *nocturnis* who made it returning to his body."

Fil followed him into the library and scooped up the envelope where she'd dropped it when the golem attacked. "Then the Hierophant made the golem and sent it after me. That's why when it saw me, it stopped fighting you and came after me again."

Spar grunted and herded her back toward the door. "Yes."

"Crap."

Pausing to shift back to his human form, Spar opened the door and glanced down at her. "You appear uninjured, but I may have missed something. If you are unable to make the drive back to Montreal, I can fly us, but we would have to leave the motorcycle here, and we would have to wait for darkness. I prefer to leave now, but I will not risk your health."

Fil felt herself soften and reached up to touch his face. "I'm okay," she reassured him. "I got yanked on and thrown around some, so I'm probably covered in bruises, but nothing serious."

"You are certain?"

His dark eyes blazed down at her, their inner fire clearly overwhelming his ability to contain it. She could read his worry in the tense set of his features and remembered the way he had claimed her the night before. She knew he felt responsible for her safety, but the uncomfortable feeling began to take hold that he might mean that "mine" business just a touch too literally.

Taking a step back, she dropped her hand and forced a casual smile. "I'm good. Promise. But heading home sounds like a really good idea. We still need to go over this stuff from Onslow, remember? I'd prefer to do that somewhere we can be pretty sure we're not going to be attacked again."

Spar's jaw tightened. He stopped her before she could lead the way into the yard and scanned the area for threats before allowing her to step outside.

"When you think of a place like that, be certain to inform me," he grumbled. "Maybe we could visit."

Chapter Twelve

Spar stood watch at the window of Felicity's apartment and brooded. Despite her protestations, he could detect the hesitation in her movements that spoke of pain. She might not have bloody wounds or broken bones this time, but he did not like the idea of her being in the slightest discomfort. Immediately upon reaching her home, he had snatched the envelope out of her hand and sent her to the bathroom. A warm soak in a hot tub should ease some of her aches, and the time apart provided him time to think.

He could feel her pulling away, or at least making the attempt. He had noticed it immediately after the golem attack, but he had written it off to the shock of yet another attempt on her life in just a few short days. The ride back on her motorcycle had afforded him no opportunity to comfort her, aside from holding her in his arms, but even then she had held herself stiffly in his embrace. She kept trying to create distance between them, and Spar would not allow that to happen.

He had known from the beginning that he reacted to Felicity in a way he had experienced with no other woman, no other *person,* in all his long life. That alone fascinated him, but once he had touched her intimately, he had begun to suspect that something greater than mere attraction might be at work.

He had believed the stories to be only that—stories. He'd heard the tales of the first Guardians, as all of his kind had. History, after all, was one of the Light's greatest teachers.

When the first Guardians had been summoned by the Guild to battle the seven demons, they had awed the world with their terrible might. For days and weeks they had battled until finally the Seven were ripped apart and cast out of the mortal realm to their abysmal prisons. Duty fulfilled, the Guardians had slept until once again the Darkness stirred and the Wardens summoned them to their task.

Over and over, the cycle repeated, but as fierce and powerful as the Guardians were, they existed only to fight a battle they did not even claim as their own. They felt no connection to the humans they defended or to the world in which they made war, and so eventually they ceased to answer the summons of the Guild. Without anger or pain or protectiveness to make them fight, they had no reason to wake, and Darkness threatened to take over the whole of the world.

Eventually, a woman stepped forward and defied the Guild by offering her aid in waking the Guardians. Despite their protests she went to the feet of the first statue and knelt, and there she prayed to the Light to aid her and return the Guardians to the mortal world to save humanity. Before the prayer even finished, a mighty crack split the air and the Guardian leapt from the stone and seized the woman, claiming her as his. She was his mate, he vowed, and for her sake and the sake of her people he would once again take up his struggle against the Seven.

One by one, women of power appeared, and one by one each Guardian found his destined mate. Each fought for her sake to banish the Darkness once more from the world, and when the threat had passed, each one demanded that the Guild release him from his duty so that he could spend the rest of his existence with his chosen mate.

From that time forward, the Guild had given each summoned Guardian the ability to feel at least the most basic of emotions—hatred for the evil of the Darkness. Canny as they were, the Guild preferred not to have to replace their warriors every waking cycle, and so in the past several thousands of years Spar had heard whispers of only a handful of additional Guardians who had found their true mates. It had become a kind of legend among his brethren, a fairy tale each of them knew yet none of them truly believed. Until now.

Spar believed Felicity might be his true mate.

He almost feared to think the words. Never had he believed he would find her. By the Light, he had not truly believed she existed, or ever would. He had looked into his future and seen war and sleep in an infinite cycle of sameness. Then one day, he would lose a battle and be destroyed, and another Guardian would be called to take his place. He had known this the way he knew how to fight or fly, something not to be questioned. But now, a different sort of future had begun to dance at the edge of his vision, and he found himself longing for it with a painful intensity.

Spar wanted Felicity, in a way that bordered on obsession. He wanted not just her body, but her clever mind, and her fierce heart, and her generous soul. Last night, he had felt as if he had tasted them, touched them, as if she had welcomed him into her and shown him the possibilities of a world without bloodshed, without the endlessly tainting blackness of the Dark. He wanted more of that, of her.

The sound of her footsteps pulled him from his thoughts, and he turned to see her emerge from the short hallway, clad head-to-toe in baggy, shapeless fabric that hid every one of her curves from his gaze. He fought the desire to smile at her tactic. Did she think every inch of her beautiful body was not already printed on his brain, ready to be called up at a moment's notice? He did not need the sight of her skin to make him want her. He didn't even need her to be present. He would want her if she were on another plane of existence, because he had already touched her, and he knew she was his.

"You ready to find out what's in that envelope?" she asked.

He watched her toes wiggle nervously inside a ridiculously fluffy pair of brightly striped socks and nodded. "Let us see what the Warden thought we should know."

For more than an hour they worked together, sorting through the thick stack of papers, skimming through the contents, and laying them out across the surface of the coffee table. When they finished, Spar stepped back to take in the story they told.

Fil sat at one end of the sofa with her legs curled up beneath her doing much the same thing. After several minutes, she leaned back and shook her head. "The only thing I get from looking at all that is creeped out. If Onslow thought this would send us some kind of coherent message, it's flown right over my head and out the window." She glanced up at him. "Do you know what it's supposed to mean?"

Spar only wished he did not. To call the envelope's contents disturbing would do them a disservice. The missing Warden had clearly spent weeks, if not months, pulling together a seemingly random collection of information. Photocopied pages of obscure texts on demonology overlapped lined pages of handwritten notes on books so old, no library would let them near the harsh light of a copy machine. Other texts appeared as printouts from online library collections, most of which possessed margins filled with questions, conclusions, and clarifications.

A handful of photographs included specimens in sepia tones, creased and faded over time, as well as at least one faded Polaroid and several computer-printed five-by-sevens. A few showed people in either posed or candid settings, while others appeared to focus on locations, either urban or scenic. A copy of what looked like an article from an academic journal called *The Psychology of the Supernatural* sat next to a handful of newspaper clippings in English, French, Spanish, German, and Arabic.

It all added up to an eclectic and puzzling collection. Unless, of course, one examined the whole through the eyes of a Warden. Or a Guardian.

Rage and dread rose within him, and Spar fought the urge to scoop Felicity up in his arms and fly her to safety. He burned with the need to find her a sanctuary, somewhere not even the slightest hint of Darkness could penetrate. But if Onslow's theory was correct, no such place existed, especially not for a human with powers beyond the ordinary and the mark of the Defiler on her skin.

He felt Felicity's gaze on him, sensed her concern, and turned to her knowing his expression would appear grim. Better to worry her than to terrify her. At least, for now.

"What is it? You understand what's here, I can see it in your face. So tell me."

Her tone was implacable, but he caught the trace of worry threaded through it. What he was about to reveal would offer no comfort.

He drew a deep breath. "The Warden wished us to know that he believes we have already failed in at least a part of our task," he said gravely. "According to what he is trying to tell us, the Order's plans have advanced farther than we feared.

"One of the Seven is already free."

Fil blinked. For a frozen moment, it was all she could do. She didn't even think she drew breath, but she knew her heart hadn't stopped, because it beat in her ears like echoing thunder, deafening her to anything else. The skin of her palm began to tingle, and she hoped like hell it was a psychosomatic reaction.

"How is that possible? I thought a Guardian was supposed to sense when one of the bad guys started to stir and step in before it got that far." Her voice cracked and croaked, but she got the question out and clenched her fists while she waited for an answer.

Spar shook his head. "I do not know. What you say is true, and the Wardens are meant to summon us from our sleep at the first sign of such a threat, and yet neither of those things happened. I can only theorize that this is why the Order has launched its war against the Guild. By thinning the ranks of the Wardens, they may have disrupted what binds us together and made it possible for them to call one of their Masters forth unnoticed."

She felt a laugh bubbling up in her throat, knew it came out just this side of hysterical. "Unnoticed? I have a hard time believing that one of the seven embodiments of ultimate evil in the universe popped up in Saskatoon or someplace one day and nobody noticed."

"And that is to our advantage."

Spar lowered himself to the sofa beside her and reached for her hand. She fought to keep it from him, but his strength easily overwhelmed her. His gentle concern, though, was what really threatened to push her over the edge.

"We have an advantage?"

"If one of the Seven had broken free of its prison of its own free will, it would have been at the peak of its strength. Nothing else could shatter the wards and safeguards that keep it contained, and a demon of the Darkness at full strength could have passed no one's notice. Without the Guardians there to battle against it, its path of destruction would already have swept wide and bloody across the land. We would have heard about it."

Fil looked up at him, at his dark, serious eyes glinting with inner fire, and struggled not to climb into his lap, curl up into a ball, and hide. She didn't know how much longer she could take this. Every time she thought she got a handle on this nightmare, something else happened to make things even worse. If she thought pinching herself would wake her up into a different, saner reality, she'd be nothing but a giant walking bruise.

Of course, after her run-in with the golem, she sort of felt that way already.

"Maybe that means Onslow was wrong, then." She tried to make the hope in her voice come off as something other than pathetic, but had a feeling she hadn't succeeded. "If we haven't seen any evidence of activity by the Seven, maybe they're still locked up where they belong."

"The evidence is here." Spar gestured to the paperwork, making her stomach sink into her ankles. "I believe the Warden invested a great deal of time into his research, and it appears he was thorough. His theory, and I agree with him, is that the *nocturnis* either discovered or developed a spell that works like the one the Wardens use to summon us from our sleep, only instead of waking the Guardians, they attempted to pull a demon onto our plane of existence. It would require a tremendous amount of power, but it could work."

"And you think it did."

"It makes sense." He picked up newspaper clipping and spread it open on her lap. "I assume that you do not read Arabic—"

"Not so much."

"—so I will tell you that this article relates the tale

of a massacre in the mountains on the northern border of Afghanistan."

"Considering there's a war on there, do you really think that has anything to do with demons? I mean, I've always considered the groups who want to subjugate their women and make war on the West to be pretty evil, but—"

He shushed her with a glance. "A place like that is the perfect cover for the *nocturnis*. As you see, the media reports that a group of militant rebels attacked a small village in the dead of night. Fifty people were slaughtered, every man, woman, and child in the village. The eldest was almost eighty, the youngest only weeks from its mother's womb."

Fil felt her heart clench. "That's unspeakably awful, but things like that happen during wars."

"And they happen when doers of evil need to raise tremendous amounts of power through the sacrifice of blood," he insisted in clear, cold words. "Nothing in the universe raises more Dark power than the spilling of human blood and the draining of a human life force. Nothing. It is the most unforgivable of acts, and one that feeds the Darkness like nothing else. Even the *nocturnis* reserve it for the rarest and most important of their rituals. The lifeblood of a single human will nourish a demon at full strength for days. Perhaps weeks. To sacrifice fifty of them could have broken through the wards of one's prison and allowed the Order to call it forth."

Fil shook her head. She understood what Spar was telling her, but she didn't want to hear it, didn't want to believe it. "If that's all it takes, then why don't they just bomb a city and break all of the Seven out at once?

Why waste time lurking in the shadows when they could have already taken over the world a thousand times by now?"

Spar gaped at her for a moment.

"What?"

He squeezed her hand. "I think we are very lucky that you are on the side of the Light, my fierce little human." He sighed. "Thankfully it is not so simple. A device like a bomb does not have the same effect. It is not simply the death of a human that is required. There is a ritual that must be performed, and the death requires the draining of blood. A bladed weapon must be used, one dedicated to the Darkness. Wholesale destruction may please the Seven, but it does not feed them the power they require. For that, each life must be taken individually, and that requires either a great deal of time, or a great many killers."

"That still sounds like something they could have tried before."

"With the Wardens and the Guardians looking on? We would never have allowed it."

Fil thought back on the things she had learned from Ella and Kees since this weird roller-coaster ride had begun. Parts of it began to click into place. "That's why they started their big recruitment drive, and why they went after the Guild." She cursed. "They were getting the manpower in place to be able to perform large-scale sacrifices, in the first case. And in the second, by taking out the Wardens, they ensured fewer people were able to interfere and made it nearly impossible to summon the Guardians to stop them completely."

Spar nodded grimly. "So I am sure they believed."

"That's almost elegant."

Fil could see the beauty of the plan. It would have required years of planning, maybe even decades. Calculating the numbers required, finding suitable recruits, and swaying them to the Dark side couldn't have been easy. At least she hoped not. She would like to think it took more than the promise of cookies to make the average person dedicate his soul to serving the ultimate evil.

Then there would have been training for all the new little minions. They would have to learn not only the proper use of magic, but also the rituals required of the Order's demonic Masters. Add in the time it took to cause as much damage to the Guild as Ella had begun to suspect, and this was no strike of blind fury. Someone had to have orchestrated it like a chess match, and that person was playing a very long game.

"The Hierophant." She snapped back to focus and looked up at Spar. "He's got to be running this, right? There has to be an architect, and if he's the leader of the Order, it has to be him behind it."

"That is my assumption."

"Then we have to find him." Resolve and weariness warred inside her. According to what Onslow had uncovered, the force behind this plot appeared to possess both patience and cunning. He wouldn't make an easy opponent. "It's like a snake. That's what the old saying says. The head is the dangerous part. Cut that off, and all you've got is dead snake."

Spar gazed at her, looking bemused. "That is an old saying?"

"Close enough." She raised a hand to stifle a yawn.

"So that's what we do. We find the Hierophant, and we stop him. Simple. We can start tomorrow."

"Simple." He chuckled. "As I said, I am grateful you choose to work with the Light rather than against us. I do not think you have set us an easy task."

"We know where to start, at least. I've seen the Hierophant, remember. I know what he looks like. That's something we can work with."

"How?"

Fatigue had begun to tug on her eyelids, making them droop. "Can I figure that out in the morning? I could really use some sleep." Another yawn threatened to crack her jaw.

If Spar nodded, she didn't see it. She didn't hear him agree, either. It didn't matter. Nothing short of the hand of God could have kept her awake in that moment. Apparently, a road trip, a fight with a golem, and coming up with a plan to save the world could really take it out of a girl.

Who knew?

Chapter Thirteen

Fil slept like the dead. Not a dream, not a snore, not a minion of evil disturbed her slumber. Not for the first six hours. When the seventh hit sometime after three in the morning, the heavy blanket of unconsciousness lifted, and she stirred enough to roll onto her back. The wall there didn't bother to protest.

Her eyes flew open, taking a few seconds to adjust to the darkness. She felt the bulk of another figure in the bed, but she didn't need to turn her head to know who it was. She could sense Spar, could have picked him out of a crowd blindfolded and deaf. He called to her senses in a way she'd never experienced before.

The last thing she remembered was her sofa and her grand plan for hunting the Hierophant. She must have drifted off right there and left Spar to get her into bed. Her own mental phrasing made her snort. So far, the man hadn't had a lick of trouble getting her to bed anytime he wanted. He was rapidly becoming an addiction.

Careful not to wake him, Fil shifted until she could look at the man lying beside her. He took up a good deal more than half the bed, but she had to give him credit for not being a cover hog. Surprisingly, that was important with him, since unlike the few other men she had slept with in her life, this one didn't pump out heat like a furnace. She knew that if she touched him, his skin would feel pleasantly warm, but heat didn't radiate off him the way it seemed to from her human bed partners.

Human bed partners.

Fil rolled her eyes in the darkness. Wasn't that just a statement of the surrealist wonderland her life had become? Now she was thinking about her past lovers in terms of their species, because the latest was decidedly not a member of her own. She wondered: Should that bother her more than it did?

No, she had plenty of objections to the current situation that didn't involve DNA. She just wasn't certain she wanted to look at them too closely. She had a feeling she wouldn't like what she found.

She knew she had been sending Spar mixed signals, and she sort of hated herself for it. She'd always hated the kind of person who blew hot, then cold, then hot again as if unable to decide on a straight course. As far as she was concerned, playing games should involve cards, dice, or little plastic timers, not emotions. Her grandparents had raised her to tell the truth, even when a white lie might be easier. Sparing a person's feelings was one thing, but leading him on was quite another.

How she could lead Spar on when she herself had no clue what path she was following only added to Fil's confusion. She could admit that she had made the first move between them. Well, the first sex move. Sure, he had kissed her outside the hospital, but when he'd had her naked in the shower, all he'd done was clean her up and tend to her wound. She was the one who had seduced him, and God help her, she couldn't bring herself to regret it.

Spar made her feel the most amazing things. Every time he touched her, she felt electricity rage through her. It was like the strange magnetic energy she'd felt every time she'd seen his statue only amplified by a thousand. She would love to chalk it up to chemistry, but even the strongest attraction she'd felt for another man looked ridiculous compared with the feelings Spar inspired. Those feelings were so intense, they scared her.

Seriously. If she'd been wearing boots, she'd have been shaking in them. Spar was the first thing in her life ever to threaten her independence. From the beginning, her grandparents had taught her to take care of herself. They'd wanted her to be a strong woman, because they had known that their ages would take them from her before she was ready. Her love for them meant she could never have been ready, even if they'd lived two hundred years, but they had realized they wouldn't be with her through adulthood, and they had planned for that.

When they had passed away during her first year of college, the pain of the loss had staggered her, but she had known how to make their final arrangements, manage her own finances, deal with her grandfather's business, and basically do everything necessary to continue to build a life for herself. She had them to thank for that.

Now, eight years later, along came someone who not just wanted but *needed* to take care of her. She understood that for Spar, a Guardian's duty could never be shirked; it was part and parcel of what made him who he was, the literal reason for his existence. Without that desire to protect her and her fellow man, he wouldn't exist, and the question for Fil now wasn't if she would be able to let him protect her, but whether she would be able to cope when he stopped.

She tried to picture her life after he left, when things went back to normal, and the gaping hole his absence created nearly stole her breath. How could the life she'd so enjoyed before look so empty now? It had only been three days, for God's sake! Three days was not enough for him to become some integral component to her happiness. She had a career that challenged, fascinated, and delighted her, a hobby that qualified more as a passion, a comfortable home, and friends who made her laugh and do and think. Before she'd stepped into the abbey, she'd been happy, really happy with the life she had made for herself. Why did that have to change?

Okay, it made sense that she might see things a little differently than before. After all, until she'd met Spar and encountered the *nocturnis,* she'd had no idea there was some sort of ongoing war between good and evil being waged before humanity's unseeing eyes; and of course now that she knew, it wasn't something she was likely to forget. She also knew now that her ability to see the special abilities of others was only the tip of the iceberg as far as the existence of magic in the world was concerned. She didn't think she'd ever be able to stop looking for it now, and every new person she met would face the scrutiny of her inner eye. Was he gifted? Not gifted? *Nocturnis?* Something else?

A new perspective she could handle—would have to handle, since she doubted she had much choice in the matter. What she didn't know was whether she could handle watching Spar turn back to stone, knowing that by the time he awoke again she might be gone. A Guardian was immortal, but Fil knew she sure as heck wasn't. If nothing else, the past few days had made that abundantly clear. One day, she would die, and Spar would live on.

Will he remember me the next time he awakes? she wondered. Or would she be some vague shadow tucked away in the corner of his mind, a sense of déjà vu that never really made itself clear?

She watched him breathing, seeing the rise and fall of his chest in the darkened room. When she was a child, she'd spent more than a few nights lying awake in the dark and wondering similar things about her mother. As much as her grandparents loved her and as clearly as they had explained that her mother just wasn't able to take care of her the way she deserved, she had occasionally wondered. What had it been about the drugs that made them more important than a child? Why had the money for a fix been more important than the money for rent or food or clothes? Why had Fil not been worth the sacrifice of an addiction?

She knew it wasn't a fair question, had known it even before she'd spent several worthwhile sessions with a counselor coming to grips with the fact that none of her questions had answers. Her job was to learn to stop expecting any and to build her life around the empty places where the answers should have been. Eventually, she was reassured, she'd find other things to fill those gaps and she wouldn't even notice them anymore. She'd thought she had done that, but now the idea of Spar winning his battle and slipping back into his enchanted sleep felt like a great big backhoe, digging up those spots in her subconscious all over again. She could practically hear the rumble of the engines in the quiet bedroom.

She wondered if Ella felt the same way about Kees. She'd seen the way the two interacted and knew there was something between them. Ella had called herself Kees's Warden, and Fil knew by now that it was a lifelong position—but for the length of the Warden's life, not the Guardian's. According to Spar, a Guardian would have dozens of personal Wardens during his life, each one handing the position on to a successor at the end of his life. How would Ella bring herself to do that? How could she grow old, knowing exactly where her lover was but never being able to talk with him, hold him, make love with him; then have to teach someone else to care for him after her death? Didn't her heart break just thinking about it?

Fil already felt a crack in hers. She knew that as long as the threat from the Seven existed, Spar and Kees would remain awake and on guard, but that wouldn't last forever. Eventually, the Light would prevail, the threat would be eliminated, and the Guardians would return to their stony forms. If the opposite happened . . . well, at least Fil wouldn't have to worry about missing Spar, because they'd both be demon chow. It almost made her wish the battle would go on forever, just because as long as it did, she could keep Spar at her side.

Hm, maybe she should give Ella a call soon, when Spar and Kees were otherwise occupied. If her friend was currently suffering from the same thoughts and anxieties plaguing Fil, maybe she'd have some advice to share on how to cope with it. If not . . . well, at least they'd each have a shoulder to cry on.

Sighing out a wry chuckle, Fil shifted to pillow her cheek in one hand and lifted the other to trace an invisible line down the muscles of Spar's forearm to the back of his hand. She knew the soft touch would wake him, but she didn't care. He'd have hundreds, maybe thousands of years to sleep during his lifetime. She had only now.

"You are awake." His voice was low and quiet and still thickened by sleep. It rumbled through her like the purr of a great cat and made her shiver. If she hadn't seduced him first, he could have had her with the sound of his voice alone. "Is something wrong?"

She shook her head and drew her fingertip back up to trail across his broad chest, stopping to explore the furrow that ran between the two sides of the hard, muscular plane. "I fell asleep so early that I just woke up. Then I saw you."

Slowly, he reached for her, giving her plenty of time to refuse, not that she had any intention of turning him away. She wanted to wince at the evidence of how she'd confused him, but she didn't want to kill the mood. She'd been pushing him away most of the day. Now she'd just have to make it clear that she'd changed her mind.

She arched into his hand, moving eagerly closer as he drew her against him. He made a much nicer shape to snuggle into than a spare pillow. He fit against her perfectly, hard where she was soft, angled where she was curved. Cuddling against him felt like coming home, yet filled her with longing for something more. She needed him to touch her.

Whether he read her mind or her expression, she couldn't tell, but his warm, rough fingers stroked down her arm, over her hip, gliding down her thigh. Even through the covers, his touch heated her skin, and she murmured her pleasure, punctuating the sound with soft kisses pressed against his collarbone.

He made a low sound of approval and reached for the edge of the blankets. He tugged them away, his gaze following every inch of bare skin revealed by the slow retreat. She knew her skin was pale enough to glow in the moonlight, but Spar didn't seem to think that was a flaw. His gaze ate her up like she was a big bowl of his favorite dessert topped with a healthy dollop of whipped cream. No one had ever made her feel as beautiful as he did, as desired. As cherished.

Bared completely, Fil shivered, not from cold, but from the heat his attention generated. Wherever his gaze touched her, she felt as if flames licked at her skin, and the thought of what it might do to her to feel his tongue follow suit had her eyes drifting shut on a moan.

Spar chuckled softly and leaned closer until his breath teased the rim of her ear. "I would pay more than a penny for those thoughts, little human, were I not filled with such vivid imaginings of my own."

Her skin flushed as dizzying possibilities danced

through her head. If the man's thoughts were anywhere near as dirty as her own, he'd be moaning, too, but instead he growled and leaned down to take her mouth with his.

The taste of him thrilled her. Warm and rich and earthy, with the mineral tang of a French white wine and the clean softness of spring sunshine, she wanted to drink him down in fast, greedy gulps. She tried, but he made no secret of the fact that this was his kiss. He controlled it from the first moment, leading, directing, conquering . . . all she could go was grab hold of his shoulders and enjoy being swept away in the storm of his making.

She gasped like a drowning woman when his lips finally slid from hers to trail along the curve of her jaw, up to her plump earlobe. He lingered there for a lifetime at least, tugging the nub of flesh with his teeth, then soothing the sting with soft strokes of his tongue. Never in her life had she understood the allure of a lover playing with her ear, but when Spar did it, it might as well have been her clit. His skillful touch sent bolts of electricity straight to her pussy, making her clench with need.

He reduced her to a keening whine when he dragged his mouth across her throat, the flat of his tongue tasting her like melting ice cream. A tender nuzzle against her breast made her shake; the feel of his hot lips closing around her nipple made her sob. He drew on the peak with strong, rhythmic pulls, then teased with clever little flicks before resuming the suction. Fil tugged desperately at his shoulders, trying to bring him over her, but he resisted with casual strength. He kept them both on their sides, facing each other, while he fed on her flesh and left indelible marks on her soul.

"Spar. Please."

She tried to curl her arms around his head, to cradle him against her breasts, to do something to alleviate the ache that threatened to drive her mad. Chuckling, he slipped easily from her grasp and continued his ruthless assault.

A rough palm stroked up the side of her knee, along the quivering line of her thigh, before drifting inward. Gentle fingertips brushed like feathers through the soft, pale curls concealing her sex before delving deeper. She arched helplessly against him, urging him to soothe the pain of relentless need.

When his fingers slid away, she almost broke, almost begged him not to leave her, but he hushed her with butterfly kisses and lifted her upper leg to drape her knees across his hip. The position left her open, exposed, and his fingers quickly returned to fill the space he had created. He slipped through her damp folds, parting her tender flesh to uncover the tense little bundle of nerves at the top of her slit.

He slid a finger across the nub, and that single touch was enough to have Fil tensing and arching as if a bolt of lightning had coursed through her. She cried out, but he swallowed the sound, his mouth returning to hers with renewed passion.

This time, he didn't just taste her, he devoured her. She felt consumed, overwhelmed, feasted upon. His tongue tangled with hers while his fingers rubbed hard, tight circles around her clit. In seconds he brought her to the edge of release, but before she could fling herself into the void, he abruptly stopped. She tried to pull her mouth from his, to berate him for toying with her, but he fisted his free hand in the hair at the back of her head and simultaneously plunged two fingers deep into her swollen passage.

She screamed into his mouth, her hips snapping forward as pleasure crashed over her. A mini climax grasped her by the neck and shook hard, but it didn't even take the edge off the hunger. Immediately it began to build once more, and Spar fed it with greedy kisses and clever fingers.

Struggling for air, she broke away from his kiss and gasped frantically. A vague thought edged with hysteria pointed out that if she'd wondered before how she could survive without him, now she should be wondering how she would survive this encounter. The man was killing her, and she couldn't wait to embrace her end.

"Open your eyes," he growled, the sound rough and feral, different from anything else she'd heard from him. "Look at me."

It took several tries to force her eyes open. When she finally succeeded, the world looked hazy and out of focus. All but Spar. He stared into her eyes with fire heating his gaze and between her legs, his touch robbing her of sanity.

"You are mine, Felicity." The words fell like hammer blows, fierce in their intensity. "My human, my woman."

She knew she should hate the primitive statements, but they resonated inside her like church bells. Her heart could detect no lie in them, nothing false, nothing to take issue with. Even her mind was silent on the subject.

And her body? Oh, her body wept a rousing chorus of hallelujah.

"Say it."

His voice was an order, a demand, a decree from on high. Within her channel, his fingers curved to stroke firmly against her inner wall, hitting the spot that made her see stars on every contact.

"Mine."

How could he expect her to speak when she couldn't even breathe? She struggled for air, struggled for a voice, struggled for a mind not shattered from the pleasure of his touch.

Suddenly it left her. His fingers withdrew, and despite their bodies pressed together, only his fist in her hair held her to him.

"Say. It."

He scraped his teeth—were those his fangs? How were those his fangs?—against her throat and thrust his hips forward. With her leg pinned above his own, the movement brought the tip of his erection to her opening and taunted her with heavy nudges.

"Say you are mine," he snarled, and Fil felt herself nodding in agreement.

"Yours," she breathed.

Then she screamed as he drove himself deep inside her.

He filled her up so full, stretching her, fucking *completing* her, the stony bastard. She was his. He had made her his, and now he pounded within her to celebrate his claim.

She could feel her muscles tightening, her pussy clenching, her whole being vibrating with the need to come. Her head thrashed, but his grip in her hair held her in place. His other hand cupped her ass, keeping her steady while he tore her world out from under her.

Their play and their positioning had started slow and tender, an exploration and sharing, but it had turned into a frank act of possession, her body his to hold and possess. She'd have given her next breath to possess him in return.

They strained together, each struggling to get closer, until it felt as if they shared the same skin. She breathed his air; his skin drank the perspiration from hers. Their hearts beat wildly but together, sharing a rhythm in perfect synchronicity.

Fil felt the claws of climax digging into her flesh, dragging her toward an explosion she thought might rip her apart. She wished that magic gave her to power to freeze them in time, so that they could always be like this, joined together, bathing in the bliss of their union, pleasure always drifting at the edge of their grasp.

Ruthlessly, he pushed her forward and she broke with a ragged cry. Her scream echoed in her head as her entire body clenched. She shook with the force of it, unable to do more than let it wash over her. Her body continued to absorb his thrusts. She felt his rhythm growing ragged, heard his breath catch, felt the rumble begin low in his chest. She tracked its progress as it built and built until it burst from his throat in a mighty roar.

She looked into his face and saw his eyes go blind a split second before they blazed with the white-hot fire she had come to associate with his magic. It bathed her in an unearthly glow as he poured himself inside her.

In silence, she lay beside him and shivered. Spar had touched more than her body, deeper than her heart. He had woven himself into the very fiber of her soul, and he would take a piece with him when he stepped back into his shell of stone.

Chapter Fourteen

Over the next week, Fil discovered she had absolutely no knack for doing tedious research. Apparently she would have made a piss-poor private detective. She did, however, appear to be developing an ability to ignore elephants in the room, eight-hundred-pound gorillas in the corner, and anything right under her nose with a skill that was sure to dethrone the reigning Queen of Denial.

Yup, that crown was hers, baby!

Spar seemed to be operating on the principle of don't-ask-don't-tell; he never brought up the status of their relationship, and she never told him that the minute he turned his back on her, she was going to sob like a little girl and crawl inside a vat of ice cream the size of a small, third-world country. The American military had nothing on the two of them.

It didn't help matters that every time Fil tried to get Ella on the phone, either Kees answered or one of them was so pressed for time, they barely managed to impart the vital information they shared before the call ended.

She had gotten not a single inkling of what Ella and Kees's relationship might be like, but if it was anything like hers with Spar, she wouldn't be surprised that it was the last thing her friend wanted to talk about.

The fact that Fil had finished a commission just before the explosion at the abbey and hadn't bothered to line another up ahead of time meant that at least she had plenty of time to brood about everything. Oh, and try to find the elusive Hierophant in a world of over seven billion people. But mostly, she brooded.

To save her sanity, she'd turned over all the information from Onslow to Ella, along with giving her friend every last detail she could remember about her vision of the Hierophant. Ella had apparently developed some mad research skills over the past few weeks, and Fil was happy to take advantage. Maybe if both of them worked on the problem, Ella would come up with a solution. She was finding nothing.

By Sunday afternoon, she had reached her breaking point. Snapping her laptop closed, she thumped it down on the coffee table and glared at Spar. He hadn't done anything in particular; in fact, he'd simply been sitting in an armchair wading through some of the resource materials Onslow had mentioned in his packet of info. He'd speculated that knowing as much about the Order's summoning rituals as possible might help in searching out their location. His lack of transgressions didn't matter, though. Fil was bored and frustrated and angry, and she still had this damned demon mark on her hand, which in the past day or so had started to itch like a bad case of poison ivy. So goddamn it, she was entitled to glare whenever and wherever she wanted to.

"I'm going for a walk," she snapped, surging to her feet.

Spar looked up at her and frowned. "It is too dangerous."

"What's dangerous is keeping me cooped up in this building like it's Alcatraz. We haven't left the damned place since the trip to Ottawa and I, for one, have cabin fever. I need some fresh air."

"Have you forgotten what happened on that trip to Ottawa? You were attacked by a golem."

"Yeah, I was the one who nearly got her hip dislocated. I remember it pretty well."

Spar set aside his papers and rose. "Then you should know that the Hierophant is unlikely to have given up his attempts to reach you. Whether he wants you ritually dead dead or just plain dead do you truly wish to risk falling into his hands?"

She lifted her head and stuck her chin out, barely suppressing the urge to slam her fist into his straight-lipped, clench-jawed face. She knew she'd just come away with a broken hand. The man's head was made of rock. Literally.

"At this point, I could do with a new set of hands," she snarled, almost surprised at the vitriol of her own tone, but the rage drove her on. "You've been putting your hands on me pretty regular for a while now, haven't you? Maybe I'm starting to get a little tired of it."

Spar jerked back as if she had punched him. The look on his face tugged at something in her chest, but it barely registered under the heavy weight of the fury that drove her.

Fil could swear the edges of her vision had begun to

turn crimson, as if *seeing red* was more than just a turn of phrase. Maybe she really had burst a blood vessel or something, to bring up another cliché, but she couldn't pull herself back long enough to care. She needed to get out of this fucking apartment and she needed to get away from that fucking Guardian. Who the hell was he to keep telling her what to do and where to go? He didn't fucking own her!

When her thoughts darted into the kitchen and danced briefly over the big chef's knife that sat in the top of her knife block, she screamed a word in Lithuanian she hadn't even remembered she knew and threw herself toward the front door. If she stayed here one more second, there was going to be bloodshed.

She felt a cold jab of terror when something inside her cheered at the idea.

"Felicity!"

She ignored him and fumbled for the doorknob, finally managing to grasp the solid metal and yank open the heavy panel. Instead of an empty landing at the top of a narrow stair, Fil found herself looking into a pretty face and a pair of warm brown eyes.

Those eyes took one look at her, darted over her shoulder to see Spar hovering behind her projecting enough worry and frustration to light up the province, and went cool and sharp in an instant. She shouldered her way into the apartment, forcing Fil back into Spar's solid body.

"She's in trouble," the woman said, her voice coolly efficient, her tone broking no opposition. "Grab her before she tries to take a swing at me."

Fil's arm was moving before the words were past the

stranger's lips, but Spar's hand darted out from around her back and caught her fist before it could make contact with the side of the woman's head. Frustration detonated inside her, and her rage became a living thing, more powerful than Fil herself. Her vision went entirely red and she lost herself in the madness.

"Tim told me she was worried, but I had no idea it was so serious. I should have come sooner."

Spar looked up from where he had Felicity wrapped in his embrace and saw the unfamiliar woman shaking her head. In his arms, his mate thrashed like a wild woman, throwing herself from side to side, kicking and growling, acting more like a wild animal than like his Felicity. He had no idea what was happening, but he believed the woman when she said Felicity was in trouble.

He fought back his rapidly escalating concern and glared at her. "Who are you, and what are you doing here?"

"My name is Wynn, and Tim Massello at the university told me he thought your girlfriend could use my help. Anything else you want to know will have to wait." She gestured to the sofa. "Get her down there and hold on to her. I have some things in my car I need to fetch. This could get messy."

She turned as if to leave the apartment. Grunting, Spar adjusted his hold on Felicity after she sank her teeth into one of his forearms, and raised his voice to be heard over her screeching. "What is going on? What is happening to my mate?"

"It's the mark, and we'll talk later about the big picture here. If you want her to get through this, let me go get my things. I can help her. I promise."

Unable to do anything else, Spar watched Wynn head back down the stairs, then returned his focus to Felicity. Her face was contorted into a mask of rage unlike anything he had ever seen before. She hissed and spat and snapped at the air like a rabid dog, all the while fighting with surprising strength to break his hold. He had her pinned against his chest, but he realized that getting her down onto the sofa might make her easier to contain. If he pinned her against the cushions and used his weight over the top of her, he could minimize her ability to move.

By the Light, he needed to know what was wrong with her. One moment, she had been working quietly on her computer, and the next she had picked a fight with him over nothing, something they had discussed and agreed on well before today. She knew that anytime she left her home, she tempted the Order to launch another attack on her. Spar knew she hated being trapped indoors, but they had agreed that when her restlessness grew too much, either he would take her to her studio, or after dark he would take her for a short flight above the city. They had made a deal, and until this afternoon Fil had expressed no dissatisfaction with the arrangement.

He had no idea what could have set her off, but if this Wynn woman could take one look and attribute this fit to the demon's mark, he knew the matter had turned grave. He had hoped that with days passing free of further visions, the danger of the mark had passed, or at least had grown no stronger. Now he very much feared the opposite.

Felicity continued to fight him, but her strength, even fueled by her raging madness, could not compare to his. He worried not about her escaping his hold, but about her hurting herself, or about him unintentionally injuring her in his struggle to keep her pinned.

When the woman called Wynn reappeared at the top of the stairs, Spar had Felicity trapped against the sofa with his own body. He held her wrists above her head in one of his hands; one of his legs pinned hers at the knee. With her relatively secured, he took his first good look at the stranger.

She stood somewhere around average height for a human female, perhaps five inches or so above five feet, taller than his Felicity. Her medium-brown hair hung in subtle waves down her back nearly to her waist, and her large brown eyes reminded him of a doe's, deep and soft and very round. At the moment, they carried an expression of worry, one that tightened her pretty features into pinched lines.

Her figure appeared well rounded at the breast and hips, but surprisingly compact elsewhere. Her baggy, wide-bottomed jeans and loose-fitting, printed top did their best to camouflage it, but a male, even a mated one, would be hard-pressed not to notice. He could also see that despite the cool weather, she wore nothing but a pair of thin sandals on her feet, and her toenails had been painted a glittering purple.

It wasn't her appearance that gave her away, though. It was the canvas sack she placed on the coffee table, and the items she began to remove. He recognized a tiny metal cauldron and the charcoal disk she wedged inside as an incense burner and could tell from the scents of several small cloth bags that they contained herbs and resins that could be burned, or perhaps even used for other purposes. As she continued to line things up atop the wooden surface, he grunted.

"You are the witch."

"Nothing gets past you, does it?" She didn't bother to look at him, just calmly continued her preparations. "I guess that's why they made you a Guardian."

Spar's shock briefly loosened his grip, and Felicity managed to tear one hand free to swing wildly at his face. He felt her nails scratch his skin and immediately resecured her, tightening his grip a fraction.

"What did you call me?" he demanded.

The woman rolled her eyes. "I don't need to see you covered in granite to recognize you for what you are, Guardian. My full name is Wynn Myfanwy Llewellyn Powe, and for seven generations the men in my mother's family have served the Light as members of the Guild of Wardens."

Spar shook with the need to grab the woman and shake her. Did she not realize the importance of what she had just told him?

"Who among your family currently serves?" he demanded, leaning toward her with a growl. "I must contact him immediately. We need to—"

"Hey, right now we need to deal with this." Wynn pointed at Felicity, still writhing on the sofa. "Do you mind postponing the discussion of my curriculum vitae until we get Felicity out of danger?"

Shame flooded him, and Spar shifted under the unfamiliar emotion. "Of course. Felicity must be treated."

"Glad we agree." Wynn twisted to move around

Spar's grip on his mate, laying the back of her hand against Felicity's forehead. She frowned when she felt the heat of the other woman's skin. "How long has she borne the mark?"

"More than a sennight. It struck her late on Friday night this week past."

"I love how you guys sound more and more medieval the more worked up you get."

He watched her reach for something on the table. "She seemed to suffer no ill effects before this. At least, nothing that affected her behavior. She did have a vision last weekend, and afterward the mark appeared to darken on her skin."

Wynn shook her head. "I am really sorry I didn't come sooner. When Tim called me and told me he knew a woman who needed a curse removed, I thought he meant someone who got a rash on her hand and didn't want to wait for an appointment with a dermatologist. I made a poor assumption, and I'm going to have to live with that for a while. If I'd contacted you right away, this would have been a lot easier. And a lot less dangerous."

Spar did not like the sound of that. "What will you do? You can remove the mark, can you not?"

"I wish. Unfortunately, it's taken root too deeply. I won't be able to remove it completely, but I'm going to sever the connection to its source."

"The source is dead. The *nocturnis* who cast the spell was murdered by one of his own. That is what Felicity saw in her vision."

"Wrong. If the source were a single person, this would be no big deal. Bippity-boppity-boop, I wave my magic wand, mark disappears, and we all go home happy for a nice smoked meat sandwich." She handed him a bundle of red silk cords. "This is a lot more complicated than that. This mark is tied not to the caster, but to the Defiler himself. Cutting the bond will not be quick or easy. You need to bind her."

Appalled, Spar refused. "I will not. I can hold her as I am doing now. I will not tie her up and leave her feeling abandoned, like some sort of prisoner. You will start without those." He threw the ropes onto the coffee table.

Wynn picked them up and handed them back. "You can't hold her for this. One, I wasn't kidding when I said it wouldn't be quick; we could be here for hours. And two, I need to be able to get to her without you getting in the way. You take up too much space where I need to maneuver."

He glared at her, using his most intimidating Guardian expression. She simply watched him and waited, hand out, red cords dripping from the sides of her palm. Muttering something foul in a dead language, he snatched the cords from her and began to wrap around his mate's slender wrists.

"Actually, my mother is entirely human, so the live-stock reference is way off."

Of course, the witch spoke Aramaic. Why hadn't he simply assumed?

It took longer to bind Felicity than it should have, and very little of that had to do with Spar's reluctance. She fought him like a wildcat, throwing herself against his grip every time he shifted, continually looking for a weakness that would allow her to escape. When he finally had her subdued with rope around her wrists, elbows, knees, and ankles, Wynn handed him additional cords, longer ones this time.

"This sofa has exposed legs. Tie her hands to one end and her feet to the other."

Spar's fists clenched until he feared they would shatter. "Is this really necessary?"

"It's for her safety, Guardian. This won't be a pleasant experience for any of us."

Silent, fuming, and aching, Spar did as she instructed. When Felicity had been fully secured, Wynn reached out and touched his arm.

"I know you want to—need to—be close to her, but I can't let you get in the way," she said, her expression grave. When he opened his mouth to protest, one corner of her mouth curved slightly upward. "If you walk around and stand at the back of the sofa, she'll be within arm's reach, but you won't be any more in the way than the furniture itself. Okay?"

He felt a rush of gratitude as he moved into position. Gazing down at his mate, he saw the way her chest rose and fell as she panted from her long exertions. Her skin gleamed with sweat, and her clothing had been torn and rumpled during their struggles. Her shirt bore several holes where buttons had been, and beneath the fabric her skin was mottled a sickly grayish color. His eyes flew back to her face, and he could see the odd color beginning to seep down from her hairline.

Wynn followed his gaze, and her jaw tightened. "Okay, let's get started."

What followed were the longest six hours of Spar's inhumanly long life. He lost track of the incenses Wynn burned and the incantations she chanted. Crystals and stones and herbs and runes all passed in front of his watchful eyes. At times she laid her hand on his mate's head or body, and at times she seemed to forget Felicity was even there as she seemingly slipped in and out of a trance-like state. What he would always remember, though, was the long strip of muslin that she anointed with several different oils before wrapping it nine times around the hand that bore the demon's mark. Spar would remember because he'd had to pry Felicity's fingers from their clenched fist and hold them while Wynn worked, and because his mate had screamed in agony during the entire winding process.

At times over the course of the afternoon and into the evening, Spar wondered that no one reported the cries to the human authorities. Had he heard them from the street and not realized what was happening above the empty storefront, he would have suspected torture at the very least, if not outright murder. Of course, he doubted many murder victims took six hours to die.

It took that long for Wynn to do her work. Watching Felicity during that time filled him with a kind of agony he had never experienced before. The fact that she continued to fight her bindings and writhe and struggle during the entire experience proved the forces at play to be inhuman. Not even the pure energy of magic could have fueled that kind of persistence for so many hours.

The tenuous trust he had in Wynn wavered for a moment when she reached to the table at the start of the seventh hour and picked up a double-edged knife. His hand shot out over the back of the sofa and grabbed her wrist.

"What are you doing?"

"Relax, Guardian. I'm not foolish enough to harm another human in your presence." She turned the knife in her hand, kissed the blade, and then offered him the hilt. "Take it."

Spar recognized the ritual blade. The athame wasn't large—only nine inches from end to end—but it gleamed wickedly sharp in the lights of the living room. The hilt had been fashioned from ebony wood turned to curve gracefully in the palm. It flowed uninterrupted to the blade with no pommel or guard to break the line between wood and metal. Despite having sat untouched on the table for hours, it felt warm in his hand.

"You won't let me harm her, so you're going to have to do it."

Spar's head snapped up, and he felt his fangs emerge even in his human guise. "What?"

Wynn watched him steadily, outwardly unafraid of his show of aggression. "I've weakened the bond, but to sever it, the poison it's infected her with has to be drained. We need to cut her hand and let the cloth soak it up." She saw the expression on his face, and her mouth curved. "Just a prick, Guardian. I promise she'll suffer no lasting harm."

Spar still didn't like the idea, something he felt certain the witch had no trouble seeing in his face and his reluctant movements. He turned to Felicity and saw to his surprise that her movements had slowed, growing less aggressive in the last several minutes. She continued to pant more like an animal than a human, but she no longer bucked and thrashed against her bonds. He felt a renewed sense of optimism that the witch might actually know what she was doing.

"You need to use the tip of the blade and prick her through the cloth right in the center of the mark. Don't disturb the wrapping otherwise. It needs to stay in place," Wynn instructed as she hovered on Felicity's other side. "The binding around the hand needs to soak up the blood. After you prick her, hand me back the athame."

He nodded that he understood her instructions, much as he was loath to carry them out. The idea of deliberately causing his mate injury went against the very fabric of his nature. If it would save her, though, he would do whatever he needed to. Taking her bound hand in one of his, he gently pried the fingers open and cradled the palm in one of his own.

With a deep breath, he pulled back and struck before he could think. If he allowed himself to hesitate, he questioned his ability to follow through. The wickedly honed blade sliced through the muslin as if it were tissue paper, and he felt the tip bite into Felicity's tender flesh. Her high, wild scream nearly caused him to drop the knife.

Color bloomed in the center of the binding, not blood-red but black as pitch. Wynn glanced at it and nodded. "Good."

Reluctantly, Spar passed back the blade. "What now?"

"Give it a minute."

Spar waited, eyes riveted to the spot where the black substance continued to stain the white cloth. Near Felicity's head, Wynn closed her eyes and began to chant. The words were lost on him, but he recognized the lilting, shifting syllables as Welsh. As she spoke her spell, the stain on Felicity's bandage spread until the very edges began to turn not black, but bright, bloody red.

Wynn's eyes snapped open and she reached forward,

slipping the blade of the knife between Felicity's skin and the soaked cloth. She sliced easily through the muslin and drew it away, handling it reluctantly by the very edges. Using the athame to shift and poke at it, she stuffed it into a black silk bag she held at the ready and tied it shut with a thin, black cord.

Immediately Spar's gaze shifted to his mate. He felt his heart stutter as he saw the clear, fair color of her skin and the calm, peaceful expression on her face. She had fallen perfectly still, her body relaxed against the ropes that bound her, no longer fighting to escape. He reached out and cupped her face in his hand, feeling her skin smooth, cool, and soft against his.

After a moment, she stirred, her lashes fluttering briefly before parting to reveal sleepy and confused green eyes. "Hm, wow," she murmured, her voice husky. Not from sleep, but from six hours of shrieking, screaming, and moaning. "That was one hell of a nap. How long was I asleep?"

Chapter Fifteen

After everything she had done for them, it only seemed polite to ask Wynn to stay for dinner. Plus, having been informed what had happened over the past several hours, Fil still had a few questions to ask. Easier to ask them with the witch still present and properly fed.

They ordered in Chinese, and over Hunan beef, Buddhist delight, and pork dumplings, Fil tried to fill in the big blank spot in her memory. "I'm still having a hard time wrapping my mind around it all. The last thing I remember is sitting on the sofa with my laptop feeling frustrated with our lack of progress in the search."

"It's not surprising." Wynn lifted a broccoli spear to her mouth with deftly wielded chopsticks. "You weren't yourself. And I mean that literally. I wouldn't exactly call what you went through possession, not in the classical sense, but your actions absolutely were not your own. Memory loss isn't unexpected."

"Doesn't mean I have to like it."

"Don't blame you."

Turning over her left hand, Fil examined the tiny, new red scar in the middle of the demon's mark. "I've already thanked you for your help, so please don't think I'm not grateful, but I kind of wish whatever you had done had erased this thing completely. I can't imagine walking around for the rest of my life with some demon's signature scrawled across my palm."

"Sorry about that, but I don't think it will last forever." Wynn sipped from a glass of cola before continuing. "Like I told the Guardian, what I did was break the bond tying you to the demon's energy. Without that, the mark has nothing sealing it in place. It should fade over time. Sorry it's not immediate."

"Hey, any improvement is appreciated. Thanks."

"You're welcome."

"And I think that after the experience we shared, you might consider calling me by my name," Spar threw in.

Wynn glanced at him and raised an eyebrow. "I didn't want to presume any familiarity."

Fil frowned. "Why not? If you grew up with Wardens in your family, you're already a hell of a lot more familiar with the whole Guardian thing than I am."

"Yeah, that's why I didn't presume." Wynn made a face. "Everything is turned upside down now, I suppose, but the way I grew up the Guardians were always held up as these figures of awe, something you treated with kid gloves and a whole lot of respect. Especially if you were just a girl."

Oh, that phrase rubbed Fil all sorts of the wrong way. "Just a girl?" she repeated.

Wynn snorted. "You really are new to this, aren't you? Let's just say that the Guild of Wardens does not have the universe's greatest track record when it comes to gender parity and equal rights."

Fil glanced at Spar. He looked uncomfortable.

"What does that mean, exactly?"

"Ninety-nine percent of those accepted into the Guild as apprentices are men. Literally. For every one hundred members of the Guild, there is exactly one woman. And trust me, it's not like there aren't women out there who are qualified, but somehow, mysteriously, they're almost always passed over in favor of men."

"What the hell is that all about?"

Shrugging, Wynn pointed her chopsticks at Spar. "Why don't you ask him?"

Fil shifted on the sofa to face the Guardian. "What the hell is that all about?"

Spar gave Wynn a dirty look. "I am not a member of the Guild. The Guardians exist separately from the Guild and do not make its rules or govern its practices."

"Um, I call cop-out." Fil poked him in the chest. "You might not belong to the Guild, but you've worked with them for, like, a thousand years. Or more. You can't tell me you aren't at least familiar with how they operate."

He sighed, as if the topic tried his patience. Fil could have told him that he hadn't even seen her trying side yet. "The Guild works on an apprentice system, which limits the number of applicants that can be admitted. Training a new Warden is an intense and time-consuming process, and each Guild member has only so much teaching he can handle in addition to his other duties. I do not know why more women are not accepted to train, only that each Warden has complete authority over whom he accepts as a student. No one can force him to turn away a female applicant, any more than one could force him to accept one."

"Yeah, they've got quite the little system going there. Very old-boy network, complete with justifications about how women are 'unsuited' to the work of a warden. Just like we were supposedly unsuited to medicine, business, and the military once upon a time."

Fil heard the bitter edge to Wynn's voice. "What about the job they claim we're 'unsuited' for?"

Wynn smiled sharply. "You know, I don't think I've ever gotten a straight answer to that question, and I've been asking it since I could talk."

"Well, what qualifies someone to apply in the first place? Is there some weird test you have to pass first? Something that requires a penis?"

"The only stated rule about becoming a Warden is that the applicant must have a preexisting magical ability of sufficient strength to cast the spell of supplication. If you can do that, you're qualified."

"And I can assume the spell doesn't involve writing your name in the snow with your own pee, right?"

"Felicity!" Spar thundered.

"What? I can't think of another reason a woman couldn't cast the same spell a man can."

"There isn't one," Wynn said. "That's why the whole thing is such a joke."

Fil narrowed her eyes and curled her lip. "I'm not laughing."

"You and me both, sister." Wynn pushed aside her plate and leveled her gaze on Spar. "Like I told the Guardian, my family has produced Wardens for the

Guild for seven generations. Magic runs pretty deep in our line. We're all witches of one kind or another. Because I'm female, a witch is all I am. If I were a man, I'd be a Warden by now."

Spar lifted his hands. "Do not hold me responsible, human. I am not the cause of your denial. I will not take the blame for it."

"Still, you have to admit it's ridiculous, Spar," Fil said. "I mean, why turn away perfectly qualified applicants? It seems to me it's time the Guild dragged its sorry ass into the twenty-first century."

"I'm not sure the Guild has an ass left to drag anywhere," Wynn admitted. "Are you guys aware of what's been happening with the Wardens?"

"You mean that finding one these days is like looking for a leprechaun and his great big pot o' gold?" Fil nodded. "Oh, yeah. We're aware. What no one can seem to figure out is when it started and how it got so far."

"No one?" Wynn latched on to the phrasing and looked curious. "Who else knows about it? Have you guys spoken to another Warden? When? What was his name? Where did you find him?"

The flurry of questions removed any doubt that the witch had a personal stake in the answers. "Who are you missing?"

"My brother, Bran. He just completed his training two years ago. I haven't heard from him in more than eight months."

Fil heard the pain in the other woman's voice and reached out to touch her hand. "I'm sorry. I wish we could tell you something, but the only Warden we've even had a line on was named Jeffrey, and my friend

Ella said she met one named Alan a few weeks ago. Jeffrey was unfortunately gone when we got to his place, and Ella said Alan was killed by *nocturnis*."

Wynn blew out a breath. "Sorry. It's just really hard not to know, you know?"

"Ella is still looking for Wardens, and she's getting better at it every day. I'll ask her to keep an eye out for Bran, okay?"

"Thanks, but who is Ella, and how is she mixed up in all this?"

Fil briefly sketched out the story of her friendship with Ella Harrow and how the other woman had been the first to stumble onto the problem with the Guild of Wardens. She and her Guardian, Kees.

Wynn's eyes went wide. "There's another Guardian awake? Oh, my Goddess, that is such bad, bad news." She looked a little green around the edges. "For two Guardians to be awake at the same time, without being summoned by the Guild . . . that spells serious, world-ending trouble."

"So we're beginning to suspect."

Fil and Spar exchanged glances. She saw his barely perceptible shrug and knew he was leaving it up to her whether she wanted to tell Wynn the rest. For Fil, there was no question. The witch had already saved her life, and her family background made her more familiar with the Wardens, the Guardians, and the Order than either Ella or herself. Heck, she probably knew more about how the Guild worked than Kees and Spar. She was a resource they couldn't afford to let get away.

Turning back to Wynn, she nibbled her lip, then just went for it. "Spar and I got some information from the

Warden we just missed finding. Jeffrey. According to what he put together—and we're inclined to believe him—he thinks one of the Seven might already have been set free."

Every drop of blood drained from Wynn's face, leaving her pale, gray, and trembling. "Please, Goddess, no."

"We don't think it's very strong right now," Fil reassured her. "Spar believes it didn't escape but was basically dragged into this plane using some really fucked-up magic the *nocturnis* concocted. Excuse my language."

"No, the Order's magic *is* fucked up. That's the technical term." The witch used a shaking hand to tuck her long hair behind her ear. "What makes you think the demon is weak for now?"

"Felicity's life represents strong evidence." Spar took her still-marked hand in his and stroked her palm with a fingertip. "Were it not, do you believe she could have survived more than a week bearing its mark?"

"If the mark belonged to another member of the Seven, it might be possible, but no. You're right. And I think that the mark used on her belongs to the Defiler probably indicates that it is the one who was summoned."

"I believe you are correct. Also the fact that the end of the world has not already been reported by the human media adds to my belief that the demon remains weak, perhaps critically so."

"True. If a full-strength member of the Seven were already among us, we'd be toast by now." She winced.

"I had a vision last weekend," Fil said. "I saw someone, a member of the Order, in some kind of basement or something. It looked like he was performing some sort of ritual, or maybe casting a spell . . . I'm not sure. Anyway, after a minute the vision shifted and I saw him enter the room of the guy who gave me the mark. He killed him, killed the guy who marked me, but before that he spoke to him, and it sounded like the first guy was the other one's boss. I think the dead guy called him the Hierophant. You know, before the part where he became dead."

"The Hierophant?" Wynn looked surprised. "Here in Montreal?"

"You don't think it's possible?"

"Anything is possible when it comes to the *nocturnis*. I'm just surprised. I've been living here for more than a year, and I never even suspected activity on that level. It makes me feel like a bit of an idiot."

"I suppose I can't be a hundred percent positive, since the ritual space was inside, and he sort of teleported into the hospital room without registering his flight path, but it didn't *feel* like he was far away. Do you understand what I mean?"

Wynn gave a slight smile. "Instinct is the basis of magic."

"Right, and my instinct said he was close by. The problem is that I have absolutely no idea where 'close by' might actually be. Heck, I'm so new at this, 'close by' in magical terms could mean Manitoba. How would I know?"

"Manitoba isn't close in any terms. Even Manitoban terms." Wynn looked thoughtful. "If we could figure out a way to locate the Hierophant, that would be amazing. Taking him out would really throw the Order for a loop. Eventually someone would step in to take his place, but in the meantime it would be chaos. And not the kind of chaos they like."

"We thought the same, but locating a single human on this plane with not even a name to aid our search . . ." Spar trailed off. "So far, it has not gone well."

"What have you tried?"

"Everything we can think of," Fil said. "Mostly stabbing around under the Internet's dark rocks and seeing if I can scare anything into the light."

"The Order keeps its business off the Net. They figured out early on it made them too easy to track. You won't catch him that way. Have you tried finding him by not looking for him?"

"Pardon?"

"I mean, by not looking for *him*. Look for what he leaves behind," Wynn explained. "If the Order managed to summon one of the Seven, you can bet the Hierophant was behind it, so he'll be right in the thick of things. He'll be the demon's chief servant, and if it really is weak, he'll be trying to feed it."

"Ew. I take it he's not bringing it Tim Hortons and poutine, huh?"

"Not so much. Demons are pretty finicky eaters, strictly blood and human souls."

Spar growled. "We should be looking for evidence of human sacrifice."

"Unfortunately."

"Ick. I was really hoping you wouldn't say that."

"It's the quickest way to find them, and the faster they're found, the fewer sacrifices they get to make," Wynn reasoned. "I can try scrying for them, but you can't rely on that. I have no idea how long it could take, since I don't know the person I'm looking for. Plus, chances are the Hierophant will have magical wards up to prevent occult prying into his business. I'm a damned fine witch, but I'm betting he's more experienced than I am, and he'll be pulling power from the Darkness. My way should be a backup plan only."

Fil groaned and let her head thump back against the sofa cushions. "Oh, good. I get to spend the next however-long-it-turns-out-to-be immersing myself in the happy fun-time of homicide reports. Yay, me."

Wynn shot her a commiserating look. "Keep an eye out on missing persons, too. Sometimes they're smart enough to hide their victims afterward."

"And you say you're mad because this isn't your full-time job?"

The witch shrugged. "We all have our quirks."

Chapter Sixteen

Fil found herself reluctant to let Wynn go, and over the next few days she wished more than once that she'd just kidnapped the other woman and kept her close. Pumping her for information while she was across town in her own apartment just took so much more effort.

The location of the Hierophant, though, wasn't what Fil kept asking about. No, all of her questions centered on the Guardians—how they were summoned, how long they worked between their periods of slumber, if they ever woke when the world wasn't in imminent peril. If Wynn guessed the reasons behind the other woman's questions, she never let on.

"They wake when the Warden they're bonded to finishes training his apprentice," the witch had explained. "It's a way of passing the torch from one Warden to the next, so the Guardian is familiar with him if the new guy has to do a summoning during his tenure. But as far as I know, it's either that, or humanity's pants are on fire. Not really much in between."

Fil found that less than reassuring. She picked up her brooding right where she'd left off, minus the psychotic, demon-inspired fit of rage, but Spar threw himself into their new search with gusto. He seemed determined to ferret out every gruesome death and every missing persons report he could get his hands on. Accessing those was pretty slow going, though. They had to rely mostly on newspaper reports, since asking the police to identify any demon attacks or ritually sacrificed humans would likely land them in jail, or the nuthouse.

Of course Fil had contacted Ricky, but even that had proved more than a touch awkward. Explaining her newfound interest in the subject of death and mayhem turned out to be a bit tricky.

"First you ask me about a bombing the police still haven't been able to explain, and now you want to know about ritual murders?" the reporter had demanded, his tone incredulous. "Girl, have you gotten yourself mixed up in something I don't want to know about? 'Cause this is starting to sound like you're founding your own terrorist cell, or something."

Fil had rolled her eyes. "Right. Me and the Taliban. I'm looking into something for a friend, Ricky, but if you aren't comfortable helping me out, just say so. I'll find another way to get the information; it'll just take me longer."

"Oh, I'm damned uncomfortable, but I'll still help. I've owed you more than one favor through the years, Fil, but I'm pretty sure this is going to even the scales. I don't want to know if you're trying to track down a serial killer or studying up to become one yourself—either way, that's a dangerous path to walk. You be careful."

She knew Ricky didn't actually believe she was out to become a killer, but she understood his warning. She was into something dangerous, she just couldn't explain what it really was. And if she'd tried, she doubted he would have believed her. After all, who went around trying to track down demons and demonic minions? It made her sound even crazier than the serial-killer angle.

If she was honest with herself, she felt pretty crazy these days, and dealing with demons, a cult of demon worshippers, human sacrifice, and the location of the head lunatic contributed to that the least. It was the guy with wings determined to save the world that made her feel like she'd lost her mind.

She tried being all Zen about it, living in the moment, not thinking about the future but savoring each moment as it came. That had lasted all of about half an hour; then Spar had mentioned something about how he would like to show Fil the cathedral he had once guarded in the Alsace. Just like that, all her tranquility went flying out the window. Hearing him talk about the future as if he could be part of hers made her want to scream. Didn't he get what it did to her to think about him leaving her?

He stepped up behind her, his movements as silent as ever, so she didn't realize he had approached until his arms drew her up against the back of the sofa. Leaning down, he nuzzled the hollow beneath her ear.

"I think it is time to take a break, little human." He pressed a kiss against her sensitive skin, and she couldn't suppress the shiver. "I am getting hungry. How about you?" Another kiss, followed by the teasing scrape of his teeth. "Or would you rather just have lunch?"

Heart aching, Felicity shrugged and scooted forward out of his grip. He let her go, but his wicked chuckle died into puzzled silence. She felt his gaze boring into her back, but she ignored it. "Go ahead and fix yourself something. I'm not hungry."

She stood and reached out to move the laptop, but Spar stepped in front of her. His hand closed around her elbow and tugged her to face him. "What is wrong? You appear angry. How have I offended you?"

Fil snorted. "I'm not offended, Spar. I'm fine. I'm just not in the mood right now."

"Not in the mood?" he repeated, scowling down at her. "You do not wish to make love with me at the moment. I respect that, but I do not care to be lied to, Felicity. Something clearly bothers you. You will tell me what it is."

"Actually, I won't." She closed the laptop with a snap and shook free of his hand. "I know it's your duty to look after me, Spar, and I know you have a great time when we have sex, but none of that makes you entitled to know every little thing that goes on inside my head, so back off."

Spar reached for her again, this time grabbing her left hand. "You sound as you did before Wynn severed the mark. Has something happened? Is its power over you returning? We should call her and ask her to come right away."

"It's not the damned mark, Spar! I can be pissed off without being under the influence of demonic juju. Just leave it alone."

"I will not leave it alone. You behave irrationally. Last night you lay in my arms and held me close to you as you slept, but now you act as if I have committed some great evil against you. If I have done something that upsets you, I deserve the chance to make it right. Since I can think of nothing of the sort, I require you to explain it to me so that I can apologize for my actions."

Fil threw up her hands. She felt like laughing, or crying, because this argument was so ridiculous and she knew she had started it. She was behaving like an idiot, but she couldn't seem to stop herself. The pain inside her wanted to be shared, and Spar, ever vigilant by her side, was the perfect target.

"You haven't done anything, Spar," she gritted out. "You haven't done anything, you haven't said anything, you haven't so much as *thought* anything. At least, not as far as I can tell. I guess I'm just in a really bad mood."

He stepped forward, reaching for her, and Fil froze. If he put his arms around her right now, she thought she might shatter into about nine billion tiny pieces.

"If you are upset, let me help," he murmured. "Let me comfort you."

"I told you, Spar, let it drop."

He let it drop. He let his arms drop, then he let his disguise drop until he stood before her in his natural form, the top of his head nearly brushing the apartment's ceiling. His sharply carved features glowered at her as he bared his fangs and tapped his talons together with a menacing click.

"You ask me to do the impossible, human," he growled, the sound even deeper than usual, more ominous. "I have revealed myself to you in every way imaginable, and yet still you would conceal yourself from me. Do you have so little consideration for me? For my feelings? Do you look at me as I am now and think of me as a monster? Is that why every time I get close to you, you find a reason to push me away?"

"No! Spar, I have never thought you were a monster." Fil bit her lip, torn between the instinct to protect herself by keeping her true feelings for him secret, and the need to let him know that no matter what he looked like, in human form or Guardian, she loved him. It wasn't what he was that was killing her, it was what she would become without him.

Empty.

She took a deep breath and tried to stop her hands from shaking by pressing them hard against her thighs. "Spar, I don't think you're—"

The sound of church bells announced that she had a phone call. She saw Spar's eyes narrow, knew he was about to order her not to answer, so she dove for the cell phone and pressed the ANSWER button as fast as humanly possible. As it was, his roar nearly drowned out her breathless "Hello?"

There was a pause on the other end of the call. "Jesus, where are you, Fil? The Granby Zoo? Did you piss off one of the lions?"

"Rick. No, sorry, that was, um, the TV. Let me just turn it down." She shot Spar a warning glance and turned her back on him to concentrate on the reporter's voice. "Hey, you got something for me?"

"I've got a reason for us to sit down and talk. Meet me at Claude's in half an hour."

Fil winced. She didn't need to run that idea by Spar to know he would object. He'd gotten even more cautious about letting her go out in public these last few days. She glanced at him, wondering if he'd blow his feathers when she told him what Rick had requested.

"Um, I'm not sure," she began, but Rick overrode her objections.

"Half an hour, Fil. You're going to want to hear this, and then I'm going to want to know why."

He hung up before she could say more.

When Fil turned back to her Guardian, she got a shock at seeing him already back in his human form, tugging at the sleeves of his dark-gray sweater. "What are you doing?"

He jerked his chin at the phone. "I hardly think your friend needs to see me in my true form over *café* and bagels."

His voice sounded clipped and cold, a tone he'd never used with her before, and Fil found she didn't like it at all. It made a fist squeeze in her belly.

"You're angry."

He looked at her. "A moment ago, we were both angry. You did not wish to talk then; I do not wish to talk now. I heard the reporter ask you to meet him. You know I cannot allow you to go alone." He waved toward the door. "Shall we?"

Felicity turned without a word to grab her jacket. How did she always manage to push away the people she most wanted to care for her? Was it some kind of curse? You'd think in the last twenty-seven years, she would have learned something about holding on to the ones she loved.

Rick waited for them in the same booth of Claude's café where they had eaten breakfast two weeks before.

This time, instead of sausage and coffee, the place smelled of french fries and beef gravy. Once again, Spar followed Fil through the crowd and tried not to look like he was angry.

He was very, very angry.

His little human threatened to drive him demented. Over and over she seemed to change her mind, seducing him, then pushing him away, drawing him in, then retreating behind a barrier he could not penetrate. He had thought after the demon's mark was severed, things had gotten a little better. She had leaned on him during that experience, and since then—while she had seemed perhaps a bit quiet—she had made no move to withdraw from him. Not until this morning.

He felt as if he had reached the top of a mountain, only to have an undetectable tremor set off a landslide that washed him right back to the bottom again. He had chosen Felicity as his mate, and there was no going back for him, but he was beginning to fear his patience with her vacillations would not last much longer. He wanted her to love him before he claimed her, but he didn't know how much longer he could wait.

A hint of his temper must have shown in his expression, because the reporter looked uneasy when he slid into the booth beside Felicity.

"Wow, he looks even more cheerful than the last time I saw you guys."

"We're both little rays of sunshine," Felicity said with a definite snarl. Spar felt a surge of satisfaction that she had not shaken off their argument, either. "You said you had something to tell me. Tell."

"Aaaaand, all those years at charm school are finally

paying off, I see." Rick set a thick red folder on the table beside his place setting, but he did not push it toward them. He laid his hand over the top and leaned toward Felicity. "You asked me to look into some very dark shit, Fil, and I did it because I consider you a friend, but the stuff I found is going to give me nightmares for a month, and I've been working the police beat in this town since before the Hell's Angels and the Rock Machine started decorating the streets with each other's blood. Are you sure you want to see this?"

Spar saw her jaw tighten and her chest expand as she drew in a slow breath. When she nodded, the motion was small, but definite. "I have to, Rick. It's important."

"No, what it is, is fucked. Up." He handed Felicity the folder and sat back in his seat. "I advise you to look at everything *before* you eat. I just had these boots shined."

Spar found the warning unnecessary though not inappropriate. The folder contained not just information, but photographs. Spar guessed the ones that appeared to be outdoors had been taken at a crime scene. Others featured metal tables and surgical instruments that identified them as autopsy photos. The images they depicted were graphic and brutal—slit throats, mutilated bodies, evidence of animal activity on some, what only an educated eye would distinguish as demon activity on others. Human authorities, he knew, would lump it in with the damage done by the animals, but Spar could see the differences.

"How many?" Felicity asked.

Her expression remained blank, but Spar could see the fast beat of her pulse in her throat and feel the distress pouring off her. She was strong, his little human, but no one with a heart could look on these images and not be affected.

"The police have only found three so far, and they're keeping it very, very quiet," Rick said. "The last thing they want is a public panic about an active serial killer." He paused. "Is that what it is?"

"Not exactly."

Felicity looked at Spar. Before she contacted the reporter for the first time, they had discussed what she would be able to tell him. The whole story would overwhelm him, if he could even be persuaded to believe it, but they could not pretend the questions they asked had been sparked by idle curiosity. In the end, they had settled on a carefully edited version of the truth.

She turned back to the reporter. "We think it's a cult. We think the murders are being committed as part of some kind of sacrifice."

"Like satanists?" Rick gave a half laugh. "Normally, I'd tell you that kind of thing only happens in low-budget horror films, but in this case the police have done some speculating of their own. There were some weird things about the bodies."

"Just the bodies? Not the crime scene?"

"The police don't have a scene. The bodies were dumped after they were killed elsewhere."

Felicity swore under her breath, another smattering of Lithuanian, Spar assumed. "Okay, so what did they find weird?"

"First?" Rick picked up a pencil and began tapping the eraser end against the tabletop. The motion had the habitually fidgety quality of a smoker in a smoke-free environment. "That there were bodies of both sexes. Most serial killers pick a gender of victim and stick to it. If he kills women, for example, and they find a dead man at one of his scenes, it's almost always because the guy got in the way. The ones who actually target couples, like the Zodiac killer in California, they tend not to be torturers. This one obviously is."

Obviously. Spar could see the evidence of many shallow cuts on the skin of the victims, wounds that would have hurt and bled but not led to death, not before the Hierophant was ready. He would have used the sacrifice's pain to season the demon's meal.

"Also, rope was found still tied to victim number two's wrists," Rick continued. "The knots were unusual, not least of all because there were seven of them. Everyone figures that was overkill for a hundred-and-four-pound teenager. They're thinking the killer tied them for ritual reasons.

"Then, of course, there's the fact that when the bodies were found, none of them was completely intact. All three had their hearts ripped out of their chests. I think that one was what clinched it. How about you?"

Felicity looked up at the reporter's biting sarcasm. "Do you think I'm laughing at any of this?" she asked quietly. "Do you think this isn't turning my stomach and keeping me up at night? Trust me, what this cult is doing has already come close to killing me, so get off your high horse, Ricky. I'm not some serial-killer groupie getting off on this horror show."

"Then why haven't you contacted the police and told them what you know? Because I know you know something." Rick's voice vibrated with anger, and Spar tensed, ready to step between the man and his mate. "Do you have any idea how desperate they are for leads? The first girl? She disappeared six months ago, and by the time they found her she'd already been dead for three. So for three months they've been working on this, and do you know what they have to show for it? Squat. This folder has as much useful information in it as the four file boxes full of junk they have down at the police station."

"I can tell you're frustrated, Rick, but I can't tell why you're taking it out on me," Fil said, her brow furrowing in concern. "What's really going on here?"

Rick threw down his pencil and grabbed his coffee mug, draining the contents in one long gulp. "You want to know what's going on, Fil? How about that I've spoken to the families of each of those dead bodies in there, and every single one of them would give a fucking limb to find out what happened to the person they loved. So forgive me if I get a little cranky when I see someone who might be able to give them some answers, and all she's interested in doing is playing all closemouthed and mysterious. It fucks with my digestion."

"Ricky! I promise you, I'm doing what I can, but you don't understand what—"

"You know what? Save it." Ricky slid from the booth and grabbed the jacket and messenger bag from the seat beside him. "Like I said before, consider us even now in the favor department, Fil. I'll see you around."

Spar did not watch the man stalk to the front of the café and out the door; he was too busy watching his mate. He saw the way the reporter's words sliced at her tender heart, and suddenly all his own anger drowned under a wave of compassion. She had been hurt by the man's words, and he couldn't stand to see Felicity hurt.

He put his arm around her shoulders and squeezed gently. "I am sorry, little one. You are right, he did not understand, but it did not give him a reason to speak to you so harshly."

"No." She shook her head and stared blankly down at the folder the reporter had left behind. "It's not his fault. It's mine. I'm the one who made him angry. I'm the reason he left. It's fine. It's no big deal."

"It sounds to me as if it's a very big deal." She'd spoken flatly, almost unemotionally, but he had heard how thin her voice had grown, how strained it sounded. "You are hurt, little one, and no matter how angry he was, he had no right to hurt you."

"I told you, it's fine."

She took a deep breath and visibly pulled herself together. When she looked at him again, her expression was clear, but a shadow lurked in her mossy-green eyes that Spar didn't like at all.

"Anyway, right now we've got bigger issues to deal with." She turned back to the folder and flipped to a photocopy of a police report. "I'm just glad Rick didn't get mad enough to take this all with him. This is going to really help us out. This even has GPS coordinates for where the bodies were found. Apparently, they were all dumped within a pretty short distance. Maybe if we took a look around out there, we could find something to lead us back to the Order."

Spar watched her for a long moment. She had shut
down again, shut him out of her emotions, but this time
the act didn't anger him so much as it worried him. It
seemed it was not he alone who caused her to close herself off, but any sense of loss or abandonment that trig-
gered it. When she was hurt, he began to understand, she
pulled back like a turtle in its shell, trying to keep the
hurt from reoccurring. But if that was the secret to her
emotional vacillation, why would she believe that he ever
intended to hurt her?

She looked at him, her brows raised, clearly waiting
for a response. Spar nodded. "Indeed. We should definitely search the scenes. Even if we find no physical
evidence, there may be traces of magic that could be
helpful."

Felicity pursed her lips. "I'm pretty good at picking
up on magic, whether it's in people or objects, but maybe
we should bring Wynn with us. An extra pair of eyes
can't hurt, and she's got training, as a witch, even if not
as a Warden. She might recognize something like a spell
or whatever that I might miss."

"Agreed."

He itched to question her as to the origins of her
emotional withdrawal response, but he sensed this was
not the time. She was still fragile after the episode with
the reporter, and he didn't want to take the chance of
provoking the anger she had felt with him earlier in her
home. His mate could be a prickly little thing. Instead
of pressing, he reached over to shut the folder and
grabbed two menus from the holder by the wall.

"Let's eat first, though," he said, handing her one.
"The only thing left in your refrigerator is lettuce and a

slightly withered carrot, and I am no rabbit. A Guardian needs meat."

She managed a ghost of a smile and flipped open her menu. "Yeah, so does a temporarily out-of-work restorationist. Haven't you ever heard the term *starving artist* before?"

Chapter Seventeen

Wynn told them she would be available by late that afternoon. After some debate about light levels and tromping through the woods after dark, they agreed to give the area a quick look that evening and reconvene tomorrow when the light was better for a more thorough going-over.

Given that the three of them wouldn't fit on the Tiger, Fil broke out her van for the trip. Spar looked at it with surprise when she pulled out of the cramped garage behind the storefront.

"This is your vehicle as well?"

"Well, it would be pretty hard to transport valuable works of art on Laurent."

"Laurent?"

Fil grinned. "My motorcycle."

Spar eyed her oddly. "Your motorcycle has a name. And it is Laurent."

"After the patron saint of Canada."

He opened the door of the hulking white van and climbed inside. "You are a very strange human."

Fil hauled herself up behind the wheel and reached for her seat belt. "Hush. Don't call me names. You'll make Josephine angry."

"Josephine?" Spar asked, then groaned. "Do not tell me. That is the name of the van?"

"Yup." She grinned and pulled out into traffic.

They found Wynn waiting outside her small apartment building, wearing worn jeans and closed-toe shoes. The tennis shoes looked old and battered and comfortable enough to cover rough terrain. She climbed into the back of the van without a word for the lack of seating in the cargo area. She just dropped to the floor, tucked her legs up tailor-fashion, and set down the bulging bag she carried with her.

"Nice ride," she said, glancing around the huge cargo space. "I could really use something like this for making deliveries. I could get everything done in one trip."

"It has its uses," Fil agreed. "Sorry it's not more comfortable for you."

Wynn dismissed her concerns with a wave. "I'm fine. So where are we headed, anyway?"

"We're going to the park."

"Mount Royal?"

Fil nodded. "That's where the bodies were found, in the woods behind the Belvedere Kondiaronk. We'll have to park at Maison Smith and walk up."

The drive to the mountain passed quietly. Wynn seemed absorbed in cataloging the contents of her sack, and Spar had been walking on eggshells even since the scene in the café. She didn't know if he thought she'd shatter at the slightest push, or if he'd just given up trying to get her to talk to him. She couldn't even decide which she'd prefer.

Not that she had time to deal with either. Being rejected by a good friend, being in love with a man who wasn't a man and couldn't stick with her through the long haul, and dealing with her own messy, tangled emotions had to take a back burner to averting the coming apocalypse. That was her story, and she wasn't just sticking to it, she'd metaphorically superglued her ass right in the middle. Dynamite couldn't shake her devotion to denial and avoidance. She embraced the duo as her new best friends.

Fil pulled the van into the lot beside the maison and parked close to the roadway that became the Chemin Olmsted. The trail would lead northeast toward the chalet at the Kondiaronk lookout, forking before it reached that point to loop around on either side. In the center grew a dense patch of forest, technically off limits to the public. According to the bylaws of the park, no off-trail activities of any kind were permitted, but people being who they were, hikers and nature lovers occasionally wandered into the heavy trees. Apparently, so did murderers.

Pulling her phone from her pocket, Fil opened the GPS app and programmed in the coordinates listed in Ricky's file. "Come on," she urged the others. "We're heading this way."

They had reached the park in the waning hours of afternoon, and dusk hovered in the background, waiting to descend. Technically, the park would close when it did, but Fil hoped it wouldn't take them too long to make a first pass over the dump site. She'd spent many happy hours in these surroundings during her life, but today the woods possessed a quiet sense of foreboding that raised the hairs on the back of her neck. She didn't want to be here after dark, not tonight.

Spar stuck close to her side as she led the way up the well-worn trail that funneled visitors toward the chalet, which boasted some of the most spectacular views of the city to be found anywhere. Once they reached the split in the trail, the right-hand path would take them to the lookout at the chalet and the left would take a long, far-from-direct path around the forest to the huge steel cross that decorated the northeastern peak of Mount Royal. After that, it would circle down and back to rejoin itself at the chalet. But it was the central path at the fork that Fil followed.

This path led into the trees before opening onto a clear area behind the belvedere most people more grandly termed "the chalet." Fil led her companions along the trail for about two-thirds of its distance before she turned off and pointed north.

"That way."

The going quickly became rougher as they moved off the gravel path and into the woods themselves. Fallen leaves and twigs snapped underfoot, almost seeming to echo in the quiet. The trio had to step around trunks, push aside branches, and forge through the occasional bramble as they followed the map to the coordinates of the dump site.

They were no longer in the open, and the shadows had deepened. The last rays of the afternoon sun didn't penetrate so deeply here, and Fil tried to tell herself that the chill that raced through her came from the dropping temperature. Given the way it intensified as they drew closer to the coordinates, her self didn't seem convinced.

"You know, Frederick Olmsted designed this park after he finished Central Park in New York," Wynn commented, her rich voice pushing away a little of the uncomfortable silence. "I've visited there once or twice, but I don't remember it being quite as wild as this."

Fil glanced over her shoulder. "You've been to New York City?"

"Sure. I mean, I grew up in the Midwest, but I think everyone makes a pilgrimage to New York at least once in their life."

"The Midwest?" Fil stopped in her tracks, surprised. Somehow, circumstances had distracted her from noticing the other woman's accent. "You're American?"

"Well, yeah. Didn't Tim tell you that?"

"No. I think I would have remembered. What are you doing living in Montreal?"

"I've been working at McGill."

"You're a professor?" Fil hoped her tone conveyed something other than skepticism. She'd figured out Wynn was a very smart woman, but somehow she couldn't see her as a college professor.

Wynn chuckled, sounding unoffended. "Goddess, no. As far as I know, they don't have a Department of Wicky-Woo-Woo." She winked at the other woman. "No, it was a temporary position assisting one of the botanists in the Department of Plant Science with his research looking into the physical properties of traditional medicinal herbs. The grant is almost up, though, so I get to say in all seriousness—my work here is done."

Fil laughed, but the sound faded almost as soon as it passed her lips. Her next step cracked a fallen twig, but what startled her was the sensation of stepping into a cold, clammy fog. The level of light didn't change, but the atmosphere did, going icy and unnaturally still. The sounds of birds and insects and little forest creatures disappeared, so that the beep of her phone indicating the approach of their destination almost made her jump.

"We're nearly there, aren't we?" Wynn asked unnecessarily. "I can feel it."

Spar touched Fil's arm. "Stay close to me."

She had no plans to argue with that. She could feel a serious case of the creeps coming on.

After only a couple more minutes, Fill pushed through a thick stand of fir trees and stumbled into a small open area, not even ten feet in diameter. It looked less like a clearing and more like a bald patch, a scar left behind by a fallen tree, which would explain the odd mess in the center of the space.

It couldn't technically be called a stump, since the tree—a fairly massive maple, she guessed—obviously hadn't been cut down. She didn't know if it had rotted until the trunk could no longer support its weight, or if it had been struck by lightning or toppled in a storm, but judging by the uneven spikes of wood sticking up out of the churned-up earth, it hadn't gone down quietly. It almost looked like it had been ripped from the ground by some angry giant, and wasn't that a comforting thought to be popping into her head? As if demons and demon worshippers hadn't given her enough to worry about.

"Right here," Wynn breathed close behind her. "Can you see it?"

Fil wished she could say no.

A miasma hung low to the ground, only a few inches beyond the ruined remains of the maple tree. For some reason, Fil had thought that if she spotted something like this, it would take the shape of a person, like a magical chalk outline of the spot where a victim had lain. Instead, she saw thick, disquieting tendrils of greenish black, the color of healing bruises or rotted flesh. They twined around one of the wooden spikes, beneath the carpet of fallen leaves, and up again into the air. The tip of one waved, as if stirred by a breeze, only there was no breeze this deep inside the forest, and the motion looked more like an animal sniffing out prey than an innocently swaying plant frond.

"I see it."

Spar grumbled. "We should take a look around in case any physical evidence remains. I trust the human authorities were thorough, but it is better to check for ourselves."

They split up to section off the ground. Fil made a point of staying away from the foul area near the trunk. She decided to begin at the edge of the clearing and work her way in toward the center. Picking up a stick, she began to search the ground, poking at rocks and shifting aside piles of leaves to be sure nothing hid underneath. She worked quickly, since they did not want to linger too long this evening. She didn't really anticipate finding anything.

She didn't think any of them would, so when Wynn made a startled noise, she expected to hear about a snake or a spider that had caught the other woman off guard.

"I think I found something."

Dropping her branch, Fil hurried to the witch's side, Spar moving close behind. The woman crouched near a tumbled pile of rocks along the tree line at the northwestern edge of the tiny clearing.

"Look."

Fil followed the tip of her pointing finger to the ordinary-looking stones. At first, she could see nothing unusual in the little arrangement. Various shades of gray, the rocks looked like . . . rocks. Some bore chunks of dirt or moss; others were cracked or chipped from weather and natural forces. It wasn't until Fil blinked and opened her other set of eyes that she understood what Wynn had spotted.

The dull glint of pyrite in a crack between two stones had disguised the glitter to the naked eye, and the swiftly fading light hadn't helped. With her inner vision, Fil could make out the edge of a woman's earring, a thin wire of gold curled into a sweeping hoop. It glowed with a subtle blush of pinkish light.

"Do you think it belonged to one of the victims?" she asked.

Wynn reached out and shifted the stones, deftly plucking the piece of jewelry and holding it up for a closer examination. "Given this right here? I think there's a decent chance." She pointed to the post, where dried blood had collected to stain the metal. "It looks like it was ripped free. You know, like during a struggle."

Fil winced in sympathy and tugged her own bare lobe. "Well, if it did belong to one of the girls, it didn't do her much good, despite the blessing."

"It was blessed?" Wynn glanced at her curiously. "I thought I felt something subtle, but it's barely enough to ping my senses. How can you tell?"

"I can see it." She told the witch about her small magical talent. "You're right that it's subtle. In fact, it's so subtle I doubt it was much more than someone saying a prayer over the pair before they gave them to her. Too bad they didn't carry something stronger. Maybe we wouldn't have had to find them out here. Or her."

Wynn nodded in silent agreement and slipped the earring into a small pouch she pulled from her bag. "I'm taking it home. I'll scry over it later. That should tell me definitely if it belonged to one of the girls. If it did, I can try to use it to trace back to the Order. If she was still wearing it during the ritual, I could get lucky and find the sacrificial site."

Fil grimaced. "Damn. So it's not here? Not even someplace close to here?"

"No. The energy here sucks, and I'm taking like three showers when I get home to wash it off, but it's not nearly gross enough for that. I think what's lingering in this site came with them when they dumped the bodies, and it clung to the remains. It's been too long for me to feel it leading back anywhere else." She rose and tucked the little bag into the bigger bag. "You feel anything different?"

"Just maybe a fourth shower."

"It will be dark in a few more minutes," Spar pointed

out. "Take one last quick look at the area, but we need to start heading back."

Fil sighed and shook her head. "I was really hoping we'd get lucky and find a great big sign reading ALTAR OF DEATH with an arrow pointing us in the right direction."

Wynn snorted. "Our lives would all be a lot easier if the *nocturnis* were only that stupid."

The trio made one last quick sweep around the clearing, but of course they found nothing. Fil could only wish things were that easy. The sole thing that changed on her second look around the clearing was her discomfort with the energy of the area. The darker it became, the less she wanted to be here. She found herself instinctively moving closer to Spar just waiting for him to give the signal that he was ready to leave.

When it came, she nearly ran back to the truck. Well, she would have, but by then dusk had well and truly settled around them, and she could barely see the trees five feet in front of her. Knowing her luck, she'd have run face-first into one and given herself a concussion.

Spar gripped her hand. "I can see perfectly clearly," he said to reassure her. "Just follow me."

Fil clung, and she had no shame in admitting it. She hadn't liked this patch of woods in daylight; she certainly had no intention of changing her mind now that everything looked dark and creepy and sinister in the twilight. She turned back to urge Wynn to stick close. Her eyes picked out the witch's pale features just in time to see her eyes go wide and her body seemingly levitate three feet above the forest floor.

"They set a trap!" Wynn shouted, struggling against the invisible force that gripped her. She tried to pull something out of her bag, but how she could find a single item in the huge sack eluded Fil. "Run!"

Fil's instincts screamed at her to obey. Oh, how her cowardly heart joined the cheer, but her mind wouldn't let her abandon the other woman. She couldn't tell if she dropped Spar's hand or he dropped hers, but all at once both of them turned on their heels and sprinted back toward Wynn. The bag the witch carried tumbled to the ground just outside the clearing.

"Wynn!" Fil cried out, but the harder her legs pumped, the farther away the witch appeared, as if she was being dragged backward through the trees.

Spar surged forward, shedding his humanity like an ill-fitting disguise. Their surroundings forced him to keep his wings furled, but his muscular stag's legs ate up distance in great bounds. Fil had to pour on every ounce of speed she could muster just to keep him in sight. Of course, when she broke through the brush into the small clearing, her vision filled with the picture of Wynn, now hanging limp and still in midair. The tendril of sick energy that had hugged the ground earlier now rose up like a malignant version of Jack's beanstalk, tall and broad and glowing with evil power. The thick stems supported Wynn's body from beneath, while the viney ends curled around her arms and legs to hold her in place.

"Holy shit," Fil panted, skidding to a halt. "Spar, what the hell is that?"

"Dead," the Guardian snarled and launched himself into the heart of the growth.

Chapter Eighteen

The chill hit him first, the clammy cold at the center of the dark energy clinging to his skin and threatening to leach the warmth from the very heart of him. Spar ignored it. He had fought demons and their minions for centuries, and he would not fall prey to their puny scare tactics. He simply reached for a tendril of power and yanked it away from Wynn's still form.

The trouble with magic was its resilience. Each tendril he touched and snapped off seemed to re-form almost before he could blink. Realizing he was making no progress this way, he reached directly for the human witch to tug her free of the spell.

Behind him he could hear Felicity shouting. He just hoped she had enough sense to stay out of the way, because he couldn't concentrate on freeing Wynn if worry kept him too busy protecting his mate.

Spar wrapped his arms around the unmoving human and tried to yank her free of the Dark magic. It stretched briefly like a rubber band before springing back into place, dragging Wynn with it. The evil here was strong, but Spar was stronger.

He cursed the surrounding trees that hemmed him in and made it impossible to spread his wings. Their huge span would never clear the encroaching trunks, but if he could get above the human, his power would give him greater leverage to tear her free. Working from the ground gave the plant-like spell an advantage.

He could have used the witch's help, too. Guardians might be magic, but they couldn't work magic the way a Warden or a talented human could. Spar could disguise himself from curious eyes and accomplish physical feats that no human could manage, or summon himself clothing or weapons, but he couldn't cast a spell, or uncast one that held another imprisoned. A witch just might be able to.

Reaching for Wynn again, he shook her this time and called her name, trying to wake her, to get her to talk to him, to help his fight. He couldn't tell if she had been injured during her struggle and knocked unconscious, or if her sleep was a side effect of the spell. Either way, it didn't matter. She failed to respond to any of his attempts to get her to open her eyes.

An ominous cracking sound reached his ears, and the ground trembled at his feet. Cursing, Spar looked down and saw the earth split open as more tendrils of Dark power pushed up through the soil. This time, the vines reached for him, as if they intended to surround him the same way they had with Wynn. They would find the Guardian not so easy to ensnare.

Summoning his spear to him with a thought, Spar brought the wickedly sharp head down and around like a scythe. The honed edge sliced though the creeping vines, but unlike live, growing plants, these screamed audibly in pain before they withered back into the dirt. He felt a brief surge of triumph until a new wave of tendrils pushed up, even more than before. They moved faster this time, twining around his limbs almost as quickly as he could cut them back.

He was managing to keep himself free, but Wynn still lay in the grip of the spell. Risking a glance in her direction, he could see the vines growing up and over her body, encasing her in a greenish-black cocoon of Dark energy. He swore and swung his spear faster.

Oh. Hell. No.

Fear had gripped Fil when she'd seen the Darkness grab hold of Wynn, but when those nasty, cancerous excuses for Audrey Two the carnivorous plant began attacking Spar, she'd had enough. Fil might not be a Guardian, and she might not be a witch, but she also wasn't a coward, and she wasn't about to sit back and watch while her new friend and her lover were devoured by the Darkness. Not on your life.

She glanced around for something to use as a tool, wondering where a nice sturdy flamethrower was when you needed one. Or maybe she was just looking for inspiration; Fil couldn't be entirely sure. Either way, the first thing her gaze landed on was Wynn's fallen bag, lying in the leaves at the edge of the clearing.

Witch or not, there had to be something inside Fil could use. As far as she could tell from watching Wynn, the witch carried everything she owned in there, possibly including her kitchen sink. It wouldn't surprise Fil at all to learn the thing had a spell on it like Hermione's purse in the last couple of Harry Potter movies.

She contemplated dumping everything out and sorting through it on the forest floor, but she didn't want to take the chance that it contained anything Wynn would absolutely refuse to leave behind. If they could get free but had to make a mad dash to safety, she didn't want to have to stop and repack everything. Instead, she took a deep breath, offered up an even briefer prayer, and stuck her unmarked right hand into the sack. No reason to take chances, right?

Her fingers closed over something fat and cylindrical. At first Fil thought she'd grabbed a candle and started to drop it right back inside, but something stopped her, some niggling in the back of her throat. Biting her lip, she pulled the item out of the bag and looked at it. In her hand she held a jar about seven inches high and three inches in diameter, made of clear glass and stoppered with a thick cork. Inside, she could see a dark, crystalline powder, and in the faint darkness she could just make out a white sticker bearing the neatly printed words DRIVE AWAY SALT.

Shit. At this point anything was worth a try.

Clutching the jar, she jumped to her feet and strode toward the center of the clearing. The green-black vine things had nearly engulfed Wynn's body by now, but Spar seemed to be doing a decent job mowing them back from himself with his flashing spear. Either way, she could see that all of the tendrils came from roughly the same area, the three-foot patch of ground around the base of the fallen tree.

Spar had explained to her how Wynn had chanted in-cantations over her sleeping form while trying to sever the bond with the demonic energy in her hand, but Fil was personally fresh out of chants. She didn't know any incantations or any spells, and all her life she'd sucked at rhyming poetry. No, she would just have to take care of this in her own fashion.

A quick twist popped the cork from the jar. Tilting it to bring the salt to the opening, Fil reached in and grabbed a hefty pinch between her thumb and first two fingers. Her arm came back like a pitcher on the mound and she bared her teeth at the twining mass of Dark power.

"Let go of my friends and go back where you came from, you nasty-assed piece of shit!" she roared, and she flung the salt hard at the base of the Darkness.

The night filled with shrill, throbbing screams as the mass seemed to draw back on itself, like a living creature touched by flame. Several loops of vine fell off Wynn's still form, loosening their hold on the witch. Excitement rushed into Fil's chest, and she hurried to pour a handful of salt into her palm.

"I said begone!"

This time, she flung a whole pile of the black salt on the earth where the tendrils had emerged. The shriek-ing grew louder, and the vines dropped Wynn to the earth with a thud. Fil winced and hoped to God the woman hadn't been seriously injured by the fall. Wasn't being relaxed and lying down supposed to help distrib-ute the impact? Still, falling twelve feet onto a bunch of rocks and tree roots couldn't have been comfortable.

Spar roared and darted forward to scoop Wynn up into his arms. "Felicity! Come!" he shouted, turning back toward the path. "Hurry!"

Like she planned to stick around. First, though, she wanted to make sure that this time nothing followed them. Shifting the jar into her right hand, she pointed the opening at the base of the retreating Darkness and threw the remaining contents of the jar onto the earth.

"And fucking stay there!" she ordered, right before she flung the jar after the salt and bolted after the Guardian.

She barely slowed down to scoop Wynn's bag into her grasp. Opening her inner vision, she let the magical glow that emanated from Spar's body light her way back to the parking lot. She saw the way he hesitated at the head of the trail and groaned.

"Šūdas!"

Even now that dark had fallen and the park had officially closed, they couldn't take the chance of Spar being seen.

"I would fly her home, but I will not leave you unguarded," he snarled, his eyes glinting with an almost feral light. Battling to save two humans had apparently gotten her Guardian all stirred up.

"Give me two minutes. With your night vision, you can keep an eye on me from here."

Spinning on her heels, Fil ran the remaining distance to the parking lot and hopped in the van. She practically left skid marks as she maneuvered the big tank of a vehicle until the rear cargo doors backed up as close to the tree line as possible. She bumped her knee on the center console as she scrambled into the back to open the doors from the inside. Leaning her head out, she put her fingers to her lips and whistled.

Within seconds Spar appeared to lift Wynn into the empty cargo area. "Stay back here with her," Fil ordered, after checking to make sure the witch still had a pulse. Thank God, she did. If she looked closely, she could even see her chest rise and fall with shallow breaths. "I'll take us straight home."

She did, managing the trip down off the mountain in record time. She didn't bother returning Wynn to her apartment, just drove the unconscious woman, the Guardian, and herself directly to Fil's building in Montreal's Latin Quarter, maneuvering the van through the narrow alley to the garage in the rear.

Once she cut the engine, the van's headlights blinked off and the building's small rear courtyard plunged into relative darkness. Lights from the neighbors alleviated the gloom somewhat, but Fil had neglected to leave any of her own lights burning, so it was dark enough not to worry about Spar making the short trip to the back door in his natural form. Between the lack of illumination and the high wooden privacy fence closing off the yard, being spotted was pretty unlikely. Fil hurried across the open space to unlock the back door, then waved for Spar to follow. It looked like this time, she got to play nurse for the unconscious witch. It was funny how quickly fate had turned the tables, right?

Yeah, Fil wasn't laughing, either.

Spar laid the witch down on the sofa where Felicity had stretched out only days before and fought back the urge to howl. At every turn, he found his mate threatened, and if the Darkness didn't kill her, she appeared to be doing a fine job trying to kill herself.

When he thought of the risk she had taken, charging at the Darkness with nothing more than a jar of salt for a weapon, he could feel his heart turn to ice in his chest. He had barely believed the sight, convinced that she knew enough to keep herself back, out of danger, while he battled for their safety. But no, not his little mate. She had thrown herself into the fray, bellowing like a madwoman, hurling profanities and black salt in nearly equal measure. If he had been human, the sight would have caused him a stroke.

Seeing her now, kneeling beside the sofa, her concern clearly for the unconscious Wynn and not at all for her own well-being, threatened to drive away what little remained of his sanity. Tugging her to her feet, he turned her in the direction of the bathroom and shoved her none too gently toward the door. "I will see to the witch. You will check to ensure you have sustained no new wounds and that the old one on your side was not reopened during our encounter. Go."

He could hardly be surprised when she dug in her heels and turned to face him, her expression a study in confusion and stubborn will. "No, I'm fine. For God's sake, I'm standing right here in front of you, walking, talking, and acting perfectly normal. Don't worry about me. Wynn is the one who's been unconscious for nearly an hour. And did you see that fall? She could be seriously injured, and we wouldn't know because she can't tell us. I really think we should take her to the hospital. Get her checked out."

"Getting her to safety was the most important thing.

If she requires medical care, we will see that she gets it. After you assure me that you yourself were not harmed or reinjured." He crossed his arms over his chest and ruffled his wings impatiently.

Felicity's mouth dropped open as she stared at him. "Really? My God, you're an idiot sometimes!" She shrugged out of her jacket with jerky movements and flung the leather to the floor. Reaching for the hem of her shirt, she yanked the material over her head and tossed it after the jacket before flinging her arms out to the sides. "There. See for yourself. The cut is fine. It's been two weeks, for fuck's sake. All that's left are some itchy scabs. Satisfied?"

That she could ask that question while she stood before him half naked, with nothing more than a scrap of lacy satin covering her beautiful breasts, told Spar she lacked a certain basic understanding of his nature. He wouldn't be satisfied until he had her pressed flat against the nearest horizontal surface while he buried himself inside her sweet flesh. Just the thought of her in danger reduced him to his most primitive instincts: protect, defend, claim. He'd done the first two, so maybe it was time for the third.

Eyes narrowing, he took a step toward her.

"Um, guys?"

The words came weakly, but the sound of Wynn's voice had both Spar and his mate snapping to attention. Felicity hurried back to kneel at their friend's hip and laid a hand over hers.

"Hey," his mate murmured with a smile. "Thank God you're awake. I was starting to get worried. How do you feel?"

The witch grimaced. "Like I just got hit by a truck. Or half devoured by a nasty *nocturnis* spell. And for some reason, my right ankle feels like someone tried to twist my foot off my leg. In fact, I almost wish they'd succeeded. It might hurt less that way."

Felicity reached down and carefully raised the hem of Wynn's jeans. From the swelling of the joint, it was clear the ankle was injured. "Crap. It could be broken. We should get you to the hospital. I bet it happened when the plant from hell dropped you."

"No, I'm pretty sure it's just sprained," Wynn said. "All I need is an Ace bandage and about seven billion ibuprofen. I'm more interested in hearing how you got the spell to let go in the first place."

"Was that a spell? I don't get why it didn't go after us when we first entered the clearing, if it was."

"It was a trap, probably set to go off if anyone with magical ability entered the area. Most likely the *nocturnis* have a password that lets them go in and out without setting it off, but when we tried to leave, it tripped the trigger. I should have seen it, but I wasn't looking. I was so intent on finding something to trace back to the ritual site that I didn't even look." She made a face as if disgusted with her own oversight. "So really, I just got what I deserved."

"Don't be an idiot," Felicity snapped. "None of us bothered to look for traps, and we should have. I'm the one who asked you to come along in case you picked up something I missed. We all saw the energy on the ground, and we all wrote it off as leftover Dark magic schmutz. You don't get to play the martyr on this one."

Wynn appeared to disagree, but she let it drop and

looked up at Spar. "I'm in your debt, Guardian. Thank you for rescuing me. The Darkness had me overwhelmed. Without you, it probably would have devoured me whole."

Spar shook his head and shot a pointed glance at Felicity. "You owe me nothing. Even had I saved you, to do so would have been no more than my duty, but Felicity is the one who freed you, not I."

"Really?" Wynn's eyes went wide, and she fixed her gaze on the other woman. "How did you do it?"

Felicity's mouth twisted in a wry half smile. "Sheer dumb luck, mostly. You dropped your bag of tricks when that thing grabbed you. Spar ran right past it into the fray, and he did a pretty good job hacking away at the tendrils, but it just kept growing and growing. I figured you must have brought something with you for emergency defense against the Dark arts, what with your Harry Potter vibe going on, so I decided to check. The first thing I grabbed was a jar labeled DRIVE AWAY SALT, which I figured sounded worth a try."

The witch laughed in surprise. "Wow, good guess. You picked the best possible 'trick' you could have used, from the sounds of it."

"Huh. Go me. So what is drive away salt, anyway?"

"Some people call it black salt or witch's salt, and that's basically what it is—just salt with some ingredients added that turn it black. Lucky for you, or for all of us really, the jar I brought with me was specifically mixed with the Order in mind. I made it to drive away demonic energy."

"How?"

"It's all in the added ingredients. The black color

comes mostly from charcoal, which I used to burn sage, rue, and benzoin. Sage is the cleanser, the purifier. It's why people for centuries have been using it to smudge houses and circles and anything else that needs to be blessed. Rue removes hexes and drives away black magic, and benzoin is a resin that also purifies, but specifically it works against demons. It's noxious to them. Once the ingredients are burned, I mix the ashes and charcoal with pure sea salt, and voilà. Black salt."

"Wow. And I just grabbed the first thing I touched. That worked out pretty well."

Wynn smiled. "Like I said before, instinct is the basis of magic."

Spar watched the two women grin at each other and fought back the need to shake sense into both of them. Did his mate not realize the chance she had taken? What could have happened if her first touch had landed on the wrong item? And the witch needed to be taught not to encourage Felicity's recklessness. His mate seemed to be having no trouble carving years off his immortality without Wynn's assistance.

"Either of you could have died," he bit out through clenched teeth, but the expressions the two women turned to him were blank.

"But we didn't," Wynn pointed out with exaggerated patience. "Fil did exactly right."

"We're fine," Felicity echoed. "All's well that ends well, and all that crap." She frowned back at Wynn. "Except for that ankle. If you're sure it's just a sprain, I'll go fetch an elastic bandage. I think I have one in the bathroom."

"Can you grab my bag, too? I think I have a jar of

everlasting ointment in there. If I rub that in before we wrap it, it should help a lot."

"You got it."

"Oh, and um, maybe you want to put on a shirt? I mean, not that we don't have all the same parts and everything, but I'm not used to hanging out with other chicks in just their bras."

Felicity's cheeks flushed a delicate pink. "Oops. Forgot about that, but it is kinda chilly in here. I'll be right back."

Spar looked at Felicity, then at Wynn, then back at Felicity. The women simply carried on as if nothing serious had happened. Wynn pulled herself into a sitting position against the arm of the sofa, and Felicity headed toward the door where she'd dropped the witch's bag as soon as they'd entered the apartment. Spar felt like he was trapped in some strange alternate universe where danger ceased to exist and female humans ruled the world.

He had to get out of there before he got trapped. Or lost his bloody mind.

"I am going up to the roof," he snarled, heading for the window that led to the fire escape in the alley. "I will check to be certain we were not followed or . . ." He slammed the window open and simply growled. "I will be on the roof."

Maybe the cool night air would clear his head. If nothing else, a little distance might save his mate the ravages of a thoroughly spanked bottom.

Chapter Nineteen

"Hm. He seemed . . . cranky."

Fil looked toward the window and frowned. "Yeah, he gets a little wound up when it comes to safety and stuff. I think this whole episode with you and me both having to go up against *nocturnis* magic might have gotten to him."

"I don't think it was the idea of *my* being in danger that upset him."

"What are you talking about? You're human; Spar's a Guardian. Trust me, he takes his duty to protect humanity against the Darkness damned seriously."

Wynn smiled. "Oh, I can see that. I just think that when it comes to you, duty isn't his only motivation."

Felicity felt another blush rise to her cheeks. Damn her über-fair complexion! "We've been together for two weeks now. Protecting me has become a habit."

"Oh, you've been 'together' all that time, have you?" The witch wriggled her eyebrows with exaggerated meaning.

"Stop it. I just mean he's gotten used to having to

haul me out of trouble. Since he woke up he's seen me zapped with a demon mark, nearly blown up by a crazy *nocturnis,* sliced up by a *hhissih,* attacked by a golem, and now going up against some weird, magical version of Audrey Two from *Little Shop of Horrors.* Of course his protective instincts have to be screaming at him that I'm one slippery step away from total annihilation."

"You really don't think there's more to it than that?"

"What else would there be?"

Wynn rolled her eyes. "Come on, Fil. You don't think I can see what's going on with you two? He looks at you like you're the one who breathed life into his stone form. And you practically eat him up with butter and jelly every time you look at him. No matter which form he's wearing. Plus, the two of you generate enough electricity to light up half of Montreal. You're madly in love with each other."

Hearing the truth from someone else's lips—or at least her half of it—felt like having a pin stuck in Fil's balloon of denial. She felt herself deflate until she collapsed onto the end of the sofa with a flubbery sigh. "God, am I that transparent?"

"Sweetie, you're in love. People are supposed to be able to see it when you're together."

"People, sure, but not him. At least, I hope not."

"You mean you haven't told him."

Fil looked at her new friend as if she'd lost her mind. "Why on God's green earth would I want to do that?"

"Why tell him you love him?" Wynn shot her the same look right back. "Um, maybe because you are, and even if he thinks he knows already, he deserves to hear it from you."

"Right, and what do I deserve? To stand back and wave him off like he's heading out for a day at the office when he turns back to stone and sleeps till after I'm dead?" She tried to keep the bitterness out of her voice, but she knew she wasn't succeeding. It went too deep for her to contain all of it. "Sure, sounds like a swell time."

"Wait. Hold on a minute." Wynn held up a hand and made a rewinding motion with her finger. "Back that up. Has Spar not claimed you? Because if he hasn't, my mojo is way off right now. You two practically vibrate at the same frequency when you're together. I could have sworn you were his."

"His what? Pal? Girlfriend? Fuck buddy? I don't think you're going to convince me that male Guardians are so different from the males of other species that just because we've had sex, I get to assume there's a happily-ever-after in store. I'm human; I get to live maybe eighty, ninety years. He's immortal; he'll live forever, long after I've not only wrinkled and sagged in all the wrong places, but turned into dust. Plus, he'll do most of it asleep and therefore completely oblivious to me and my *un*-immortalness. Shakespeare should have given *Romeo and Juliet* such a tragic ending."

"But he's told you that's not the way it works, right?"

"He doesn't need to tell me anything." Angry and feeling chilled by more than the temperature in the room, Fil swiped her shirt up off the floor and tugged it back on. "I know there's no future for the two of us, so falling in love with Spar would be the dumbest thing I could possibly do."

"You've already done it, sweetie. Will denying the truth really help?" Wynn cut her off when she tried to answer. "No, save it. It looks like there are a few things Spar still has to explain to you, and like an idiot male, he's already left it longer than he should have."

"If you keep on with the cryptic bullshit, I'm going to wrap your ankle in poison ivy leaves instead of the elastic bandage," Fill threatened.

"Gah, you've got a nasty streak." Wynn shook her head. "Sorry, but this is Spar's news to share, not mine. Just trust me when I tell you that you're not doomed to a lonely life of misery, okay? There are things about the Guardians that you clearly still haven't learned, but it's Spar's place to fill you in. If I did it and I'm wrong, I'd only make things worse for you."

"Comforting. Thanks." Fil shot the witch a sour look.

"Hey, I'm not at my best right now. I've got a sprained ankle and bruises out the wazoo, plus I can still feel those nasty-assed vines on my skin. I'm not sure there's a loofah big enough to scrub that memory away." She shuddered delicately.

"Sorry." Frustrated but exhausted, Fil pushed to her feet. "You dig out your ointment. I'll go fetch the bandage. I think I have a bag of frozen peas around, too. That should help your swelling some."

"Thank you. I mean it, Fil." Her earnest tone had Fil pausing to glance at her from the hallway. "Don't let the bastards get you down. Or Spar, either. I really don't think he's going to break your heart. I promise."

Fil feared it might already be too late. "Don't worry about me. Start thinking of ways to use that earring we found to hunt these *nocturnis* assholes down. No matter what happens, watching Spar hack them to bits is sure to put at least one smile on my face."

By the time Spar crawled back into the apartment, Wynn had disappeared and Fil was tucked in her bed, lying still under the blankets. When he saw the light from the window glinting off her open eyes, he knew she wasn't asleep.

"Where's the witch?" he asked quietly. He had resumed his human form in the living room, and now had the bother of removing his clothing before he climbed in to join his mate.

"In the guest room, hopefully asleep. She's got a pretty badly sprained ankle, and some amazingly colorful bruises, but other than that she assures me everything is in working order."

"I am glad she did not try to leave."

Fil snorted. "Who says she didn't try? I practically had to sit on her to keep her here once we got her ankle wrapped. She insisted she could call a cab and be fine at home by herself. She had some plan to get right to work scrying with that earring."

Spar grunted and stretched out between the cotton sheets, already warmed by his little human's feminine body. He tugged her against his side and tried to ignore the brief hesitation before she snuggled into him. "It is good that you stopped her. She will require rest in order to perform such a difficult task. Tomorrow is soon enough for her to begin."

"That's what I said."

Feeling his mate's curves pressed against him had

its predictable effect on Spar's body. He felt himself begin to harden, but once again he felt distance between himself and his Felicity. No longer did it feel like a purposeful barrier she erected to keep him away, but he still perceived something separating them. The sensation troubled him.

"What is wrong?" he asked, his voice soft and tender.

He reached out to brush a strand of hair from her cheek and couldn't resist tangling his fingers in the pale, silky mass. During the day she habitually pulled the long, blond fall into a ponytail, leaving only a fringe of short bangs to frame her pretty face, but at night he had come to love seeing it tumble around her shoulders. The curtain of it reached down to her shoulder blades, a straight, shining waterfall of the palest yellow sunlight. When she leaned over him and let it drift along his skin, he wanted to freeze time and just wallow in the ticklish joy of it.

She shook her head, rubbing her cheek against his chest in the process. "Nothing. I'm just tired."

He could hear the shading in her words, not a lie, but not precisely the truth. Part of him wanted to push her, sick of allowing her to hold him at arm's length, but he could still see her face in the diner earlier, when her friend had accused her of vile things and then stalked away as if disgusted with her. The image had seared itself in his memory, clear and sharp as broken glass. The greater part of him would do anything to spare her pain, so once again he kept silent. There would be time, he promised himself. After they dealt with the Hierophant and his plans there would be time to deal with whatever troubled her. Until then, Spar would simply do his best to keep her safe, and to demonstrate to her that he loved her, every part of her, including the ones that she hid from him.

Hooking a finger beneath her chin, he urged her to lift her face to his. He swept her lips with a gentle kiss, needing to prove to her that she was cherished. She responded eagerly, parting to lure him within. He couldn't resist the invitation and moved to taste her, savoring the spiced-wine sweetness of her mouth. He could drink from her lips for a lifetime, never hungering for other nourishment, never coming up for air. This little human completed him. She filled in the places he hadn't known were empty, and he wallowed in the heady sensation.

Her arms wrapped around him, her little hands stroking his back, pausing to knead with the strength that always surprised him. She felt so tiny and delicate in his arms that he tended to forget his mate had a core of molten steel in her, flexible enough to bend, but strong enough to carry the weight of the world. She tried to do just that far too often for his liking.

He traced his own fingers lightly along her spine, feeling the way the butterfly touch made her shiver and arch against him. Her back was highly sensitive, and he recalled one recent evening when he'd traced every graceful inch of it with fingers and lips and tongue. She had melted beneath him and begged him to take her before he was through. Tonight, he had no plans to take; all he desired was to give.

He should have known she would never let him get away with it. He chuckled against her throat as she brought her hands forward to caress his chest, fingers playing with his nipples in a way that made him bite back a moan. It hadn't taken his little mate long to find every place on his body that sent his head spinning, and she apparently loved to tease all of them until he lost control and took her like the beast he was. Not tonight, though. Tonight he would not simply have her or she him. Tonight, they would love.

Pressing her back against the softness of the mattress, he moved over her, supporting himself on his elbows, allowing her to carry only a fraction of his weight. Immediately, her thighs parted to cradle his hips, her legs coming up to wrap around his waist and press him to her. All he had to do was touch her, and she gave herself. He never had to ask for her touch or her attention, because she lavished it on him without reserve. This was the only time Spar felt no barriers between them, when they came together like this. During their lovemaking, she dropped the walls, closed the distance, and simply loved him. He had to find a way to persuade her to do it all the time.

His hands glided over her with tender purpose, seeking out all the spots that made her sigh, that made her shiver. He loved the way her breath hitched when she gasped, the low throaty timbre of her moans. When he hit a particularly sensitive patch of skin, her whole body would tense, then tremble, then melt beneath him. It made him feel like a god and only made him crave to feel it again.

Getting enough of her wasn't even the remotest possibility. He craved her even in his sleep, those short periods when he closed his eyes and let himself dream of her. It wasn't like the slumber he experienced when the magic took him, and he could easily have done without it, but he knew she required rest so he took advantage of the times when she slept by lying beside her and letting her fill him up like water in an empty cup. Every night the cup refilled, and every night his thirst only grew.

The warm wetness between her thighs bathed him in heat and made him ache to have her. The more he touched, the more liquid she became, until he wanted to dive into her like his own personal sea. His hands skimmed down her sides and hers clenched tight on his hips, trying to pull him inside. With a groan, he gave up his resistance and joined them.

Her breath shuddered out against his ear, his name a whisper of need and pleasure and tenderness. Immediately she clamped around him, her body designed so perfectly for his. The tight clasp sent his senses reeling, robbing him of everything but the feel of her, hot and slick and welcoming.

When he began to move, she lifted into his thrusts, her body undulating in graceful waves beneath him. He rocked into her, his rhythm slow but relentless, pushing both of them steadily along to the inevitable conclusion.

He thrust and she parried, he stroked and she caressed. Together they lost themselves in the power of their desire, becoming not him and her but them, a new being made of passion and respect and love.

He would have made it last forever if he could. He knew he'd never get enough of her, never find a greater perfection than his body in hers, her arms around him, their breath mingling in sweet tangles of heat. But nothing could hold back their pleasure.

It crashed over them together, a tidal wave of ecstasy

that dragged them under before shooting them back to the surface, limp and spent and one.

Spar barely had the energy to shift himself to the side to keep from crushing his mate before he collapsed atop her in a heap of satisfied Guardian. When he pressed his lips a final time against her brow, he saw her eyes drift shut and sleep claim her. For now, it could have her, but soon enough the universe would know that Spar's claim trumped all the others. When a Guardian claimed his mate, he would face the depths of the Darkness and give up his measure of eternity to keep her.

Chapter Twenty

First thing in the morning, Wynn insisted on going home. Insisted at the top of her lungs, to be honest, and she didn't flinch when Fil turned up her own volume to match. Neither of them paid any attention to Spar's pained wince, but each recognized when she had met an opponent she couldn't bully into submission. It was one of the things that cemented their friendship.

"I can't do the scrying until I get home. I need my tools, I need my altar, and I need the peace and quiet," the witch insisted. "No offense, sweetie, but since I met you *peaceful* has not been an appropriate adjective to describe my life."

"You'd be surprised how many people tell me that," Fil muttered. "I guess that means you won't let us hang around and stand guard while you work, either?"

"What part of 'peace' did you not understand?" Wynn gave her an exaggerated stare. "Plus, Goddess knows how long it will take me to actually see something. Scrying isn't like casting a normal spell. Whatever I ask to see, I still have to wait for the vision, and although I've had it come in minutes, I've also had to wait days. Sometimes even weeks. You are not going to hang around watching my TV and eating my snacks for that long. It would spell the end of our friendship. Hell, of any friendship!"

"I'm not sure we have weeks, Wynn."

She sighed. "I know. I'm praying it won't take that long, but to have you stand guard around me and wait would just be silly. Besides, my apartment is warded tighter than a tick. I'll be safe there, I promise."

"You realize I'm holding you to that, right?"

"*Mais oui,* as you francophones say."

Fil didn't find the wink that accompanied the statement as reassuring as she was sure Wynn had intended. Which probably had something to do with the new habit she developed of pacing around the apartment in circles that drove Spar to the brink of insanity.

"Little one," he repeated daily, usually more than once, "wearing yourself into exhaustion will not hurry the process. Wynn's vision will come when it comes. Sit and try to focus on something else."

On the third evening, he pretty much lost it.

"For the sake of the Eternal Light, woman, *sit! Down!*"

Fil shot him a glare. "I can't! What the hell is taking her so long? I know she said this wasn't instantaneous, but it's been three days! The Order could have killed someone else by now. Shit, they could have killed another dozen people. We have to find them."

Spar grasped her shoulders to hold her in place. "We all know the dangers, Felicity. Do you think Wynn does not take this seriously?"

"Fil," she corrected, mostly out of habit at this point. She'd given up any real hope of getting him to stop using her full name. "I know she's taking it seriously, I'm just so frustrated. I'm sick of looking over my shoulder every five minutes, and I'm sick of worrying what else the *nocturnis* are going to do before we can stop them. If they manage to restore the demon to its full strength, we'll be screwed, especially with Ella still having trouble finding the rest of you Guardians."

She dropped her head to his chest—which was almost as good as banging it against a brick wall—and smacked him ineffectually with the flat of her left hand. "And I'm sick of having this stupid mark still clinging to my skin. You know, for the last year or so I'd been giving some serious thought to getting a tattoo, but I think this thing has turned me off the idea of permanent body art in a big way."

Spar raised her hand to his lips and pressed a kiss to the center of her palm. "I cannot say I can blame you for that. Try to remember what Wynn said. It will fade eventually. You must be patient."

"Yeah, you can see how well I'm doing in that department."

He hugged her. "It is difficult for all of us. Come, you need a distraction. You will show me once again how to play this game called poker. Only this time, you will show me the tricks your grandmother taught you."

Fil appreciated his effort, really she did, but the fact that he actually won a couple of the hands they played demonstrated exactly how much trouble she had concentrating on anything else. For some reason, the tension always got worse after dark, too. Maybe she was just that superstitious, but she couldn't help thinking that every time the sun set, the Order got a little closer to bringing about the end of the world. Intellectually, she realized evil could operate in the daylight just as well as in the dark—well, she realized it now, since Spar had patiently explained to her that vampires did not really exist—but her subconscious still equated black magic with the hours of darkness.

Who had known she was such a traditionalist?

When the phone rang just after nine that night, Fil practically flew across the apartment to answer it. If this wasn't Wynn with good news, she really was going to lose her mind.

"Hello?"

"Fil? Hey, it's Rick."

She nearly dropped the phone. "Rick?" Out of the corner of her eye she saw Spar glance at her curiously. "I . . . I, uh, didn't expect to hear from you."

"Yeah, I know. I wanted to apologize for that, for the way I yelled and walked out on you at the café. I know you're not some sicko, I just—" He paused. "I let that stuff get to me, and I took it out on you. I'm sorry. Really."

Fil felt a rush of relief. He had hurt her the other day, but it made it better to know he didn't really think of her the way he'd said. She didn't want to lose his friendship permanently. "Thanks, Ricky. I appreciate that."

"Good." She heard shuffling in the background. "Listen, I found some more information I think might help you out. Something about where the police are looking for the actual crime scenes. Can I stop by and show you?"

Did the police have a lead on the ritual site? A jolt of adrenaline hit her at the thought. Maybe it wouldn't matter that Wynn's scrying was taking so long. If the police had a solid lead, even if they'd just narrowed it down to half a dozen locations, Fil could be more than happy to schlep her way to every single one of them to check it out. It was the closest they'd gotten so far.

"You want me to meet you at Claude's?" she offered.

"No," he said. "I've already eaten dinner, and anyway I'm almost on your side of town already. I'll swing by your place. Half an hour okay?"

Fil didn't even bother to check with Spar. If he was okay with Wynn's visits, she was sure he'd be fine with Rick's. "I'll be here. You know where to find me."

"I certainly do. *À bientôt, chère.*"

She hung up with an excited grin. "Ricky said he got some more info from the police. They may have leads on the ritual site. Well, the murder site, I'm sure they're calling it. He's on his way over with the details."

Spar frowned. "I am not sure I like that. He upset you the last time you met with him. He accused you of callousness toward the death of the sacrifices." He crossed his arms over his chest. "I will not allow him in your home if seeing him will upset you."

"*You* won't allow him in *my* home?" Fil shook her head. If she thought Spar would remain part of her life over the long term, she would so have corrected that little statement right there, but at the moment she couldn't see the point of expending the effort on the inevitable fight. "Whatever. He apologized for that, and I forgave him. I understood where he was coming from anyway. Rick might enjoy playing the hard-boiled, eternally skeptical crime reporter, but inside he's a big softie. Stuff like those murders really gets to him. I'm not surprised he was upset by all the questions I was asking."

Her Guardian grumbled. "If he makes you sad again, I will not be held responsible for the detachment of his limbs from his torso."

"Ew!"

His grin flashed a hint of fang.

"Down, boy."

Eager anticipation had her nearly laughing when the phone rang a second time. Without checking the caller ID, she snatched it up and answered. "Nice, Ricky. What happened? You forget the address already?"

"I think someone is trying to get inside my apartment!"

Fil froze. She recognized Wynn's voice even though the woman spoke in an urgent whisper, but those were definitely not the words she and Spar had been hoping to hear when the witch finally called. "Wynn, what do you mean? What's going on?"

Spar straightened, immediately focusing on her. He must have heard the concern in her voice, because he rose from his seat at the table and began to shimmer the way he did before he changed forms.

"Someone's trying to break in. Felicity, I need help! You have to send Spar. It's the Order! I know it is!"

"Wynn, calm down," Fil urged, waving at Spar to hurry up and change. This sounded like a job for the winged avenger Guardian, not the sadly untalented gambler Guardian. "We'll come for you, I swear. Just do whatever you can to shore up those wards. We're on our way."

The line went dead and Fil felt her heart skip a beat. "It's Wynn. She said the *nocturnis* are at her house trying to break in. She needs your help. You have to get over there."

"No, *we* have to get over there. You know that you are not to stray from my sight."

"Are you kidding me?" Fil demanded. "Do you really think we have time to fight about this right now?"

Spar's eyes narrowed at her attempt to mimic his deep, gravelly voice. "So far, the *nocturnis* have had no reason to track us here, but we cannot assume that they do not know we are here. We cannot assume this place is safe. We had no reason to believe they knew of Wynn's location, either, but she is currently under siege." He shook his head. "I will not knowingly leave you in danger and undefended. You will come with me where I can ensure you will not be alone and vulnerable to attack."

"*Šūdas!*" Fil yanked on her ponytail. "You're being an idiot *and* wasting time. Wynn needs you. I'm safe here. Besides, Rick is already on his way over. I can't just leave him to arrive to an empty apartment. He'll think I'm blowing him off."

"Call and tell him to come another time."

"Spar, get your ass out the window and go save Wynn!" she yelled at him. "Not only is she our friend, but she still needs to try to find the location of the ritual site, especially if Ricky's leads don't pan out. We can't count on the human authorities to know where to find the *nocturnis*. We need Wynn. Besides, I won't be alone if Ricky is here. Now go!"

She could see Spar warring with himself and cursed again. Marching over to the fire escape window, she flung open the sash and practically threw him outside. "Go save my friend! Ricky will be here any minute, and I vow on the spirit of Laurent—the saint *and* the motorcycle—that I will call if I sense the slightest danger. You can take my cell phone."

She tucked the phone into the waistband of his leather kilt-thingie and shooed him. "Now go! Save the day! Don't make me sing the *Underdog* theme."

Spar growled something she didn't really want a translation for, grabbed her arms, and hauled her to him for a bruising kiss. Then he climbed onto the fire escape's metal railing and launched himself into the night sky. Fil closed the window after him and locked it for good measure. The man had such good hearing, especially in Guardian form, he'd probably be listening to make sure she did it. He really was that paranoid.

Gazing around the living room in the sudden silence, Fil realized that this was the first time since that night at the abbey that she had been entirely alone. It actually struck her as a little creepy.

Rubbing her hands over her own arms to chafe some warmth into them against the sudden chill that struck her, she sank onto the sofa and frowned. She hoped Ricky would arrive soon, not so she wouldn't be alone, but to keep her mind off what might be happening to Wynn. At least, that was what she told herself.

She felt like an idiot if she let herself think about it. Fil had been on her own for almost ten years, since her grandparents had died, and she'd never had a problem being alone. She possessed a strong streak of independence, something she knew drove her Guardian crazy at times, and she'd always enjoyed her own company.

Maybe being an artist gave her something of a solitary nature, but this was the first time in years that she could remember being unhappy to be left sitting alone in an empty apartment. Knowing that Spar wouldn't be with her forever, she told herself to get used to it. This wouldn't be the last time she found herself left in solitude.

Right, because depressing herself was a terrific idea, given her current frame of mind.

Fil snorted and reached for the remote control. She wasn't a big television watcher, but at the moment the idea of filling the room with talking voices appealed to her, even if no one else was really there. The illusion would suffice for the time being, and Ricky would arrive at any moment for something a touch more genuine.

She had barely settled on a station playing reruns of familiar British sitcoms when the knock rattled the apartment door. Relieved to have her visitor arrive to ease her agitation, she flung open the door with a smile on her face.

"Good timing," she greeted her friend, then felt her smile die. Ricky stood on the landing at the top of the stairs, but he hadn't come alone, and the face of the man standing slightly behind him made every hair on the back of Fil's neck stand up and vibrate.

"Well, hello there, little mousey," the Hierophant purred. "I've been looking for you."

Chapter Twenty-one

Spar flew to Wynn's apartment in a small four-story row house as fast as his wings would carry him. Just minutes after leaving Felicity's fire escape, he landed on the witch's roof and frowned. He had expected to find fire and brimstone waiting for him, the wail of police sirens, or the screams of Wynn and her neighbors, but the building seemed peaceful and quiet, nothing out of the ordinary to disturb the crisp night air. He could see not a single *nocturnis,* couldn't even sense the presence of an evil threat. He felt absolutely nothing.

Something wasn't right.

Pulling Felicity's cell phone from his belt, he called Wynn even as he lowered himself to the fire escape outside her apartment window. Part of him hoped she wouldn't answer, because what woman under attack by demonic cultists stopped to answer her phone?

"Hello?" When she picked up the call, the witch's voice was calm and even as always, not a trace of the urgency she had used with Felicity.

"Wynn, are you harmed? Are the *nocturnis* still here? I am at the window. Let me inside."

"Spar, is that you?" She sounded confused but unhurt, and he could see those emotions in her face when she appeared at the window with her phone pressed to her ear. "Hold on."

She disconnected the call and slid open the window. "What *nocturnis* are you talking about? And what are you doing here? Where's Fil?"

Fear and rage like nothing he had ever experienced crashed over Spar like a tsunami, and the metal platform beneath him trembled when he cursed in the foulest terms he could conjure. "It was another trap. A diversion. You called Felicity moments ago, sounding terrified. You said *nocturnis* were attempting to enter your apartment."

"No, I didn't. Spar, I swear it."

"I believe you. I heard a few words, though, and the caller sounded exactly as you sound. Felicity was convinced. She sent me to rescue you. They must have used magic to mimic your voice." He flapped his wings and prepared to launch himself back into the sky. "I have to return to her. They might even have her by now."

"Wait!" Her urgent tone and tight grip caught him before he could fly. "I'm sure it was a trap, but I *was* just about to call you two. That's how I can be a hundred percent certain it couldn't have been me on the phone, because about ten minutes ago I just came to. From the vision. Spar, if they've taken her this is even more important. They'll want to make her the next sacrifice, but now I know where we can find them."

His lips curled back, exposing the sharp length of his fangs, and his talons ached with the need to rend *nocturnis* flesh. "Tell me. Now."

Fil came to on a rush of adrenaline, moving from blankness to full awareness so fast, it left her dizzy. Or maybe that was the blow she'd taken to the back of her head. At this point, it was hard to tell. The cold and dark filled her with a sense of déjà vu that brought the memories of her vision rushing back, but when she opened her eyes this time, she found herself not in a damp, dank basement, but lying in the bottom of a motorboat while freshwater spray misted against her face.

Moaning, she reached up to touch the already swollen lump at the rear of her skull. She winced when the light brush of her own fingers sent her blistering headache straight past agonizing and on to debilitating. Between the pain in her head and the motion of the water, she forecast vomit likely within the next thirty to sixty minutes.

"She's beginning to wake. Tie her hands."

Someone grabbed her shoulder and roughly rolled her onto her belly before dragging her hands to the small of her back. If only the bastard had put his shoes within range of her mouth, she'd have decorated them real nice for him. Rough hemp bound her wrists together with her hands pointing toward the opposite elbows. She gritted her teeth and concentrated on taking slow shallow breaths through her nose.

She couldn't see much of anything. Her head hurt too much to do a lot of thrashing around, and it was dark out here on the river. She assumed that's where they were, cruising somewhere on the St. Lawrence. She hoped she hadn't been down long enough for them to speed the entire way to Lake Ontario. Judging by the blackness of the night, she doubted it. They couldn't have gotten to her more than an hour or two earlier.

God, she felt like an idiot. The Hierophant had shown up at her door and all she'd been able to do was gape at him while he instructed his minion to knock her senseless. She should have at least slammed the door in his ugly face. She doubted it would have kept him out for long, but it might have given her a chance to run. Or to dial her cell phone.

When Spar found out about this, he was going to kill her. He'd probably have to resurrect her dead ass to do it, since she doubted the Hierophant had come all the way to her apartment and kidnapped her so they could munch popcorn together and watch a *Big Bang Theory* marathon. She figured his plans for her had more to do with ceremonial knives and demonic overlords. Joy.

It stung to know that Ricky had been involved in her kidnapping, but recalling the vacant expression on his face while the Hierophant had instructed him to clock her a good one, she wondered if he might be under some kind of mind-control spell the *nocturnis* had concocted. Maybe it was wishful thinking on her part, but her friend hadn't looked like himself, and no matter how mad he'd been at her the last time she'd seem him, she could never believe that the Rick Racleaux she'd known for almost fifteen years would knowingly hand her to someone who intended to rip her heart out of her chest. In her brain, the equation simply did not compute.

When she tried to turn her head, though, the agony

that followed made the math just a touch easier. If his heart really wasn't in the whole human-sacrifice thing, did he have to hit her so hard? A pulled punch would have been as good as an olive branch, given the present circumstances.

Those circumstances really were going to make her hurl if they stayed on the water much longer. Not that hurrying toward their destination sounded like a great idea, considering what she assumed was going to happen when they got there, but getting off the water and onto solid land held a very strong appeal. Mostly to her stomach.

Her head cast a different vote. When the bow of the speedboat ran aground on a sandy bottom, the force of the impact sent her sliding forward and tapped her injured head gently against the hull. Once again the world went gray, and she felt her grip on awareness slipping, but hey—unconscious of reality meant unconscious of pain, right?

When she came to, she'd have to remember count her frickin' blessings.

The second time she awoke had less to do with the flood of hormones in her bloodstream and more to do with the impact of a hard shoulder to the gut as she was lifted and tossed over it to be carried. She promptly opened her mouth and spilled the contents of her stomach down the back of someone's legs. Was it wrong that when she'd finished heaving, she laughed?

Her captor seemed to think so. He immediately cried out in disgust and threw her to the ground, sending her landing half on top of her own pool of vomit.

Thankfully, that half wasn't anywhere near her face, or she'd probably have puked again.

Jesus, she just knew she had a concussion, and these bozos kept slinging her around like a sack of potatoes. If they didn't start being more careful with her, they'd find her dead of a brain bleed or intracranial swelling before they got her anywhere near their precious altar. And wouldn't that just piss off the big boss?

Fil moaned, less for the effect of playing the helpless captive and more because her head just fucking *hurt*. At least if she'd been in the NHL, they'd have let her go lie down in a dark room for fifteen minutes before making her exert herself any. These jokers started kicking her in the side and ordering her to get to her feet. Did she look like some kind of Woman of Steel to them?

"I'm not touching her," someone snapped, and from the proximity of the voice she guessed it was the guy she'd barfed on. "It's bad enough she got puke all over the hem of my robe, but now she's covered in it. If she can't walk, let the reporter carry her. He'll never know the difference."

Another man chimed in—not barf boy, but not the Hierophant, either. No way would all of these bodies have fit in the tiny motorboat, so they must have been waiting here. Wherever "here" was. "No, I can't stomach the smell of it. She needs to be cleaned off before we bring her into the circle, or I'll vomit myself."

"Throw her in the river. That should wash off the worst of it, and it's not like it matters if she catches cold."

Oh, no, it mattered, but no one paid any attention to her struggles. Given how weak she felt, she couldn't really blame them. She doubted she could fight off a demonic kitten at the moment, which was why she landed in the river water without so much as a scream.

That was a good thing, really, because it meant she had her mouth closed and didn't end up swallowing a gallon of *eau de rivière* that she would then just have to vomit back up. Once had been enough for the evening. With her hands bound behind her back, she couldn't swim, but the part of the water she'd landed in was shallow enough that she was able to get her feet under her without too much effort. She considered pushing herself farther out into the current, slow though it was near the city, just to escape, but hard hands reached in and hauled her out before she could act on the thought. Maybe the cold had slowed her reflexes: The river felt icy against her skin.

So did her soaking-wet clothes, once she made it back onto dry land. They acted like a personal air-conditioning system, wicking the heat from her body and leaching it into the surrounding atmosphere. Couple that with the breeze off the river and she could feel her internal temperature plummet. She began to shake, and the stubborn part of herself just hoped the bastards who had kidnapped her wouldn't mistake it for fear. Right now she was too damned cold, too damned angry, and in too damned much pain to be afraid. She'd save that for when the knives came out.

"Enough dawdling." This time the Hierophant spoke. Fil would never forget the sibilant hiss of his voice, the almost effeminate tenor that had greeted her at the top of her stairs. "If she's conscious she can walk. Bring her."

Hands roughly grasped each elbow, positioning her between two of the cultists as they began marching up the narrow beach into the trees. A quick look around confirmed her suspicions. She'd been taken to one of the tiny, unnamed islands that dotted the river north of the city, mostly forgotten compared with their larger, better-known neighbors. Here, the chances of anyone stumbling on their activities was remote—remote enough that Fil knew looking for help would prove useless. She was on her own, at least until her Guardian realized what had happened and flew to the rescue. She had utter confidence that Spar would come for her; she just had to pray he came in time. Until then, her survival rested in her own hands.

She allowed herself to be guided deeper into the trees while she assessed her captors. In addition to the Hierophant and Ricky—who continued to stare blankly straight ahead and trail the Hierophant like a robotic puppy—the group contained six male figures in dark hooded robes. They looked like escapees from a medieval monk convention. All but two wore their capacious hoods drawn up and forward, obscuring their features. Barf boy and one other had pushed the fabric back to drape around their necks in a sort of cowl.

The Hierophant looked just as she remembered him from her vision. Of average height, he had the slim, undernourished build of a computer geek, along with the accompanying pale, pasty complexion. He looked to be somewhere in his thirties, that indefinable kind of stage that only indicated adulthood, with no sign of youth or age to pin it down further. He wore his black hair a touch too long to be called short, and too short to be called long. Everything about him screamed unremarkable, until you looked at his face.

He had sharp, thin features that might have been called aristocratic or even handsome if the taint of evil hadn't been scrawled so plainly across them. His narrow lips wore a tight curve that spoke of cruelty, the kind that said he enjoyed the sight of pain, and enjoyed causing it even more. He made Fil's skin crawl. The other cultists she hated on principle, but for this man her hatred was visceral, curling in her gut and rattling like a snake on the alert, angry and poisonous.

She stared at his back as he led the way through the trees. As the vegetation thickened, they had to walk single-file, though one of Fil's captors made sure to keep a firm grip on her arm and walk so closely behind her she could practically smell what he'd had for lunch wafting forward over her shoulder.

She could see that they followed some sort of rough path across the uneven ground, which hinted this was undoubtedly the location Wynn had been searching for. Everything indicated they'd been using it for a while. She supposed the island had been an ideal location, far away from prying eyes and unlikely to come under scrutiny from the authorities. Basically the perfect setting for acts of unspeakable evil.

Fil preferred not to participate in those acts, so she needed to start coming up with a plan. Fast. She doubted the island was big enough that their little march would take much longer, and if they intended to strap her to some kind of bloody altar, her chances of not dying would likely decrease dramatically. Time to get moving.

When she saw the trees begin to look sick and stained, bare of leaves and darkened as if charred by invisible flames, she knew they were getting close to the ritual site. Taking a deep breath, she faked tripping over a root in the path and made sure to stumble hard into the man in front of her. The unexpected impact threw him off balance and she had the brief, satisfying image of his smacking into another *nocturnis* and sending the whole line of them tumbling to the ground like dominoes. Of course, it didn't happen that way, but her unexpected "fall" wrenched her forward so suddenly that the man holding her loosened his grip for a fleeting second. It was all she needed.

She yanked against him with all her strength, using her entire body weight to add to the force her movement. She felt his fingers tighten their grip even as they slid over her dripping skin. If she'd been wearing long sleeves, he probably would have caught her by her clothing, but she was out of his grasp and into the trees before he could finish swearing at her.

There weren't a lot of places she could go on the tiny island, and she knew they'd catch up with her before long. They knew the area infinitely better than she did, and they were the ones with the motorboat. Running had been a delaying tactic, something to give Spar just a little more time to discover where they had taken her, because she knew he'd be searching, and she knew he would never stop until he found her. To help him out, she would stall for all she was worth.

Fil quickly discovered that keeping her balance while running through heavy woods with her hands tied behind her back should qualify as an Olympic sport; it was that difficult. Her shoulders jerked every time she swerved to avoid a tree trunk or jumped over a stone or root because she instinctively wanted to put out her hands to assist her movements. If she lived through this, she was going to need a massage in the worst way.

"She can't get far. Split up and find her. We have a schedule to keep."

She heard the Hierophant's orders and could tell he sounded more annoyed at the bother of recapturing her than worried by her escape attempt. He knew as well as she did that there was nowhere for her to go.

Behind her, the *nocturnis* crashed through the brush like elephants. She began to alter her course based on the sounds around her, keeping the noises of pursuit behind her. She also tugged and twisted at the rope around her wrists, attempting to loosen the strands and work herself free. She could do a lot more to save herself if she weren't tied up, and if she could manage to get out of the rope, it would be worth it to double back toward the beach where they'd landed. With her hands free, she could start the boat's motor and get herself back across the river. For now, though, she just needed to concentrate on staying out of the bastards' clutches.

Pulling and twisting against the rough hemp quickly began to rub her skin raw, but she thought she could feel a little more give in the bindings. Pausing to draw breath, she crouched down among the branches of a young evergreen and peered into the darkness. It didn't take long to convince her that staying on the move was a better idea.

Hearing footsteps drawing closer, Fil quickly rose to her feet and took off again through the bushes. She heard cursing and knew her pursuer had gotten closer to her than she really wanted to think about. She'd have to be more careful, more on guard if she wanted to stay free long enough for Spar to reach her.

She wished she knew how long she'd been unconscious and how long it had taken to transport her unconscious body from her apartment to the island. Either that, or that she'd remained a Girl Scout beyond the first cookie drive. Didn't they teach kids how to do stuff like tell the time by gauging the position of the stars in the sky? Or did that only work with the sun? Hm, she'd probably been right when she'd told Grandma that the Scouts weren't for her. Clearly, she'd have made a lousy one.

At this point, all she could do was guess. Judging by how far north they had traveled on the river and the need to maintain discretion when transporting kidnap victims through the streets of a major city—or so she assumed, speaking as one herself—she thought it must be closing in on midnight. Did that mean ritual sacrifices didn't have to be timed to specific points on the clock? So much for tradition and symbolism. Fil was learning something new every day.

Today, she'd like to learn how not to die. That would be great.

Fil wasn't one to follow the phases of the moon, but she didn't remember seeing one in the sky above the beach, and the thick, heavy quality of the darkness all around her indicated they were under a new moon at the moment. It would make hiding easier, but avoiding anyone sneaking up on her that much more difficult. Well, unless she dropped her shields and really looked.

Putting on a burst of speed, she did her best to widen the distance between herself and her pursuers before she paused again, this time leaning against the bole of a young maple tree. Closing her eyes for a moment, she took a centering breath and then opened them to take a new look around her. She couldn't say she liked what she saw. Thin mists of blackish green and dirty red drifted through the trees, lending the woods an unnatural glow. Wherever the vapors touched, the trees and plants seemed to shudder and withdraw, bending as far away from the foul air as their roots would allow.

If just the remnants of evil could do that, Fil figured it explained the appearance of the trees she'd seen before. Closer to the ritual site, the power of the Order's evil must act like poison to every living thing around. The thought stirred her anger. The forest hadn't done anything to deserve this desecration, but then again, neither had any of the people the *nocturnis* had killed and dumped in the woods on the mountain. Neither had the villagers in Afghanistan, or Ricky, or Fil herself. She supposed that was the real definition of evil— the very lack of discrimination in what was venerated and what was destroyed.

A flicker of malignant light peeked through the trees to Fil's right, and she darted left. She thought that way led toward the outer edge of the island, and she'd prefer not to be herded that way, figuring the cover would thin out beside the water, leaving her more exposed. She'd have to double back around to stay out of sight.

The sharp crack of a branch had her veering again, away from the source of the sound and back toward the deeper woods. She could feel blood beginning to trickle over her wrists beneath the rope that bound her and tugged harder; if she was lucky, maybe the stuff would act like a lubricant to help her slip free. She thought she was making progress when something grabbed her ponytail and jerked suddenly backward.

She flew off her feet and back onto her bound hands. The impact on the already sore joints and raw skin forced a strangled cry from her throat. She could feel dirt and bits of leaves sticking to the bloodied wounds she'd created during her struggles and wanted to laugh when she found herself hoping she lived long enough to develop an infection. Hello, hysteria.

"What an utter waste of time," the Hierophant sneered, wrapping the length of her wet tail of hair around his hand and using the grip to haul her to her feet. "As you can see, you've accomplished nothing but to increase the pleasure I'm going to take in making you suffer before you die, bitch."

"Bitch?" she bit out as he began dragging her back toward the center of the island. "I'm not the one resorting to hair pulling. Is this going to turn into a catfight? You're not going to whip out some acrylic nails and try to scratch up my pretty face, are you?"

He ignored her—well, except for a particularly nasty tug that made her scalp scream along with her already aching head. The exertion of her run had not helped her concussion symptoms one little bit.

She had to walk bent over and twisted because of the grip he held on her ponytail, and she fought back new waves of nausea. She'd already seen that all barfing did was make her miserable. She doubted this guy would be as squeamish as barf boy if she puked on his robes, though if he didn't lay off the hair pulling and head jerking, they were both going to find out.

He led her back toward the twisted dead and dying trees until the forest opened up into another clearing. The Order seemed to like these spots, although in contrast with the area in the park where they had disposed of their victims, this open area had clearly been stripped bare by men. Or at least at their direction. Whether they'd cleared the vegetation themselves or used magic or the labor of some kind of demonic minions, Fil didn't care to speculate. All she knew was that as soon as they entered the clearing, the rich, fresh, earthy smell of the forest turned to a putrid stink, like death and rot and burning sulfur. It made her wonder if all those stories about hell being a pit of fire and brimstone might not be pretty damned accurate.

Several torches impaled in the earth illuminated the edges of the clearing, and a stone-lined pit contained a roaring bonfire near the center. For a moment, Fil blinked, blinded by the sudden change of light. Pain stabbed through her skull.

The ground here appeared as either bare, blackened earth or patches of some kind of lichen-y, mossy growth that reminded her less of a plant and more of the slimy, poisonous algae that occasionally grew on ponds not exposed to enough sun or fresh water. She thought at least some of the smell came from that, because to her other vision it glowed with the same greenish, purplish, blackish light that had emanated from the plant that tried to eat Wynn. It made Fil wish fondly for another jar of black salt.

The foul carpet climbed the sides of tree trunks and up the faces of a pair of stone blocks placed facing each other roughly five feet apart. Between them a thick slab of paler stone stretched like a tabletop. She didn't need to inspect it for bloodstains to recognize an altar for human sacrifice. Some things didn't require little labels for identification purposes.

Her heart leapt into her throat as she realized she stared straight at the site of her own imminent murder. Digging her heels in, she gave one last mighty wrench against her binding and felt a surge of adrenaline as one hand slipped free of the ropes. It felt like she left every inch of her skin behind to do it, but she didn't care. With her hands free and her life on the line, she intended to fight like the fucking demon they wanted to feed her to.

Fil would not make this easy. She would show the Hierophant and all his fucked-up sidekicks that not everyone stood helpless in the face of Darkness.

Some of them had the Light on their side.

Chapter Twenty-two

Spar fought the need to roar his impatience with the delay. Every fiber of his being shook with the need to act, to spring into the sky and soar straight to the island Wynn had pinpointed as the sacrificial site. She'd resorted to throwing a cast-iron skillet at his head to get his attention.

"It would be the height of macho stupidity to fly in there alone like some tragic hero," the witch had told him. "You'd intend to save her, but there's no way. Do you really think the Hierophant is acting alone? You know as well as I do that when it comes to working magic this big, they'll be using an entire inner cell. That's a minimum of seven of the most skilled black mages they have, one of whom we think is the leader of the entire Order. *Plus,* quite possibly, the Defiler itself. You know taking that on alone would be a suicide mission. If you want to kill yourself, fine, but at least give Fil a fighting chance."

Spar had laughed. "And you think that if I bring you

along, sprained ankle limiting your movements, your assistance would turn the tide? Do not be ridiculous. You might be a witch, but you are not a Warden and are completely unprepared for this kind of battle. You would only serve to distract me and get us both killed."

"That's 'an amazingly powerful witch' to you, buddy," she snapped, her eyes narrowed, "but no, that isn't what I think. What I think is that the only chance we have of saving Fil, let alone stopping the Hierophant, is to marshal *all* of our resources. Every last one of them. That means we need the other Guardian here, and the Warden-in-training. That's our only shot at making this work."

"Kees and Ella are in Vancouver, all the way on the other side of the bloody continent. Shall we send the Hierophant a polite note and ask that he please postpone killing my mate until we have had time to put together a plan to attack him most effectively?"

"Once again, Mr. Tall, Grumpy, and Sarcastic, no, I'm not saying anything of the kind. You said Ella had been studying Warden magic? Well, I have, too, when I could get my hands on it without raising suspicions. Neither of us may be full-fledged members of the Guild, but I think that if we work together, even long-distance, we can put together a portal spell and open a bridge between Vancouver and Montreal. We could have another Guardian and a magic user who has already proven herself in battle here within the hour. Don't you think that sounds better than running off half-cocked into the face of certain failure?"

"Do you think we have an hour?"

"I think we have more than one. It's barely ten thirty. If they want to do this right, they'll time the sacrifice to the Demon's Hour at three. That will let them raise the most concentrated burst of power."

"And if you're wrong?"

Her jaw clenched. "If I'm wrong, then we're already too late."

Spar had relented. Reluctantly. He knew he stood a better chance in any battle with one of his brothers at his side, especially when outnumbered and facing one of the Seven, no matter how weak it might be. Still, every minute that passed with Felicity in the hands of his enemy sliced at his soul like a razor. He felt himself going mad, and handed the responsibility for the call to Wynn, along with Felicity's cell phone. It already had Ella's number programmed in.

He couldn't concentrate on the words Wynn and Ella exchanged. He merely knew that the fifteen-minute conversation lasted fifteen minutes too long. He heard the discussion of magic circles, incenses, herbs, amulets, and candles and tried to resist the urge to tear Wynn's building apart brick by brick with his bare hands. He ground his teeth together until his fangs threatened to snap off at the roots, and his wings quivered with the need to spread and catch the currents of the crisp night air.

He took to pacing through the small apartment, ritual room to bedroom to living room to kitchen to dining room and back again, until his circling drove Wynn as crazy as Felicity's had driven him. Shouting his name, she dragged him back to her ritual room and pointed to a spot against the wall.

"Sit there and for the Goddess's sake, keep quiet. It's showtime, and since this is a first for both me and Ella, I'm going to need to concentrate." She frowned and rolled her shoulders as if loosening up before a workout. "Of course, feel free to cross your fingers. I figure it can't hurt."

He would have crossed his eyes if she told him to; anything to move this faster and get him closer to feeling his mate safe in his arms once more.

Seeing magic take shape was nothing new to Spar, but he noticed that Wynn's magic had a different feel to it than he remembered from the Wardens in his past. Instead of opening a channel to the magic, like raising the floodgates of a dam, the witch seemed just to remain as she was and let the magic soak into her like a sponge. By the time she cast a circle using the inscribed pentagram on the floor as a guide, she almost glowed with a soft-green light the color of spring leaves. He'd seen the sick and bruised purplish green of the Dark magic at the dump site, and this light seemed to wash the other from his memory, leaving behind the taste of cool water and delicate herbs.

He saw her bless and consecrate the circle with the traditional trappings of witchcraft—salt, water, fire, and air—and heard her invite the powers of the elements and the gods into her sacred space. She did so deliberately, respectfully, but quickly, and Spar knew she hurried for his sake, and for Felicity's. Gratitude filled him, joined by excitement when she moved on to the work of the circle and began to chant the spell to open the portal.

The words meant nothing to him. He couldn't focus on them when he had his gaze fixed so intently on the air in the western side of the circle. He realized that the longer Wynn chanted, the more the air became visible, beginning to shimmer and glow with magical energy.

Wynn fed more power into her voice, the volume increasing, the intensity building. She directed the palms of her hands toward the mass of waving air and began to draw them outward, as if stretching the diameter of the disturbance. The portal took on a recognizable shape, like an oval doorway, and inside the air went thick and gray and opaque, like a foggy horizon. The witch's chant rose again, and her voice turned from a supplication into an audible command. With a final shout, she stomped her uninjured foot against the wood of the floor. The sound seemed to echo through the portal.

An instant later Spar gave a hoarse gasp of welcome as Kees stepped out of the mist and into the circle. Immediately he edged to the side to allow a petite human female to follow him through.

"Wow," Ella said, wearing a grin bigger than the Cheshire cat. "That beats commercial air travel any day! We should go into business, Wynn. You know, after we finish saving the world."

Fil kicked and bit and clawed like an angry badger. No way was she going to cower and sob and play the helpless damsel while some psycho fucker strapped her to a great big rock and sliced her into demon sashimi. Hell no. Felicity Shaltis had been raised to fight her own battles, and fight them she would, down to her final breath.

Not that she'd turn down some help if it arrived, of course. She was stubborn, not stupid.

She knew down to her pinkie toes that Spar was coming for her. She felt it. Not only was the Guardian incapable of deserting a human under his care, but the big hunk of granite cared for her; she knew he did. Even if he would have to leave her when this was all over, he would never leave her in the middle, so she knew he was on his way. If he could just hurry, though, that would be good.

To be honest, Fil didn't know how much fight she had left, physically, anyway. Every time she struggled, her head throbbed even harder, and she'd noticed over the last little while that keeping her balance had begun to pose unanticipated challenges. When anything jarred her head, the edges of her vision began to go gray and blurry, and she was starting to get scared that she might end up passing out and missing her own execution. Wouldn't that be a bummer?

She gagged when the Hierophant released her ponytail with a shove, sending her sprawling to the ground at the feet of another *nocturnis*. At least this time, she was able to catch herself with her hands, so when she predictably retched once again, she didn't land face-first in the ick. Of course, the only thing left in her stomach at this point was bile, so it wasn't that big a mess. Was that the kind of small mercy she should start being thankful for?

"Resecure her," the leader ordered, his lips curving in a smile of anticipation. "And bring forward the reporter."

Once again, Fil found herself being roughly tied in more of the scratchy hemp rope. This time, her hands were secured in front of her, but the coils bit more tightly into her raw and bleeding flesh, and the cultist tied her ankles as well. She supposed they figured since she was right under their noses, they would be able to see if she wormed her way free again. The sad part was, they were probably right.

Watching helplessly, she saw one of the *nocturnis* guide Ricky toward the altar stone with no more than a hand on his shoulder. Her old friend didn't even protest as he was ordered to stretch out on his back and ropes were draped across him, binding his shoulders, arms, waist, hips, knees, and ankles to the cold stone.

"Wonderfully obedient, isn't he?"

Fil nearly jumped out of her skin as the Hierophant's words came to her from just inches away. She'd been deposited in a heap at the base of a withered pine tree, and the man crouched beside her, his gaze fixed on the preparations at the altar.

"Of course, he has no idea what he's doing, just as he had no idea when I had him call and ask to meet you at your apartment," he continued, sounding casually pleased with himself. "It's amazing how easily controlled some minds are. It barely took any effort to strip away his reason and put blind obedience in its place."

Fil swallowed another mouthful of bile. "Is that how you found me? You used Ricky to lead you to my home?"

"Of course not." He chuckled. "I knew exactly where you lived before I contacted Mr. Racleaux. You weren't all that hard to find, you know. Not while you wear the Master's brand."

The Hierophant reached out and used the tip of a glinting silver knife to pry open the fingers of her left hand. He scratched the blade over the lines of the mark still visible on her palm and smiled a truly nasty smile.

"I'm sure you thought you were safe once the witch

cast her little spell, didn't you? Well, it was inconvenient not to be able to just bring you to me with the tie to the Master, but even with that severed, I could still find you. This glows like a beacon, if you know the correct way to look. It just took me a bit longer this way to realize the Hierophant's plans."

Fil's head reeled, this time with shock instead of concussion symptoms. "The Hierophant? I thought *you* were the Hierophant," she choked out.

The man beside her laughed. "Oh, dear me, no, Felicity, my love. How could I be the Hierophant? Our leader is one with the Master, a position I would not presume to take myself. He guides us from the right hand of the Defiler, much the way the pope leads his merry band of deluded fools he calls the church. No, consider me more in the way of a cardinal. An adviser to the Hierophant, but no more, I'm afraid. Yes, it's quite a fitting analogy, and I do look so very fine in red."

With that, he dug the knife into her palm until blood welled to the surface. Laughing, he dragged a finger through the crimson fluid then raised it to his face and painted it across his cheekbones in wide stripes of carnage. Felicity curled her lips and spat right in his eye.

The backhand caught her by surprise, toppling her to her side and turning the world briefly black. She didn't completely lose consciousness, because she could hear the *nocturnis* moving about, hear the Hieroph—no, the cardinal—hear him barking orders to his fellow sociopaths. She retained the ability to hear and to smell and to touch, but she couldn't see until the darkness lifted. She found herself on her side facing the trees, trying desperately to summon the strength to pull herself back up into a sitting position.

And damn it, if even that felt like the equivalent of climbing Mount Everest on her knees, how the hell was she supposed to get herself out of this mess?

For the first time, Fil felt the urge to give in to fear, not just for her own sake, but for Ricky's. Even if the man was still under some kind of spell, he didn't deserve what the Order had in store for him. He didn't deserve to suffer and die so that some group of sick fucks could pretend they'd have a place reigning in hell after the Darkness consumed the world.

Biting back a sob, Fil stared into the woods and willed Spar to come to her.

"It's nearly two, sir," she heard a man say. Barf boy, maybe? "We should begin if we hope to wake the Master and have him prepared to receive the sacrifice at the proper hour."

"Yes, by all means, let's get started," the cardinal said, his tone jovial, even excited. Clearly this was a man who enjoyed his work. "Time waits for no one, does it?" He snapped his fingers. "Wakey, wakey, Mr. Racleaux. It's time for you to rejoin us."

A sense of deep dread overcame her, and Fil rolled herself over to face the altar once again. She wasn't close enough and didn't have the correct angle to catch a glimpse of Ricky's face, but she could see the way he suddenly lurched against his bonds.

"What the fuck is going on?" she heard her friend shout. "Where the hell am I? Who are you people?"

"We're your liberators, Mr. Racleaux," the cardinal

purred. "We're going to liberate your soul and make a much better use of it than you've done so far. Shall we get started?"

He raised his arm and Fil caught the way the blade of his knife reflected the firelight for a moment before he brought it swinging down in a violent arc. Then she heard the echo of a scream, and she couldn't tell if it was torn from Ricky's throat, or from hers.

Chapter Twenty-three

Spar flapped his powerful wings as he flew high above the city of Montreal and coasted out over the river that bordered it. Wynn clung to his neck and waist, muttering something about crashing and dying and about 206 broken bones. He tried to ignore her. She felt wrong in his arms, but she had insisted on joining the coming battle, sprained ankle or no. When Ella had begun arguing on her side, he had given up and agreed to carry her to the ritual site.

Beside him, Kees flew with a similar armful, but he seemed more than content to have his mate wrapped around him as they soared toward the small, unnamed island Wynn had identified. Ella appeared to fit against the other Guardian as if she had been made just for him, and Spar felt the stab of envy straight into his heart. He knew what it felt like to hold his mate that way, and he only hoped he would be fortunate enough to feel that again.

"Look!" Kees shouted to gain his brother's attention,

pointing down to the glow of fire visible from the air though a break in the island's thick tree cover. "I think we've found our *nocturnis*, brother."

A growl was Spar's only reply. He began to spiral his flight path in toward the clearing, grunting when the witch in his arms leaned forward and sank her teeth in his shoulder.

"What in the name of the Light was that for?" he demanded.

"Well, I wasn't going to let go of you long enough to smack you upside the head," Wynn shot back. "You can't just fly in there and give them a clean shot at you, for the Goddess's sake. Haven't you ever heard of the element of surprise? We have to sneak up on them."

"Let Kees and Ella sneak up on them. I think they will be sufficiently surprised when I land on their heads and crush their puny human bodies into jelly."

"Fine, but if one of them uses a lightning bolt to blow your head off, don't say I didn't warn y— Aaaaaaahhhhhh!"

Her words trailed off into a shriek of terror as Spar inverted his body and began a tight death spiral toward the light that glowed from inside the tight ring of trees.

At first, Fil thought she heard the sound of an eagle screaming as it swooped down on its prey. Then she thought it might be Ricky, screaming again as the cardinal inflicted yet another wound to join the dozen or more he'd already given to the helpless reporter. Almost as quickly she realized Ricky's cries had turned into pleading sobs that begged for mercy his captors didn't possess, and eagles didn't normally hunt at night.

Something else had to have made that noise, and it sounded like a woman.

"Someone is coming!" barf boy shouted, looking around nervously.

"Who?" one of the others demanded, sounding less than impressed. "The Guardian? Even if he saw through our little impersonation, so what if he comes? There are seven of us here, and once the boss finishes off the re- porter, the Master will be wide awake and ready to hear our call. One Guardian against all of us?" He snorted. "I like our chances."

Fil didn't, not when a bolt of blue-white light rained down from the sky, swallowing up the braggart and barf boy in a giant magical bubble. Finally, the cavalry had arrived.

The clearing erupted in a mass of confusion, shout- ing, and general chaos. Into the thick of it sailed not one, but two battle-ready Guardians, each looking like a par- ticipant in an Emote the Rage contest. With his spear in hand and feathered wings spread wide, Spar looked like one of God's avenging angels on the warpath. The figure she assumed had to be Kees appeared more like a demon, but knowing he was on her side made her take his bat-like wings, fangs, and heavy curving horns in stride. Better with her than against her, she figured.

The two of them landed in unison, the solid thunk of their feet hitting the earth the sweetest sound Fil could imagine. Their wings kicked up a small storm of dirt and dried leaves, and even away from the action Fil had to squint against the debris. She could see well enough to make out that the Guardians hadn't come alone. Wynn and Ella jumped to the ground as well, Ella immediately squaring off against the *nocturnis* while Wynn scanned the area looking for her. She gave a hoarse shout and nearly sang a chorus of hallelujah when the witch's eyes locked on her.

"Oh, my God, did you send down the magic bubble?" she demanded when Wynn knelt at her side. "Because that was kind of awesome. I'm going to have to make you teach me that."

"Nope, that was Ella. And I want to learn it, too."

Fil quickly turned to present her bound hands. "Can you get me out of these? Quick."

The witch drew a knife from her bag of tricks, which this time was draped across her front like a sling. "I came prepared."

Wynn sawed through the ropes, careful not to slice off any more of Fil's skin than she'd already managed to shed herself. She couldn't stop herself from tugging impatiently, and even before the last loop sprang free, she was yanking her hands apart and reaching for the ties around her ankles.

"Aaaaaghhhh!"

The pained cry had Fil's head jerking up and toward the altar. While Kees and Spar battled the *nocturnis* and Ella cast spells around the clearing like a wild woman, the cardinal had turned back to Ricky and plunged his knife deep into the other man's belly.

"Shit! Ricky!"

"Here! I'll go."

Wynn shoved the knife into Fil's hand and began limping across the clearing toward the altar.

"Oh, of all the idiotic noble gestures to come up

with at a time like this . . ." Fil trailed off and hacked madly at her final bindings.

In seconds she had herself unbound and darted past Wynn, intent on getting to her friend. She knew Spar would take care of the rest of the cultists, but she couldn't leave Ricky at the cardinal's mercy. She had to get him free and see how badly he'd been hurt. If there was a chance to save him, she would take it.

"Fil, stop!"

She ignored the witch's shout but dodged out of the way just in time to see a limp, robed body land on the ground she'd stood on a second ago. Another *nocturnis* down reassured her that the Guardians had things under control, but the cardinal still stood beside the altar, arms raised, bloody dagger clutched in his hand.

As she neared the stone slab, she could make out the sound of his chanting rising above the noise of the battle. She couldn't make out the words or understand what he was saying. The language definitely wasn't English, but it didn't sound like any other language she'd ever heard. Not French or Spanish or even Lithuanian, it had a harsh, guttural, menacing sound that made her skin pucker with goose bumps as she approached.

When she got within ten feet of the altar, Ricky turned his head, and she nearly stumbled as she caught a glimpse of his face. His eyes had swollen shut beneath the crosses carved across the sockets, as if someone hadn't tried just to blind him, but to X him out of existence. Shallow slices ran bloody trails across his cheeks and into the skin of his forehead: The sick fuck with the knife had carved the same symbol that desecrated her palm. It was horrifying to look upon, and rage and pity warred inside her.

Snarling, she pulled the rage forward and threw herself the last ten feet to the altar. She reached up for the knife, her only thought to rip it out of the cardinal's hand and see how he liked it buried in his withered black heart, but she hadn't counted on him being so strong.

He pushed her aside with alarming ease and laughed with maniacal glee. "Stupid girl! You cannot stop the Master and you cannot stop me. We will have our time upon the earth, and the world will grovel at our feet. All hail Uhlthor, the Defiler! Come now, thou fearsome Master, and feast upon that which I have offered you!"

The knife came down again, but Fil screamed in furious denial. She flung herself forward, her only thought to stop that knife from ending her friend's life once and for all. She hadn't actually intended to take the blow herself, but her momentum carried her up over the top of the altar and placed her right shoulder in the path of the blade.

Oh, sweet Jesus, the pain!

The knife sank deep, the angle biting into her flesh high in the rear before driving forward and down with brutal force. She felt the shock of the impact and heard the snap as her collarbone fractured from the strain. A scream tore from her throat, one she hadn't even realized was coming until she heard it high and sharp and vibrating with agony. Beneath her, Ricky groaned, and behind her the cardinal shrieked in fury and disbelief. No one had died upon the altar, not yet anyway, and his Master was going to be missing his breakfast right about now.

Poor baby.

All around them, the air filled with a mighty crash, a sonic boom that shook the ground and left Fil's ears ringing. As if she hadn't already checked off enough boxes on the minor traumatic brain injury self-evaluation list. The sound of rock breaking quickly followed, and Fil's second sight showed tendrils of absolute blackness emerging from new cracks in the stone beside Ricky's head.

Guess who was coming to dinner?

Fil screamed again as the cardinal yanked the knife out of her back and prepared to stab again. She didn't think, didn't plan, didn't reason; she just reacted. Even before the tip of the blade cleared her skin, she rolled to her back and raised her left hand, catching the blade in her fist as it descended a second time.

Oddly, she felt the sharp edges slice through her skin, felt the blood well up and begin pouring forth to stain the demon's mark, but she didn't feel the pain. Instead, she felt heat, white-hot and searing as she braced her arm with all her strength and stared up into the eyes of evil.

"I will hail no demonic filth, you piece of shit, but I will gladly serve you up on your Master's altar like buttered toast with raspberry fucking jam," she hissed.

With a jerk and a twist, Fil used her grip on the knife to yank the cardinal off balance and flipped her body, reversing their positions to leave the cardinal draped across the bloody altar atop his intended sacrifice. Scrambling backward, she slid to the earth and watched, both thrilled and horrified, as the tendrils of Darkness closed around the cardinal's struggling form and began to feast.

Fil's head spun and throbbed and she clutched her right arm uselessly to her side while blood dripped from the left in a steady trickle. She felt three miles past used up, but she could see Ricky's foot twitch and she stumbled forward, intent on pulling him free. Then hands closed around her shoulders, and even without pressing down they pinned her in place.

"No, you can't." Ella's familiar voice came to her, firm and steady. "It's too dangerous."

"And it's too late," Wynn added, urging all of them back from the sacrificial altar. "Your friend is already gone."

Fil blinked and tried to focus on the shapes among the blackness, but the tendrils had grown, twining together into a throbbing, squirming mass of evil. Nothing could survive that desecration, she realized, and her heart broke at the thought of Ricky, his soul devoured to feed that evil. All because of her. If she hadn't used him to get information, he never would have gotten mixed up in this, never would have seemed like a useful pawn in the Order's psychotic game. How was she supposed to live with that?

She trembled as the grief and pain and fatigue threatened to overwhelm her. Her shoulder, thankfully the left one, bumped against Ella as she swayed on her feet. "Oh, my God, how hurt is she? She's about to pass out!"

"She needs a hospital. Now."

Wynn's voice came from a long way away, miles and miles, as Fil's vision once again began to blur around the edges. This time she saw bright sparks in front of her eyes as consciousness began to fail her.

"What about the demon?"

"That's not the demon, it's just feeding tendrils. The demon is somewhere else, probably guarded by the rest of the Order. Spar and Kees will take care of it."

The ground rushed toward her.

"Holy shit, Fil!"

She knew nothing but blackness.

Damn it, not again.

Chapter Twenty-four

". . . at least another twenty-four to forty-eight hours, and that's assuming she regains consciousness soon with no signs of disorientation or more serious injury. Your fiancée was badly hurt, Mr. Livingston. I hope the police are able to find whoever did this to her."

Fil didn't particularly care if anyone ever found the remains of the Montreal cell of the Order of Eternal Darkness, but if they did, she hoped they found them in pieces. Tiny, charred bloody ones. With bugs crawling all over them.

Groaning, she forced her eyes open, tempted to pant from the exertion as if she'd just run a four-minute mile. Never in her life had she felt so exhausted and so filthy and in so much wretched discomfort. If she was in the damned hospital, the least the bastards could do was pony up the good medications.

"Felicity."

She tried to turn her head, but just the intent was enough to make her cry out. She'd recognize Spar's voice anywhere, could even tell by the timbre that it came from his human, not his gargoyle, chest, but when she tried to look at him, some sadist with a white coat and a penlight leaned over her and pried her eyelid up with a thumb.

"Miss Shaltis, do you know where you are? Can you tell me how you're feeling?"

Since rolling her eyes was beyond her, Fil let the doctor check her pupillary reactions and satisfied herself by giving him the finger in her head. "I'm in a hospital," she tried to answer, but the only thing that came out was "hospital" and that sounded like it had been croaked out by a dying frog.

"Good. And how are you feeling? Any pain?"

"Buckets full."

"On a scale of one to ten. One being no pain and ten being the worst pain you can imagine."

Since she could imagine a lot of things, including the feel of a knife slicing through her flesh and bone, Fil winced and settled for the low end of the scale. "Seven and three-quarters."

"Okay, I'll send a nurse right in with some pain meds. You've had a hell of a night. Multiple stab wounds, a broken collarbone, three broken bones in your hand, numerous contusions and lacerations, a mild case of hypothermia, and one hell of a concussion. Your fiancé said you were attacked by some kind of strange, violent cult. Do you remember anything about what happened?"

Well, she certainly didn't remember Spar asking her to marry him, but she doubted that's what the doctor meant. "Some," she managed, figuring the truth was none of his business. "Still kinda foggy."

"That's not surprising, given the severity of your

head injury. Someone is going to be checking up on you regularly through the night to make certain you can be roused and that you respond appropriately and without confusion, okay?"

"Okay." Hell, she'd have told him to send in the Spanish Inquisition so long as they brought those pain-killers he'd promised along with the rack and the thumbscrews.

"You're a very lucky woman, Miss Shaltis, but you're going to need time and rest to recover completely." The doctor pocketed his little light and stepped back from her bedside. "The police have asked to speak with you, but I've instructed them to return in the afternoon, after you've had some time to get your bearings. Until then, try to relax, and I'll send that nurse right in."

"Thank you."

Her eyes drifted shut, the effort required to keep them open simply too much for her to manage. She heard the click of the door closing, then a whisper of air before fingers settled tenderly against her cheek. Spar. Moving just didn't seem like an option, so she couldn't lift her hand to cover his, and she couldn't turn her head to press a kiss against his hand; she settled for leaning into his touch just a little and whispering his name into the quiet.

"Spar."

"I love you, Felicity." His voice washed over her, almost enough to take the pain away, and she felt her lips curve into a smile.

"Love you, too," she whispered, and slipped back into unconsciousness.

*　*　*

Fil woke again to the feel of something tugging on her arm and opened her eyes to see a nurse adjusting the IV line that ran from the pole next to her bed to the inside of her elbow. Within seconds, the claws of pain that had begun to flex into her withdrew, and blessed relief flowed through her veins. Also known as morphine. She sighed and let herself relax.

"Oh, good, you're awake and not grumbling at me," the nurse teased. "What a nice change of pace. I'm Jamie, by the way. I bet your fiancé knows by now not to try and wake you when you're sleeping. You can be a real bear about that."

Looking around, Fil realized the sledgehammers inside her skull had been downgraded to rubber mallets, and she no longer wanted to puke every time she moved. Progress! Unfortunately, she could also see that other than Jamie the nurse, she was alone in the hospital room.

"Where did he go?"

"Just downstairs, hon," Jamie hurried to assure her when she saw Fil's frown. "Your friends stopped by for a visit and they convinced him to pop by the cafeteria to get something to eat. He hadn't left your side in almost twelve hours! Poor guy needed to get some food before he fell down. A guy that size needs a lot of fuel."

Fil relaxed and gave the other woman a smile. "You're right. I'm glad he's eating."

She was, now that she knew he hadn't left for good. Losing him might be inevitable, but she hoped they'd at least have time for her to get back on her feet and jump his bones one last time before the threat passed and he slipped back into his stone sleeping bag. She wasn't ready to let him go.

Jamie patted her arm and stepped around the end of the bed. "I'll be back later, hon, but just buzz the desk if you need anything."

"Thanks."

She watched the nurse bustle over and open the door, then step back with a laugh.

"It looks like your entourage is back, Felicity. You're quite the popular girl around here." Jamie shook a finger playfully at the group gathered outside. "Now, you all be careful not to tire her out. She needs to rest, not party, so in fifteen minutes I'm coming back and kicking you all out."

Fil heard the familiar sound of Spar's growl followed by the nurse's hasty amendment. "Not you, Mr. Livingston. Of course you can stay as long as you'd like. Excuse me, I need to, ah, I'll check back later."

Ella pushed her way into the room, laughing all the way to her side. "Fil, you need to put a leash on your guard dog before he bites one of the staff here. He's been a grouch the whole time."

Fil reached up to return her friend's careful hug. "Hey, you're okay, right? You guys weren't hurt?"

Wynn stepped up to the foot of the bed and rubbed Fil's foot reassuringly through the blankets. "We're all fine. You got plenty hurt for the lot of us. Well, my ankle's still sore and swollen, but nothing new. You're the one we've all been worried about."

"Well, I'm fine," Fil assured her, then made a face. "Okay, actually I'm not so much fine as I am beat to shit, but I'm recovering, so that's the pretty much the same thing, right?"

"It is not." Spar's growl sounded fierce, a perfect

match for his scowl as he settled himself carefully onto the bed at Fil's hip. "You are seriously injured, Felicity. In fact, you nearly died. You are never to do such a reckless thing as throw yourself in the path of a murderer ever again. Do I make myself clear?"

Fil looked from her Guardian's expression of stubborn command to the rest of the group. Behind Spar, Kees stood with one arm wrapped around Ella and his chin bobbing in vehement agreement. Ella herself was rolling her eyes and elbowing her lover in the ribs, while Wynn looked straight at Fil with one eyebrow cocked and her lips pursed in an obvious bid to keep from laughing.

"Yes, I think we're all clear there," Fil drawled, deciding to see the humor in the big warrior's obvious concern. It was either that or bean him over the head with her IV pole for acting like an overprotective idiot. "But since I don't plan to get kidnapped by another murderer for as long as I live, I don't think that's going to be a hard promise to keep."

"Good." Spar's face softened, and he leaned in to brush a soft kiss over her forehead. "I will hold you to your word, little human."

"Speaking of murderers, though, what happened to the *nocturnis*?" she asked. "I mean, aside from the cardinal."

"The cardinal?" Spar frowned. "You mean the Hierophant?"

Fil shook her head, then winced and went back to keeping still. "No, that wasn't the Hierophant. I thought he was because of what I saw in my vision, but it turns out I was wrong. He told me the Hierophant wasn't here in Montreal and told me he was sort of an adviser to the Hierophant, like a cardinal to the pope. That's why I called him that."

Spar and Kees exchanged glances. "That is unfortunate," Kees grumbled. "We had hoped that with him dead, the Order would be weakened, but if he was merely a member of the high priesthood, the impact of his death will be much smaller. The cell here will suffer, but the Order's plans will likely continue without much interruption."

Her heart sank. "So what did we really accomplish then? The Hierophant is still alive, and before I lost it, I remember hearing Wynn say that wasn't even the demon that ended up killing Ricky and the cardinal, so we basically failed."

"That is not true," Spar said, grasping her chin and forcing her to meet his gaze. "We might not have killed the Hierophant, but we removed one of his counselors, and we destroyed the inner circle of the Montreal cell. For now, the Order will not be able to act within this city at least. No more bodies will be found in the park, because no one else will die here. That is something."

"But the demon is still out there. We weren't able to send it back to the prison it crawled out of."

"If the demon was never here, then we never had the chance to do so," Spar reasoned. "It appears that the cell here was funneling power to the Defiler through a remote connection. The demon itself remains in hiding and guarded by the cult. While that means we did not force it back to the abyss, it also means it still lacks the strength to confront us. Believe me, if it had been able, it would have joined us on that island and attempted to consume us all. With so much magical power gathered in one place, it would not have been able to resist. That means we still have time."

Kees nodded. "Time to continue locating the rest of the brethren and to gather whatever Wardens might still remain to our sides."

Ella glanced at Wynn with a sympathetic expression. "No leads yet on your brother, I'm afraid, but I promise I won't stop looking."

Wynn offered a crooked half smile. "I know, Ella. Thank you."

"On a more positive note, I do have some interesting information about a statue that sounds very familiar." Kees and Spar looked at Ella hopefully. She just continued to grin at Wynn. "How do you feel about checking it out for me?"

The witch looked surprised. "Why me?"

"A little birdie told me you're not from around here, that you actually live in Chicago," Ella said. "Don't you think it would be a good time now to take a trip home?"

"You think there's a Guardian in Chicago?"

"I think that's just exactly what I want you to find out."

Fil enjoyed seeing everyone, especially seeing them all alive and unhurt, but she didn't protest when Jamie returned to shoo them out. They had made their plans— Wynn would tie up the loose ends of her position at the university and head back to Chicago as soon as possible, while Kees and Ella returned to Vancouver to pick up the trail of the missing Wardens—but Fil needed time alone with Spar. She needed to have him to herself for a little while longer.

And she needed to tell him what was really in her heart.

She waited while he closed the door behind her visitors, smiling at him when he returned to her side. Rather than perch on the narrow slice of mattress at the side of the bed, he pulled up a chair and sat, leaning forward to clasp Fil's hand in his.

She squeezed his fingers and tried to swallow past the lump in her throat. She had so many things she wanted to tell him. She wanted him to know that her heart was his, that it didn't matter how much or how little time they would have together, that it didn't matter that she knew he would have to leave her one day. Fil needed him to know that she was tired of being afraid of what life would be like without him. All she wanted to do was savor each moment they had together and store up the memories to keep her warm when they had to part.

None of the words would come, though. All she was able to manage was a whispered, teary, "I love you."

"And I love you," he murmured, "sweet little human. I will love you until the end of time. So why do you cry? Does love not make you happy?"

"Of course it does," she sniffled. "It makes me ecstatic, but it also makes me miserable, because one day you're going to be gone, and my heart is going to shatter into a billion tiny pieces that will never fit back together again."

Already feeling the cracks, Fil turned her face into her pillow and wept.

"Felicity. Felicity, sweetness, no. Hush."

She felt his arms come around her, felt him gather her up and slide into the bed to cuddle her in his lap.

She clung to him like a kitten, curling her fingers into his skin and holding on tight. Her tears soaked though the material of his shirt, turning the light-gray color almost slate. He held her gently to him and pressed his cheek against her hair. He crooned soft, soothing non-sense words and simply stroked and petted her until she lay limp and exhausted, but quiet, in his arms.

"Now," he murmured, shifting to lean back until he could look into her swollen, red eyes. "What is this ridiculous belief you have that makes you think I would ever leave your side? I have claimed you as my mate, Felicity. You are mine, and I will be by your side for the rest of our lives."

A fresh wave of tears threatened, and Fil had to bite her cheek to force them back. "You know as well as I do that's impossible, Spar," she said, forcing the words past the tightness in her throat. "You might be immortal, but I'm not, and one of these days you're going to win this battle and go back to sleep until the next time you're summoned. I love you, and I'm going to keep loving you even while you're sleeping, but I'm going to get old, and eventually I'm going to die."

"As will I, my sweet mate. I will not return to sleep, not now that I have found you. Like the first of my kind, I will remain with you until we each have grown old, and we will pass from this life together."

Hope made Fil lift her head, but confusion made her shake her head at Spar. Then, of course, pain made her grimace, but she was too tough to let that keep her from dragging an explanation from her cryptic Guardian.

"Spar, what are you talking about? Since when do you get a choice about sleeping and waking? I thought

Guardians could only wake when they were summoned, and that they *had* to go back to sleep as soon as the threat they were summoned to face had been defeated. For Pete's sake, you're the one who explained it to me! Well, you and Ella."

"And did Ella not explain to you the story of the first Guardians?"

"What. Bloody. Story?" She gritted the words out through clenched teeth.

"Ah, perhaps this will make everything clear."

Pulling her back against his chest, Spar cradled Fil in his arms and proceeded to blow her mind. He told her the story of the first Guardians, about how their stony hearts had not cared about the humans they had been summoned to protect, and about how after many battles, their apathy had led them to ignore the summons of the Wardens. He explained how the Darkness had threatened to take over the whole of the earth until one day a woman of power had knelt at the feet of a Guardian and prayed to the Light to wake the protectors of humanity once again. He explained how the Guardian had broken free of his statue-cage and claimed the woman as his mate, and he explained how the same thing happened until nine Guardians had claimed nine human women of power as their own.

Then, while her jaw practically bounced off her knees, Spar explained how when the battle was won, those first Guardians refused to return to sleep and be parted from their mates. He told her how the Guild had been forced to release them from their service and summon new Guardians to take their place.

"From that point on, anytime a Guardian has found

his true mate and claimed her as his, the magic has released him from his service and granted him a mortal life to live with his beloved."

Fil heard the words, but she could hardly believe them. After all the time she'd spent trying not to love him, fearing the pain she would feel when he left her, now he was telling her that he didn't have to leave? That they could be together for the rest of their lives?

"Are you serious?" she asked, her voice trembling almost as hard as the hand she lifted to his face. "Can you really stay with me? Can we really be together like normal people and have a life together? No crazy naps and stone sleeping bags?"

Spar chuckled and pressed a kiss to her palm. "I am serious. You are my mate, Felicity, and even the power of the Light must bow to the ultimate magic of love."

She felt a smile begin to stretch her lips as her heart threatened to burst inside her chest. "You love me," she breathed, and she wanted to laugh with the sheer, encompassing joy of it.

"And you love me," he answered, his own smile wide and bright and full of promise for their future together.

Their wide-awake future.

"I do," Fil said. This time she did laugh, the sound bubbling up like springwater, fresh and pure and clean. The look in her eyes, though? She had a feeling that might be just the slightest bit dirty. "Want me to show you how much?"

Spar chuckled and a glint of fang peeked out from between his lips. "I do, but I want you to get well even more, little one. That way, once you have recovered from your injuries, you can show me with great—"

He stole a heated kiss.

"—attention—"

Another, and this one had her toes curling inside her hospital-issued gray socks.

"—to detail."

His final kiss left her breathless, with her head spinning from more than a simple, if pesky, concussion. Only the way the pain of her injuries bit through the blessed veil of her mediation when she reached to wrap her arms around him returned her to sanity.

"Fine," she pouted, seeing the way his eyes narrowed when he detected the signs of her discomfort in the lines around her eyes and mouth. "But if I'm going to have to wait, I expect you to be coming up with some creative ways to show me how much you love me back."

Spar chuckled and rose, shifting to deposit her gently back on her hospital bed. "Oh, sweet little human," he purred, bracing his hands on either side of her head and leaning over her with his expression full of love and heat. "I have existed for more than a thousand years. I have ways of showing you that you couldn't possibly have dreamed existed."

"Hm, I can hardly wait."

He kissed her softly, his mouth lingering on hers for a moment before he brushed his lips across her cheek in a touch full of tender promise. "Patience, my love," he whispered. "We have a lifetime together to explore."

"A lifetime," Fil echoed, sighing happily. "That might do. To start."

Don't miss these novels of The Others from
New York Times bestselling author
Christine Warren

Hungry Like a Wolf
Drive Me Wild
On the Prowl
Not Your Ordinary Faerie Tale
Black Magic Woman
Prince Charming Doesn't Live Here
Born to be Wild
Big Bad Wolf
You're So Vein
One Bite with a Stranger
Walk on the Wild Side
Howl at the Moon
The Demon You Know
She's No Faerie Princess
Wolf at the Door

And look for her novellas in the anthologies

The Huntress
No Rest for the Witches

From St. Martin's Paperbacks